一天一篇短日記

寫出英文強實力

從零開始也OK的「填空式」英文日記句典

シンプル穴埋め式 365日短い英語日記

mami 著　林以庭 譯

人人都能輕鬆開始、持續下去的英文短日記

　　許多人都嚮往能用流暢的英文寫日記、記錄生活，但實際動筆且能長久維持習慣的人屬於少數。

　　對初學者來說，要把日常生活中大大小小的事用英文寫下來並不是一件容易的事，甚至有些人連日記應該要寫些什麼內容都沒有概念。

　　本書就是設計給這些「想嘗試用英文寫日記卻無從開始、無法持續」的人們。

　　為了讓不擅長英文的人也能維持寫英文日記的習慣，我整理出下列兩大學習方法：

　　① 已備有三百六十五天的英文短日記

　　② 從單字填空開始入門

✎ 已備有三百六十五天的英文短日記

　　本書一開始就準備了三百六十五天的英文日記，都是像下圖中的基礎英文短句，有豐富的單字和片語讓你做搭配，可以輕鬆運用到各種情境中。

　　本書是從一名二十歲後半的女性視角出發，集結了一整年分量的日記。內容包含工作、戀愛、理財、美妝時尚、家事、節日、季節等多樣化的主題，可以抱持著閱讀小故事的心情來學習相關英文字詞。

　　這個日記雖然是從女性視角出發的，但為了包羅大多數人都能感同身受的日常小事，我把訪問許多人而得來的主題都寫進了內容裡。此外，這個日記並沒有固定星期幾的概念，內容可以更加廣泛而充實。因此，無關性別或年齡，相信所有讀者都能感同身受，產生「確實會碰到這種事」、「我心裡也常常暗自說這種話耶」這樣的心情。

　　我認為大多數想嘗試用英文寫日記卻遲遲沒有開始的人，只是不知道從何下筆而已，大家可以參考這三百六十五天的日記，用了哪些單字和文法？記錄下哪些事情？進而掌握英文寫作的訣竅。

✎ 從單字填空開始入門

這本書並不只是單純的英文日記，我特別設計出「填空日記」的方法。

I   **too much last night.**
昨晚喝太多了。

But I'm   **today, so I think I'm gonna relax at home...**
反正我今天休假，在家好好放鬆好了⋯⋯

I always end   **spending holidays like this.**
我每次放假總是這種模式。

         , I'm gonna do something fun this weekend!
好吧，這個週末來做點開心的事吧！

只需要在句子挖空的地方填入一個單字，即便是憑空寫英文日記會感到手足無措的人，也可以毫無壓力地去猜想語意。設想一些常用詞語，不要死背，而是在腦海裡自然浮現。挖空的這些詞語不光是能寫在日記裡，更能用在日常會話之中，每個人都可以輕鬆自在地開始寫日記，並且有效率地學會這些重要的英文表達方式。

若是覺得上面的單字填空乍看之下很簡單，實際上卻沒把握要填什麼單字的話，大家可以把填空日記當成一個小遊戲，邊玩邊學怎麼寫英文日記。

英文日記的教學書往往會將重點擺在「寫作」上，但本書除了寫作技巧之外，更注重的是以日常對話中也能運用到的實用性句型為主。

　　大家覺得如何呢？如果活用上述的本書特色，感覺是不是自己也可以養成寫英文日記的習慣呢？凡事以「好像滿簡單的」、「試試也無妨」的心態開始是最理想的。我一開始嘗試用英文寫作的時候也常常抱頭苦思，但自從轉換心態，把重點先擺在「簡單、簡短」後，就不再繃緊神經，可以輕鬆愉快地表達出自己的想法了。

　　如果這本書可以成為一個契機，讓大家動筆，輕鬆愉快地寫英文日記的話，對我而言，就是再高興不過的事了。

mami

① 四月 1
新人來了
New employees joined us

② 中文日記

今天來了幾個新人。

而我負責帶其中一個新人。

我有辦法好好教會他嗎……

總之,盡力就對了!

③ 英文填空日記

Today we've got some new ＿＿＿＿＿.
今天來了幾個新人。

And I'll be taking ＿＿＿＿＿ **of one of them.**
而我負責帶其中一個新人。

But I don't know if I can teach him ＿＿＿ …
我有辦法好好教會他嗎……

Anyway, I'll do my ＿＿＿ **!!**
總之,盡力就對了!

④ 英文日記

Today we've got some new employees.

And I'll be taking care of one of them.

But I don't know if I can teach him properly.

Anyway, I'll do my best!!

⑤

— — — — 常用單字片語集 — — — —

new employee
新進員工、新人
employee 指的是「員工」,加了一個 new 代表「新進員工」。

take care of ～
照看～
「照料」、「看顧」的意思。

properly
好好地、適當地、正確地
「好好地、適當地、正確地」的意思。

I'll do my best.
我會盡力。
do one's best 指的是「努力、盡力」的意思。

16

①日記標題

當天日記的標題，讀者可以從目錄中挑選自己有興趣的日記標題並閱讀當天的日記內容。

②中文日記

描述日常生活的中文日記，大家可以試著邊讀邊思考自己會怎麼用英文描述。在這個階段還不需要想得太複雜，快速瀏覽中文後，稍微想一下英文就好。

③英文填空日記

英文填空日記裡的每個空格可以填入一個英文單字，大家可以試著對照中文版本並思考合適的英文單字。只需要思考一個單字而已，相信對大家來說不會太難。

④英文日記

前面「③英文填空日記」的空格部分以不同顏色標示，檢查看看自己有沒有答對吧。

⑤常用單字片語集

從「④英文日記」中精選一些可以運用在其他情境或日常生活的單字及片語，記下這些表達方式，可以做為寫日記時的參考。

按照這些步驟，一天一篇日記，學習起來就沒有壓力了。

APRIL
4月

MAY
5月

JUNE
6月

JULY
7月

Contents

AUGUST
8月

SEPTEMBER
9月

OCTOBER
10 月

NOVEMBER
11 月

Contents

DECEMBER
12 月

JANUARY
1 月

FEBRUARY
2月

MARCH
3月

Contents

APRIL

I took my sister to Harajuku today.
今天我帶妹妹去原宿了。

It was her first time there, so she was really having fun.
這是她第一次來，所以她逛得很盡興。

She liked the bubble tea.
她尤其喜歡珍珠奶茶。

We had to wait in a long line, though...
不過排隊要排很久就是了⋯⋯

1 新人來了

New employees joined us

中文日記

今天來了幾個新人。

而我負責帶其中一個新人。

我有辦法好好教會他嗎……

總之，盡力就對了！

英文填空日記

Today we've got some new ____.
今天來了幾個新人。

And I'll be taking ____ of one of them.
而我負責帶其中一個新人。

But I don't know if I can teach him ____ …
我有辦法好好教會他嗎……

Anyway, I'll do my ____ !!
總之，盡力就對了！

英文日記

Today we've got some new employees.

And I'll be taking care of one of them.

But I don't know if I can teach him properly.

Anyway, I'll do my best!!

------------------------------ 常用單字片語集 ------------------------------

new employee
新進員工、新人
employee 指的是「員工」，加了一個 new 代表「新進員工」。

take care of ～
照看～
「照料」、「看顧」的意思。

properly
好好地、適當地、正確地
「好好地、適當地、正確地」的意思。

I'll do my best.
我會盡力。
do one's best 指的是「努力、盡力而為」的意思。

2 天氣比想像中暖和
Warmer than I thought

中文日記

今天比想像中還暖和。

早知道就不應該穿這麼厚的外套。

我都流汗了。

好想要一件春天穿的外套喔。

英文填空日記

It's warmer than I _____ today.
今天比想像中還暖和。

I shouldn't have chosen this _____ coat.
早知道就不應該穿這麼厚的外套。

I'm _____ .
我都流汗了。

I _____ a new spring jacket.
好想要一件春天穿的外套喔。

英文日記

It's warmer than I thought today.

I shouldn't have chosen this thick coat.

I'm sweating.

I want a new spring jacket.

常用單字片語集

warmer than I thought
比想像中還暖和
比較級＋than I thought 就是「比自己想像中還要～」的意思。

I shouldn't have done ～
我不應該～
should（應該～）的否定形＋「have ＋過去分詞」就會變成「我不應該～」。

sweat
流汗
sweat 本身是動詞，但常會搭配進行式，變成 I'm sweating. 來做使用。

thick
厚的
反義詞「薄的」會說 thin。

花粉害我鼻子好癢

The pollen makes me feel itchy

吼，我的鼻子好癢呀！

這個時期又來了！

眼睛好癢，完全沒辦法化妝。

花粉症真的好煩呀！

Ugh, my nose ⎯⎯⎯⎯⎯⎯!
吼，我的鼻子好癢呀！

This season is ⎯⎯⎯⎯⎯⎯ again!
這個時期又來了！

My eyes are also ⎯⎯⎯⎯⎯⎯, so I can't wear any makeup.
眼睛好癢，完全沒辦法化妝。

I really hate ⎯⎯⎯⎯⎯⎯ fever!
花粉症真的好煩呀！

Ugh, my nose tickles!

This season is here again!

My eyes are also itchy, so I can't wear any makeup.

I really hate hay fever!

------------------------------ 常用單字片語集 ------------------------------

My nose tickles.
鼻子發癢
tickle 有發癢的意思。

itchy
癢
和 tickle 的意思一樣，但 itchy 是形容詞，
記得前面一定要加上 be 動詞。

wear makeup
化妝
也會說成 put on makeup。

hay fever
花粉症
我們會說 I have hay fever.（我有花粉症）。

4 今天好睏

Sleepy today

中文日記

今天一整天都好睏啊！

一定是我昨晚熬夜看電視害的。

韓劇真是開始看就停不下來啊……

好想快點回家！

英文填空日記

I've been sleepy　　　　　day today!
今天一整天都好睏啊！

Because I stayed　　　　so late watching TV last night.
一定是我昨晚熬夜看電視害的。

**　　　　I start watching Korean TV dramas, I can never stop…**
韓劇真是開始看就停不下來啊……

I wanna go home　　　　!
好想快點回家！

英文日記

I've been sleepy all day today!

Because I stayed up so late watching TV last night.

Once I start watching Korean TV dramas, I can never stop…

I wanna go home now!

常用單字片語集

all day today
今天一整天
all day yesterday 就是「昨天一整天」。

stay up late
熬夜
stay up late -ing 就是「熬夜做某件事」的意思。

Once I starting, ...
一開始～就……
日常對話中的常用片語，學起來會很實用喔。

I wanna go home now.
好想快點回家。
now 一般指的是現在，但我們經常會以「立刻」來表示「快點」的語感。

和朋友去賞花

Cherry blossoms with friend

中文日記

今天我和朋友去公園賞櫻了。

超美的！

下次我也想看看晚上點燈的樣子，

一定很漂亮……

英文填空日記

Today I went to the park with my friend to see cherry _____.
今天我和朋友去公園賞櫻了。

It was so _____!
超美的！

Next time I wanna go see the ones _____ up at night.
下次我也想看看晚上點燈的樣子，

Must _____ amazing...
一定很漂亮……

英文日記

Today I went to the park with my friend to see cherry blossoms.

It was so beautiful!

Next time I wanna go see the ones lit up at night.

Must be amazing...

常用單字片語集

cherry blossom
櫻花
cherry blossom tree 就是「櫻花樹」的意思。

so beautiful
超美
想強調「超級、非常」的時候可以在形容詞前面加上 so 或 very。

lit up
點燈
lit 是 light 的過去分詞。

must be ～
一定會～
例句是省略掉 It must be amazing. 的 It。

6 和主管一起跑業務
Accompanied my boss

中文日記

今天和主管一起去 A 公司開會。

我們討論了新專案。

目前為止都還滿順利的。

接下來應該會很忙吧。

英文填空日記

I went to A Company with my boss to _____ a meeting today.
今天和主管一起去 A 公司開會。

We _____ the new project.
我們討論了新專案。

It seems to be going _____ so far.
目前為止都還滿順利的。

It's gonna be busy from _____ on.
接下來應該會很忙吧。

英文日記

I went to A Company with my boss to have a meeting today.

We discussed the new project.

It seems to be going well so far.

It's gonna be busy from now on.

- - - - - - - - - - - **常用單字片語集** - - - - - - - - - - -

have a meeting
開會
這時候搭配的動詞是 have。

discuss
討論
注意 discuss 後面不要加上 about 等介系詞。

go well
順利、順遂
工作場合上很常用的片語。

from now on
接下來
也可以說 from now 就好。

21

妹妹來找我玩

My sister is visiting me

明天妹妹就要來東京了。

她預計要住兩晚。

我要帶她去哪裡晃晃好呢？

她那麼喜歡逛街，原宿應該是不錯的選擇。

Tomorrow my sister is _____ to Tokyo.
明天妹妹就要來東京了。

She will stay here for two _____ .
她預計要住兩晚。

Where should I take her _____ ?
我要帶她去哪裡晃晃好呢？

Maybe Harajuku would be good because she _____ shopping.
她那麼喜歡逛街，原宿應該是不錯的選擇。

Tomorrow my sister is coming to Tokyo.

She will stay here for two nights.

Where should I take her around?

Maybe Harajuku would be good because she loves shopping.

常用單字片語集

be coming to ～
（預計）要來～
be -ing 表示未來即將發生的事。

stay for two nights
住兩晚
過夜會用 night 來表示，two nights and three days 就是「三天兩夜」的意思。

take ～ around
帶～到某處晃晃
描述「帶人到某個地方」時會用的片語，也可以用 show ～ around。

Maybe ～ would be good.
～應該是不錯的選擇。
日常對話常常用到的表現，使用 would 會帶有一種「應該還可以」的不確定語氣。

和妹妹一起在東京觀光

Sightseeing with my sis

中文日記

今天我帶妹妹去原宿了。

這是她第一次來，所以她逛得很盡興。

她尤其喜歡珍珠奶茶。

不過排隊要排很久就是了……

英文填空日記

I   my sister to Harajuku today.

今天我帶妹妹去原宿了。

It was her first   there, so she was really having fun.

這是她第一次來，所以她逛得很盡興。

She liked the   tea.

她尤其喜歡珍珠奶茶。

We had to wait in a long line,   …

不過排隊要排很久就是了……

英文日記

I took my sister to Harajuku today.

It was her first time there, so she was really having fun.

She liked the bubble tea.

We had to wait in a long line, though…

---- 常用單字片語集 ----

take ～ to ...
帶～到……
對話中常常會用到的基本句型。學起來吧！

have fun
盡興
跟 enjoy 是同樣的意思。可以說 Are you having fun?（你玩得盡興嗎？）

bubble tea
珍珠奶茶
也可以說 pearl milk tea 或 boba tea。

～ , though
～可是
這裡是當作副詞來用，但有時候 though 也可以做為連接詞。

黃金週的計畫
Plans for Golden Week

中文日記

今年黃金週的期間，我和沙織打算要去紐約，

所以我們今天擬了一些計畫。

我們兩個都愛逛街、愛吃美食，所以非常期待！

因此我得好好存錢才行！

英文填空日記

_____ this Golden Week, I'm going to New York with Saori,

今年黃金週的期間，我和沙織打算要去紐約，

so we _____ some plans today.

所以我們今天擬了一些計畫。

We _____ love shopping and eating, so we are very excited!!

我們兩個都愛逛街、愛吃美食，所以非常期待！

I have to _____ money for that!!

因此我得好好存錢才行！

英文日記

During this Golden Week, I'm going to New York with Saori,

so we made some plans today.

We both love shopping and eating, so we are very excited!!

I have to save money for that!!

常用單字片語集

during ～
～的期間
during summer（夏天的期間）、during the daytime（白天的期間）等，用法有很多。

we both ～
我們都～
當人數超過兩個人時，則使用 we all ～（我們都～）。

be excited
期待
在形容雀躍、興奮心情的時候常常會用到。

save money
存錢
可以說 save money for ～（為了～存錢）。

比起賞花……

Rather than cherry blossoms viewing...

中文日記

一邊賞花的時候，

一邊吃頓好料也不錯呀。

因為有很多攤販，

一時還不知道要挑哪個才好呢。

英文填空日記

It's also nice to have   food,
一邊賞花的時候，

**   seeing cherry blossoms.**
一邊吃頓好料也不錯呀。

There were a lot of food   ,
因為有很多攤販，

so I couldn't choose   one to try.
一時還不知道要挑哪個才好呢。

英文日記

It's also nice to have delicious food,

while seeing cherry blossoms.

There were a lot of food stands,

so I couldn't choose which one to try.

常用單字片語集

delicious
美味的
吃到美味的東西時最常使用的單字。

while -ing
一邊～
while 這個單字指的是「在～的時候」，有
很多種用法。

food stand
攤販
可以用這個單字表達常見的小吃攤或攤販。

which one
哪一個
Which one do you like?（你喜歡哪一個？）
是常見的用法。

今天休假
Day off today

昨晚喝太多了。

反正我今天休假，在家好好放鬆好了……

我每次放假總是這種模式。

好吧，這個週末來做點開心的事吧！

I   too much last night.
昨晚喝太多了。

But I'm   today, so I think I'm gonna relax at home…
反正我今天休假，在家好好放鬆好了……

I always end   spending holidays like this.
我每次放假總是這種模式。

**   , I'm gonna do something fun this weekend!**
好吧，這個週末來做點開心的事吧！

I drank too much last night.

But I'm off today, so I think I'm gonna relax at home…

I always end up spending holidays like this.

Alright, I'm gonna do something fun this weekend!

----------------------- 常用單字片語集 -----------------------

drink too much
喝太多
例句中使用的是 drink 的過去式 drank。

I'm off today.
我今天休假。
常會誤用成 Today is off.，但 I'm off today. 或 Today is my day off. 才是正確的喔。

always end up -ing ～
總是～
end up -ing ～有種「到頭來還是～」的意思，時常會搭配 always 一起使用。

alright
好吧。
alright 有很多種意思，這裡是傾向「好，來吧！」的感覺。

12 新的一週又開始了

Another week has started…

中文日記

唉，新的一週又開始了！

連假過後上班總是沒有幹勁啊。

但還是得打起精神來！

好，在那之前，我還是先來杯咖啡再休息一下吧……

英文填空日記

Oh nooo,　　　　week has started!!
唉，新的一週又開始了！

It's　　　　hard to get back to work after a long weekend.
連假過後上班總是沒有幹勁啊。

But I gotta　　　　myself!!
但還是得打起精神來！

Well, before that,　　　　me take a little coffee break…
好，在那之前，我還是先來杯咖啡再休息一下吧……

英文日記

Oh nooo, another week has started!!

It's always hard to get back to work after a long weekend.

But I gotta push myself!!

Well, before that, let me take a little coffee break…

常用單字片語集

It's always ~ to ...
……總是～
這裡 always 的後面要接形容詞。

gotta ~
還是得～
gotta 是 got to 的結合，想用比較隨興的語氣表達「還是得～」的時候，常常會使用這個詞。

push oneself
打起精神來、努力
push oneself 直譯的話，就是「推自己一把」，語感上來說更貼近「鼓舞自己」、「努力」的意思。

let me ~
我還是先來～
let me do ～其實是「先讓我～」的意思，但也可以用在「我還是先來～」這種自言自語的時候。

27

13 在客戶公司裡巧遇大介

Ran into Daisuke

中文日記

今天去 A 公司的時候，竟然遇見大介了！

他是我的高中同學。

太巧了吧！

我常常會到 A 公司去，搞不好還會碰到他呢。

英文填空日記

When I visited A Company today, I _____ into Daisuke!

今天去 A 公司的時候，竟然遇見大介了！

He is one of my _____ from high school.

他是我的高中同學。

What a _____ !

太巧了吧！

I _____ see him again cause I visit A Company often.

我常常會到 A 公司去，搞不好還會碰到他呢。

英文日記

When I visited A Company today, I ran into Daisuke!

He is one of my classmates from high school.

What a coincidence!

I might see him again cause I visit A Company often.

常用單字片語集

run into ～
巧遇～
描述和某個人湊巧碰見的情況。

classmate
同儕、同學
也可以說 We were in the same high school.
（我們讀同間高中）。

What a coincidence!
太巧了吧！
這是常用句型，把整句記下來吧。

might ～
搞不好～
用來描述一件不確定的事。

14 打掃浴室
Cleaning the bathroom

中文日記

今天我打掃了浴室。

排水孔卡了一堆頭髮！

因為我的頭髮很長，動不動就會卡住。

我以後應該要更常清理。

英文填空日記

Today I _____ **the bathroom.**
今天我打掃了浴室。

And I found a lot of hair in the _____ **!!**
排水孔卡了一堆頭髮！

Since I have long hair, it's easily _____ **in there.**
因為我的頭髮很長，動不動就會卡住。

I should clean it more _____ **.**
我以後應該要更常清理。

英文日記

Today I cleaned the bathroom.

And I found a lot of hair in the drain!!

Since I have long hair, it's easily stuck in there.

I should clean it more often.

常用單字片語集

clean the bathroom
打掃浴室
也常說 clean the room（打掃房間）。

drain
排水孔
浴室以外的排水孔一樣是用這個單字。

be stuck
卡住
stuck 是 stick 的過去式、過去分詞。

more often
更加頻繁
often 是「頻繁、經常」的意思。

15 奶奶打電話來了

Call from grandma

中文日記

今天奶奶打電話給我，

她說：「東京應該還很冷吧？

小心別感冒了！」

奶奶啊，東京跟大阪氣溫差不多啊。

英文填空日記

My _____ just called me today and said,

今天奶奶打電話給我，

"It's _____ cold in Tokyo, isn't it?

她說：「東京應該還很冷吧？

Be _____ not to catch a cold!"

小心別感冒了！」

Grandma, there's not much _____ between Osaka and Tokyo.

奶奶啊，東京跟大阪氣溫差不多啊。

英文日記

My grandma just called me today and said,

"It's still cold in Tokyo, isn't it?

Be careful not to catch a cold!"

Grandma, there's not much difference between Osaka and Tokyo.

常用單字片語集

grandma
奶奶
比 grandmother 更口語化的說法。

still
還
在討論天氣「還很冷」、「還很熱」的時候可以用這個單字。

Be careful.
小心
也可以只說 Careful!。

difference between ～ and...
～和……的差別
考試也會常常出現的固定句型。

放假閒閒沒事做

Nothing to do…

中文日記

我今天休假。

但沒事做！

我在想要不要去散散步……

不過外面好像有點冷……

英文填空日記

I'm   today.
我今天休假。

But I have   to do!
但沒事做！

I'll go   a walk maybe…
我在想要不要去散散步……

But it's   cold outside…
不過外面好像有點冷……

英文日記

I'm off today.

But I have nothing to do!

I'll go for a walk maybe…

But it's kinda cold outside…

常用單字片語集

I'm off.
我休假。
也可以說 Today's my day off.。

have nothing to do
沒事做
將 nothing 改成 something 的話，就會變成「有些事要做」。

go for a walk
去散步
take a walk 也是相同的意思。

kinda
有點
將 kind of 縮短後的口語用詞。

爸爸傳簡訊來了
Got a message from dad

中文日記

爸爸傳簡訊來了，

問我：「下次什麼時候回來？」

我上個月才剛回去過啊！

所以我回他：「我還不知道。」

英文填空日記

My dad just   me like,
爸爸傳簡訊來了，

"When are you gonna come back home   time?"
問我：「下次什麼時候回來？」

I just went   home last month!
我上個月才剛回去過啊！

So I said, "I don't know   ."
所以我回他：「我還不知道。」

英文日記

My dad just texted me like,

"When are you gonna come back home next time?"

I just went back home last month!

So I said, "I don't know yet."

常用單字片語集

text
傳簡訊
用手機傳送的訊息，我們會用 text 而不是 mail。

next time
下次
這個片語前面不用搭配 in 或 on 這些介系詞，要多加留意。

go back home
回家
一般會用 go back to ～來表示「回去～」，但 go back home 的 home 前面是不用加介系詞的。

I don't know yet.
我還不知道。
yet 通常會和完成式一起使用，但也會像這樣和現在式一起使用。

18 在 A 公司看見大介

Saw Daisuke at A Company

中文日記

我去拜訪 A 公司的時候，

看見大介在工作的樣子。

他看起來很專注，

所以我就沒有跟他搭話，直接離開了。

英文填空日記

When I　　　　　A Company,
我去拜訪 A 公司的時候，

I saw Daisuke　　　　　.
看見大介在工作的樣子。

He　　　　　very serious,
他看起來很專注，

so I left there　　　　　talking to him.
所以我就沒有跟他搭話，直接離開了。

英文日記

When I visited A Company,

I saw Daisuke working.

He looked very serious,

so I left there without talking to him.

常用單字片語集

visit ～
拜訪～
～可以填人名、公司名或地點。

see 人 -ing
看見某人在～
see 的過去式是 saw，屬於不規則變化。

look ＋形容詞
看起來很～
可以搭配各式各樣的形容詞。

without -ing
沒有～
非常實用的片語，最好記起來。

33

買到的草莓酸死了

Sour strawberries

今天突然很想吃草莓，

所以我就買回家吃了。

結果超級酸的！

有種被騙了的感覺。

I　　　　　like eating strawberries today,
今天突然很想吃草莓，

so I bought some and ate　　　　　home.
所以我就買回家吃了。

But those were too　　　　　!
結果超級酸的！

I felt like I was　　　　　off.
有種被騙了的感覺。

I felt like eating strawberries today,

so I bought some and ate at home.

But those were too sour!

I felt like I was ripped off.

常用單字片語集

feel like -ing
想～
feel 的過去式是 felt，屬於不規則變化，要多加留意。

at home
在家裡
go home（回家）這個片語的 home 之前不用加介系詞，但「在家裡」的時候就要補上一個 at。

sour
酸的
sour cream 指的就是「酸奶油」。

rip off
騙人、詐欺
be ripped off 是「被騙了」，語感上有「被敲詐」、「很虧」的感覺。

20 跳電了
Blew a fuse!

中文日記

昨天跳電了。

因為我同時用了吹風機和微波爐。

我還得去重開總電源，

要在烏漆墨黑的房間裡走路有點恐怖啊。

英文填空日記

I　　　　　 a fuse yesterday.
昨天跳電了。

Because I used two appliances at the　　　　　 time.
因為我同時用了吹風機和微波爐。

I had to go　　　　　 it on,
我還得去重開總電源，

though it was kinda　　　　　 to walk in the dark room.
要在烏漆墨黑的房間裡走路有點恐怖啊。

英文日記

I blew a fuse yesterday.

Because I used two appliances at the same time.

I had to go turn it on,

though it was kinda scary to walk in the dark room.

常用單字片語集

blow a fuse
跳電
a breaker trips 也是相同的意思。

at the same time
同時
很實用的片語，直接記下來吧。

turn on
開啟
常用在開啟電燈或電源開關的時候，要特別注意 it 擺放的位置。

scary
恐怖的
當主詞是人的時候，要改成 I'm scared.。

公司的電腦怪怪的

Something wrong with the PC

中文日記

唉，我的電腦怪怪的！

偏偏我今天積了很多要做的事。

完蛋了！

明天得接著繼續做了。

英文填空日記

Urgh, there's something　　　　 with my computer!
唉，我的電腦怪怪的！

Today I have a lot of work　　　 up,
偏偏我今天積了很多要做的事。

but I'm　　　　 !
完蛋了！

I'll carry them　　　　 to tomorrow.
明天得接著繼續做了。

英文日記

Urgh, there's something wrong with my computer!

Today I have a lot of work piled up,

but I'm stuck!

I'll carry them over to tomorrow.

常用單字片語集

There's something wrong with ～ .
～怪怪的。
可以用來形容機器故障或狀態不佳。

piled up
堆積
piled up 是「堆積」的意思，可以用來表示累積不少工作的狀態。

I'm stuck!
完蛋了！
用來形容束手無策的情況。

carry ～ over to...
接著繼續～
這裡的 carry 有「帶著、接著」的意思。

經痛讓我好煩躁

Irritated with a period pain

中文日記

我今天經痛。

但是我忘記帶止痛藥了。

我在生理期的時候都會很煩躁。

好想快點回家躺著休息呀！

英文填空日記

I'm having   .

我今天經痛。

But I forgot to bring a pain   today.

但是我忘記帶止痛藥了。

I always get irritated easily when I'm having my   .

我在生理期的時候都會很煩躁。

I wanna go home and   down now!

好想快點回家躺著休息呀！

英文日記

I'm having cramps.

But I forgot to bring a pain killer today.

I always get irritated easily when I'm having my period.

I wanna go home and lie down now!

--------- 常用單字片語集 ---------

have cramps
經痛
經痛的正確說法應該是 menstrual pains，
但在日常對話中會用 cramps。

pain killer
止痛藥
多指頭痛藥或止痛藥。

have one's period
生理期
「我現在生理期。」也可以說 I'm on my
period.。

lie down
躺下
lie down on the bed（躺在床上）是很常用
的片語。

長痘痘了
Oh no, pimples!

中文日記

額頭長痘痘了！

最近作息不是很規律。

這可能就是原因吧……

得調整一下才行。

英文填空日記

I've got pimples on my ⎯⎯⎯⎯⎯!
額頭長痘痘了！

My life has been ⎯⎯⎯⎯⎯ these days.
最近作息不是很規律。

Maybe that's ⎯⎯⎯ …
這可能就是原因吧……

I have to ⎯⎯⎯⎯⎯ it.
得調整一下才行。

英文日記

I've got pimples on my forehead!

My life has been irregular these days.

Maybe that's why…

I have to fix it.

常用單字片語集

forehead
額頭
日常對話中經常會提到身體部位，好好記下來吧。

irregular
不規律
regular（規律的）的反義詞。

that's why
這就是原因吧
要小心不要和 because 搞混了。

fix
調整
通常用來指「修理東西」，但「調整生活習慣」也是用這個動詞。

資料跑到哪裡去了？

Where did it go!?

中文日記

糟了，我把那張紙放到哪裡去了？

我以為我放在桌上！

是不是有人拿走了呢？

我找不到啦！

英文填空日記

Oh my god, where ___ I put the paper!?
糟了，我把那張紙放到哪裡去了？

I thought I ___ it on my desk!
我以為我放在桌上！

Did ___ take it?
是不是有人拿走了呢？

I can't ___ it!
我找不到啦！

英文日記

Oh my god, where did I put the paper!?

I thought I put it on my desk!

Did somebody take it?

I can't find it!

常用單字片語集

did I 〜 ?
我〜了？
也可以說 I wonder 〜，但這個句型是最簡單實用的。

put 〜 on...
把〜放在……上面
put 有「擺」、「放」的意思，可以搭配各種介系詞來使用。

Did somebody 〜 ?
是不是有人〜了？
自言自語或是詢問所有人的時候，都可以這麼說。

I can't find it!
我找不到！
也可以省略主詞，直接說 Can't find it!。

今天的運勢是……

Today's fortune

中文日記

今天早上看新聞的時候，

新聞說我的星座今天運勢很好！

我的幸運物是茄子！

呃，我不敢吃啊……

英文填空日記

When I was watching the news _____ morning,

今天早上看新聞的時候，

they said that my _____ today was lucky!

新聞說我的星座今天運勢很好！

My lucky _____ is eggplant!

我的幸運物是茄子！

_____ , I can't eat it...

呃，我不敢吃啊……

英文日記

When I was watching the news this morning,

they said that my horoscope today was lucky!

My lucky charm is eggplant!

Oops, I can't eat it...

------------ 常用單字片語集 ------------

this morning
今天早上
除此之外，還有許多用 this 表示時間、日期的片語，像是 this week（這個星期）等。

horoscope
星座運勢
可以把這個單字和自己星座的英文一起記下來喔。

lucky charm
幸運物

oops
哎唷、呃
口語對話經常會出現的感嘆詞。

26 咖啡灑到桌上了
Spilled coffee

中文日記

我把咖啡灑到桌上了！

還好重要文件沒有遭殃。

呼，幸好。

我得更加小心才行！

英文填空日記

I   my coffee on the desk!
我把咖啡灑到桌上了！

But I didn't   it on my important documents.
還好重要文件沒有遭殃。

**   , what a relief!**
呼，幸好。

I've gotta be   careful!
我得更加小心才行！

英文日記

I spilled my coffee on the desk!

But I didn't get it on my important documents.

Phew, what a relief!

I've gotta be more careful!

常用單字片語集

spill
灑
打翻飲料時會用的動詞。

get ～ on...
波及……
get 除了「拿取」以外還有很多種意思。

phew
呼
鬆一口氣時會使用的感嘆詞。

be more careful
更加小心
要注意 more 擺放的位置。

頭髮好毛躁
Messy hair

我的頭髮今天好毛躁啊！

一定是因為昨晚沒把頭髮吹乾……

我怎麼能頂著一頭亂髮去上班呀！

還是紮起來吧。

My hair is   today!
我的頭髮今天好毛躁啊！

Because I didn't   my hair last night…
一定是因為昨晚沒把頭髮吹乾……

But I can't go to work with this   hair!
我怎麼能頂著一頭亂髮去上班呀！

I'll   it back for now.
還是紮起來吧。

My hair is messy today!

Because I didn't dry my hair last night…

But I can't go to work with this ruffled hair!

I'll tie it back for now.

常用單字片語集

messy
毛躁
也可以用來表示「雜亂」。

dry one's hair
吹乾頭髮
dry（烘乾、吹乾）這個動詞也可以用在頭髮以外的東西上。

ruffled
雜亂的
這個單字也可以取代 messy。

tie back
紮在腦後
也可以說 do a ponytail（綁馬尾）。

收到朋友的喜帖
Invitation for a wedding ceremony

中文日記

今天我收到朋友的喜帖了！

她的婚禮要辦在六月六日！

我一定會參加的！

好好奇還有誰要去喔。

英文填空日記

Today I got an _____ letter from my friend!
今天我收到朋友的喜帖了！

She's going to have a wedding _____ on 6th June!
她的婚禮要辦在六月六日！

I'll _____ go!
我一定會參加的！

I wonder who _____ will go.
好好奇還有誰要去喔。

英文日記

Today I got an invitation letter from my friend!

She's going to have a wedding ceremony on 6th June!

I'll definitely go!

I wonder who else will go.

常用單字片語集

invitation letter
邀請函
invite（邀請）這個動詞也經常用到。

wedding ceremony
婚禮
ceremony（典禮）可以和許多單字組合在一起。

definitely
一定
和 absolutely 是相同意思。

else
其他人
else 常接於 how、what、where、who 等詞之後，表示「其他、別的」，如 who else、what else。

健康檢查有問題
Something wrong with my checkup results

中文日記

我之前做了健康檢查，

檢查結果好像有點問題。

必須再重新檢查一次，

我有點擔心。

英文填空日記

I had a medical ⬚⬚⬚⬚ a while ago,
我之前做了健康檢查，

but there was ⬚⬚⬚⬚ wrong with my results.
檢查結果好像有點問題。

I have to go take it ⬚⬚⬚⬚.
必須再重新檢查一次，

I'm a bit ⬚⬚⬚⬚ now.
我有點擔心。

英文日記

I had a medical checkup a while ago,

but there was something wrong with my results.

I have to go take it again.

I'm a bit worried now.

- - - - - - - - - - - - - - - 常用單字片語集 - - - - - - - - - - - -

medical checkup
健康檢查
只說 checkup 也通用。

There is something wrong.
有點問題。
經常會加上 with，變成 There is something wrong with ～（～有點問題）。

again
再一次
常用單字，有「重新、再一次」的意思。

be worried
擔心
也可以加上 about ～，變成「擔心～」。

被外國人問路

A foreigner talked to me

中文日記

今天有個觀光客用英文跟我搭話。

聽起來像是在問路，

但我完全聽不懂他的英文。

要是我能流利地説英文就好了……

英文填空日記

Today one tourist _____ to me in English.
今天有個觀光客用英文跟我搭話。

He seemed to be asking me _____,
聽起來像是在問路，

but I didn't understand his English _____ all.
但我完全聽不懂他的英文。

I wish I could speak English _____…
要是我能流利地説英文就好了……

英文日記

Today one tourist talked to me in English.

He seemed to be asking me directions,

but I didn't understand his English at all.

I wish I could speak English fluently…

常用單字片語集

talk to ～
和～搭話、說話
也可以説 speak to ～。

ask directions
問路
direction 是「方向」的意思，通常會用這個片語來表示問路。

at all
完全
會和否定句一起使用。

fluently
流利地
順便把它的形容詞 fluent（流暢的）一起記下來吧。

MAY

5 月

Such nice weather today!
今天天氣真好！
I'll get off one station before and take a walk!
我要提早一站下車，走一走！
I haven't been doing any exercise recently,
最近都沒運動，
and it's good to burn calories!
這樣還可以消耗卡路里呢！

今天好忙
Busy day today

中文日記

今天真是忙碌的一天呀！

兩個會議、一個報告，上門的客戶還不少。

累死人了！

好想快點回家好好休息呀！

英文填空日記

_____ a busy day today!!
今天真是忙碌的一天呀！

I had two meetings, one presentation, and a _____ of visitors.
兩個會議、一個報告，上門的客戶還不少。

I'm _____ !
累死人了！

I wanna go home and have a _____ now!!
好想快點回家好好休息呀！

英文日記

Such a busy day today!!

I had two meetings, one presentation, and a lot of visitors.

I'm exhausted!

I wanna go home and have a rest now!!

------------------------- 常用單字片語集 -------------------------

such a ～ day
真是～的一天
用 It was such a busy day. 也可以。such a ～是個很常用的片語，可以記下來。

a lot of ～
很多的～
many 也是同樣的意思。

be exhausted
非常疲憊
比 tired（累）還要更疲勞的說法。

have a rest
放鬆、休息
take a rest 也是同樣的意思。

準備旅行的行李

Packing for my travel

中文日記

我現在正在準備去紐約旅遊的行李。

該帶什麼衣服去才好呢？

這還是我第一次去紐約。

期待到睡不著覺啦！

英文填空日記

Now I'm   my stuff for the NY trip.
我現在正在準備去紐約旅遊的行李。

What   of clothes should I take?
該帶什麼衣服去才好呢？

It's my first   to go to NY.
這還是我第一次去紐約。

I'm   excited to sleep!
期待到睡不著覺啦！

英文日記

Now I'm packing my stuff for the NY trip.

What kind of clothes should I take?

It's my first time to go to NY.

I'm too excited to sleep!

常用單字片語集

pack one's stuff
收拾行李
stuff 是指「東西、物品」。

what kind of ~
什麼樣的~
What kind of food do you like?（你喜歡吃什麼樣的食物？）是對話中常出現的句型。

It's my first time to ~ .
這是我第一次~。
也可以說 I go to NY for the first time.（我第一次去紐約）。

too ~ to...
太~沒辦法……
一般對話中經常用到的句型，記下來吧。

我們來啦！紐約！

雖然有點涼，但天氣很好！

該做什麼才好呢……逛街？

我還要買些伴手禮給家人呢！

**　　　　　　 we are! New York!**
我們來啦！紐約！

It's a little bit　　　　, but the weather is nice!
雖然有點涼，但天氣很好！

What should we do　　　　… shopping?
該做什麼才好呢……逛街？

I gotta buy some　　　　 for my family, too!
我還要買些伴手禮給家人呢！

Here we are! New York!

It's a little bit chilly, but the weather is nice!

What should we do first… shopping?

I gotta buy some souvenirs for my family, too!

------------------------------ 常用單字片語集 ------------------------------

Here we are!
我們來了！
抵達目的地的時候經常說的台詞。

chilly
微涼
cold 是「冷」的意思，但還不到寒冷的程度的話，就可以用這個單字表達「微涼」的感覺。

first
先
也經常用來當作「首先」的意思。

souvenir
伴手禮
觀光景點的伴手禮專賣店就會在看板上寫這個單字。

提到購物就不能錯過紐約

Shopping is a must in NY

中文日記

到了紐約，

第一件事就是逛街啦！

所有知名品牌都聚集在這個城市了。

我的錢包可能要大失血了……

英文填空日記

When you ____ in NY,
到了紐約，

the ____ thing you gotta do is shopping!
第一件事就是逛街啦！

All the famous brands are ____ in this city.
所有知名品牌都聚集在這個城市了。

I think I'm gonna ____ my money…
我的錢包可能要大失血了……

英文日記

When you arrive in NY,

the first thing you gotta do is shopping!

All the famous brands are gathering in this city.

I think I'm gonna blow my money…

- - - - - - - - - - 常用單字片語集 - - - - - - - - - -

arrive in ～
抵達～
連同介系詞一起記下來吧。

The first thing you gotta do is ～.
第一件事就是～。
日常生活中經常用到的實用句型，整句一起記下來吧。

gather
聚集
無論是表示人、物品還是店家的聚集，都可以用這個單字。

blow one's money
噴錢、錢包大失血
用 blow（噴飛）來表示花了很多錢。

紐約好多高雅的咖啡店

Fancy cafes in NY

中文日記

紐約好多高雅的咖啡店呀！

我想去那間我在雜誌上看到的店！

他們的蛋糕看起來超好吃的！

希望到時候不會大排長龍。

英文填空日記

There are so many　　　　　cafes in NY!

紐約好多高雅的咖啡店呀！

I wanna go to the one I　　　　　in the magazine!

我想去那間我在雜誌上看到的店！

The cakes there　　　　　really good!

他們的蛋糕看起來超好吃的！

Hope they're not　　　　　up.

希望到時候不會大排長龍。

英文日記

There are so many fancy cafes in NY!

I wanna go to the one I saw in the magazine!

The cakes there looked really good!

Hope they're not lining up.

常用單字片語集

fancy
高雅、時髦
除此之外，也可以說 cool 或 trendy 等。

saw
看到
see（看）的過去式，屬於不規則變化，要多加留意。

look good
看起來很好吃
看見食物想表達「看起來很好吃」的時候經常會這麼說。

line up
排隊
line 做為名詞是「列」的意思。現在進行式加上 ing 的時候要注意拼字。

五月 6

最後一天，真不想回日本

Only one day left!

中文日記

天呀，已經是紐約旅遊的最後一天了嗎？

只剩一天了！

時間過得太快了吧！

我還有好多想去的地方呀！

英文填空日記

Oh my god, it's already the ⎯⎯⎯ day in NY!?
天呀，已經是紐約旅遊的最後一天了嗎？

Only one day ⎯⎯⎯!
只剩一天了！

Time passed ⎯⎯⎯ so quickly!
時間過得太快了吧！

I ⎯⎯⎯ have so many places to go!
我還有好多想去的地方呀！

英文日記

Oh my god, it's already the last day in NY!?

Only one day left!

Time passed by so quickly!

I still have so many places to go!

常用單字片語集

the last day
最後一天
「第一天」則是 the first day。

only ～ day(s) left
只剩～天
剩餘天數是複數時，要改為複數形的 days。

pass by
經過
「從旁邊經過」也是用這個片語。

still
還有
要注意不要和 yet 混用了。

53

紐約太棒了！

NY was amazing!

中文日記

噢，紐約真是太棒了！

自由女神像比我預期中的還要大。

每間店和餐廳都很好。

千萬別問我花了多少……

英文填空日記

Oh my god, NY was　　　　　!

噢，紐約真是太棒了！

The Statue of　　　　　was bigger than I expected.

自由女神像比我預期中的還要大。

And the shops and restaurants were　　　　　nice.

每間店和餐廳都很好。

Don't ask me how much I　　　　…

千萬別問我花了多少……

英文日記

Oh my god, NY was amazing!

The Statue of Liberty was bigger than I expected.

And the shops and restaurants were all nice.

Don't ask me how much I spent…

常用單字片語集

the Statue of Liberty
自由女神像
結合 statue（銅像）和 liberty（自由），就是 the Statue of Liberty（自由女神像）了。

bigger than I expected
比預期中的要來得大
使用比較級 bigger than ～的表現手法。

all nice
都很好
nice 的部分可以變更成其他形容詞。

how much I spent
我花了多少
spent 是 spend 的過去式。

該面對現實了

Back to reality

中文日記

該回歸現實了……

我有好多事要做。

真好奇我今天可以幾點離開公司呢……

我想回去紐約了！

英文填空日記

to reality now…
該回歸現實了……

I've got a lot of   to do.
我有好多事要做。

what time I can leave the office today…
真好奇我今天可以幾點離開公司呢……

I wanna go   to New York!!
我想回去紐約了！

英文日記

Back to reality now…

I've got a lot of things to do.

Wonder what time I can leave the office today…

I wanna go back to New York!!

- - - - - - - - - - - - 常用單字片語集 - - - - - - - - - - - -

back to reality
回到現實
表達「從快樂的情境被拉回現實」的常見表現手法。

I've got a lot of things to do.
我有好多事情要做。
也可以說 I have ～。

wonder ～
真好奇～
I wonder ～省略掉主詞的說法，日常對話中經常出現。

go back to ～
回去～
只要在 go to ～（去～）加上一個 back 就會變成「回去」的意思。

55

一整天的文書作業
Desk work the whole day

今天一整天都在處理文書作業。

長時間坐在電腦前面，肩膀好僵硬。

聽說瑜伽能緩解肩膀僵硬，

我今天要不要去上個瑜伽課呢……

Today I spent the   day doing desk work.
今天一整天都在處理文書作業。

I get   shoulders by working on the computer for long hours.
長時間坐在電腦前面，肩膀好僵硬。

I   yoga is good for stiff shoulders,
聽說瑜伽能緩解肩膀僵硬，

so I'll go   lessons today…
我今天要不要去上個瑜伽課呢……

Today I spent the whole day doing desk work.

I get stiff shoulders by working on the computer for long hours.

I heard yoga is good for stiff shoulders,

so I'll go take lessons today…

常用單字片語集

spend the whole day -ing
一整天都在~
可以用來表達「一整天都在做某件事」。

I heard ~ .
聽說~。
可以用來表示「聽說」、「好像」。

stiff shoulders
肩膀僵硬
也可以說是 stiff neck。

go take lessons
去上課
省略了 go to take lessons 的 to。

五月 10 又遇見大介了

Bumped into Daisuke again

中文日記

我又碰巧遇見大介了。

稍微聊了幾句，

約好下週末要一起去喝酒。

好期待下週末喔！

英文填空日記

I bumped _____ Daisuke again.
我又碰巧遇見大介了。

We just had a _____ ,
稍微聊了幾句，

and _____ to go for a drink next weekend.
約好下週末要一起去喝酒。

_____ wait for the next weekend!
好期待下週末喔！

英文日記

I bumped into Daisuke again.

We just had a chat,

and promised to go for a drink next weekend.

Can't wait for the next weekend!

- - - - - - - - - - - - - - - - - - - 常用單字片語集 - - - - - - - - - - - - - - -

bump into ～
碰巧遇見～
跟 run into 同樣意思。

have a chat
聊幾句
用來表示沒有特定目的的談話。

promise to do ～
約好要～
也可以說 make a promise。

Can't wait for ～ .
好期待～。
省略了 I can't wait ～ . 中的主詞 I，是更口語化的說法。

一口氣追完劇

Watching TV dramas all at once

中文日記

週末終於來啦！

我今天一整天都要窩在家裡！

現在正打算一口氣看完預錄好的電視劇。

晚點叫個披薩外送好了……

英文填空日記

_____, the weekend!!
週末終於來啦！

I'll _____ home all day today!!
我今天一整天都要窩在家裡！

Now I'm watching the recorded TV dramas all _____ once.
現在正打算一口氣看完預錄好的電視劇。

I think I'll order pizza _____ later…
晚點叫個披薩外送好了……

英文日記

Finally, the weekend!!

I'll stay home all day today!!

Now I'm watching the recorded TV dramas all at once.

I think I'll order pizza delivery later…

常用單字片語集

Finally, the weekend!!
週末終於來啦！
省略了 be 動詞，是更加口語化的說法，日常對話中也經常這麼說。

stay home
窩在家裡
跟 relax at home 是同樣意思。

all at once
一口氣
「一次看完電視劇」，即「一口氣追完劇」的意思。

pizza delivery
披薩外送
如果是其他食物外送可以說 food delivery。

五月
12

去上瑜伽課

Yoga day

中文日記

今天我去上瑜伽課了。

其實我在紐約大吃大喝以後變胖了一點點。

今天的課程累死人了！

但為了要瘦下來，我得堅持下去……

英文填空日記

Today I _____ to do yoga.

今天我去上瑜伽課了。

_____, I gained some weight cause I ate too much in NY.

其實我在紐約大吃大喝以後變胖了一點點。

The lesson today was _____ me!

今天的課程累死人了！

But I gotta keep it _____ to lose some weight…

但為了要瘦下來，我得堅持下去……

英文日記

Today I went to do yoga.

Actually, I gained some weight cause I ate too much in NY.

The lesson today was killing me!

But I gotta keep it up to lose some weight…

常用單字片語集

actually
其實
也可以用 to be honest，但情境並沒有那麼嚴肅，所以通常用 actually 就可以了。

gain some weight
變胖了一點點
也可以用 put on 代替 gain。

killing me
非常累、疲憊
直譯是「簡直要殺了我」，但一般會用在「煎熬、疲倦」的情況。

keep it up
繼續努力、堅持
在鼓舞別人的時候也可以說 Keep it up!（加油！）

13 下班後和同事吃飯

Dinner after work

中文日記

今天下班之後，我和同事去吃飯了。

吃吃喝喝了一頓，超開心的。

那間店的東西真的很好吃！

下次我想帶爸媽去吃吃看。

英文填空日記

Today I had dinner with my colleagues   work.
今天下班之後，我和同事去吃飯了。

We   and drank a lot. It was really fun.
吃吃喝喝了一頓，超開心的。

The food there was   !
那間店的東西真的很好吃！

I wanna   my parents there next time.
下次我想帶爸媽去吃吃看。

英文日記

Today I had dinner with my colleagues after work.

We ate and drank a lot. It was really fun.

The food there was amazing!

I wanna take my parents there next time.

- - - - - - - - - - - 常用單字片語集 - - - - - - - - - - -

after work
下班之後
如果是放學，就可以說 after school（放學之後）。

amazing
很好吃
原本只是表示「很棒」的單字，但在形容食物很美味的時候也可以用這個詞。

eat and drink
吃吃喝喝
想表達「吃喝、飲食」都可以用這個片語。

take ～ there
帶～去
要留意不可以寫成 to there 喔。

14 今天有點熱

Kinda hot today

中文日記

今天有點熱！

白天幾乎不需要穿外套了。

不過聽說明天會降溫到十度以下……

得小心不要感冒了。

英文填空日記

It was _____ hot today!
今天有點熱！

I actually didn't need a _____ during the daytime.
白天幾乎不需要穿外套了。

But it's going to be _____ than 10 degrees tomorrow.
不過聽說明天會降溫到十度以下……

I should be _____ not to catch a cold.
得小心不要感冒了。

英文日記

It was kinda hot today!

I actually didn't need a jacket during the daytime.

But it's going to be less than 10 degrees tomorrow.

I should be careful not to catch a cold.

常用單字片語集

kinda
有點、稍微
將 kind of 縮短後的口語用詞。

jacket
外套
一般通稱「外套」為 jacket。

less than ～
～以下
也可以用在氣溫以外的情況，表示「比～還少」的意思。

be careful not to ～
小心不要～
要特別留意 not 擺放的位置。

影印機怪怪的
Something wrong with the copy machine

公司的影印機怪怪的。

得聯絡維修人員來修理。

偏偏今天有很多要處理的工作，

好煩躁啊！

There's something   with the copy machine in the office.
公司的影印機怪怪的。

I have to call   to fix it.
得聯絡維修人員來修理。

I have a lot of work   do today,
偏偏今天有很多要處理的工作，

and this   me so irritated!!
好煩躁啊！

There's something wrong with the copy machine in the office.

I have to call someone to fix it.

I have a lot of work to do today,

and this makes me so irritated!!

常用單字片語集

There's something wrong with~.
～怪怪的。
可以用在形容機器故障或狀態不佳的時候。

call someone to fix
聯絡維修人員
「叫個能修理的人」，即「聯絡維修人員」的意思。

have a lot of work to do
有很多要處理的工作
把 work 改成 things 就會變成「有很多要做的事」。

make me irritated
感到煩躁
直譯會是「讓我很煩躁」，但可以用來表達「好煩躁」的心情。

和朋友一起 BBQ

BBQ with friends

中文日記

今天和朋友一起 BBQ 了。

沙織找了好幾個朋友來，

大家人都很親切！

我也玩得很開心。

英文填空日記

Today I a barbecue with my friends.
今天和朋友一起 BBQ 了。

Saori invited of her friends,
沙織找了好幾個朋友來，

who were very nice!
大家人都很親切！

I a great time.
我也玩得很開心。

英文日記

Today I had a barbecue with my friends.

Saori invited some of her friends,

who were all very nice!

I had a great time.

常用單字片語集

have a barbecue
BBQ（烤肉）
也常説 barbecue party（烤肉派對）。

some of one's friends
某人的一些朋友
只有一個朋友的話，就是 one of one's friends。

all very nice
人都很親切
注意 all 擺放的位置。

have a great time
玩得很開心
在表達「很開心、很愉快」的時候可以用的片語。

倒垃圾
Take out the trash

中文日記

我這個笨蛋！

我又忘記拿垃圾出去丟了！

這已經是這個月第三次了……

為什麼我每次都會忘記呀！

英文填空日記

I'm such an ＿＿＿＿！
我這個笨蛋！

I forgot to ＿＿＿＿ out the trash again!
我又忘記拿垃圾出去丟了！

This is the third ＿＿＿＿ this month...
這已經是這個月第三次了……

Why do I ＿＿＿＿ forget this?
為什麼我每次都會忘記呀！

英文日記

I'm such an idiot!

I forgot to take out the trash again!

This is the third time this month...

Why do I always forget this?

常用單字片語集

I'm such an idiot!
我這個笨蛋！
such a ～是「我這個～」的意思。

forget to ～
忘記～
還有類似 Don't forget to take out the trash!
（別忘記倒垃圾！）的表現手法。

take out the trash
倒垃圾
take out 是「拿出去」的意思。

Why do I always forget this!?
為什麼我每次都會忘記呀！
日常對話中經常會用到，可以把整個句子一起記下來。

五月 18 又吃太撐了

Ate too much again

中文日記

昨天又吃太撐了！

但我也沒辦法呀，

因為是吃到飽嘛……

明天再開始減肥吧……

英文填空日記

Yesterday, I ate too   again!!
昨天又吃太撐了！

But I couldn't   it,
但我也沒辦法呀，

because it was   …
因為是吃到飽嘛……

I'll   on a diet from tomorrow…
明天再開始減肥吧……

英文日記

Yesterday, I ate too much again!!

But I couldn't help it,

because it was all-you-can-eat…

I'll go on a diet from tomorrow…

常用單字片語集

eat too much
吃太撐
too much 可以活用在各式各樣的句子裡。

I can't help it.
我也沒辦法。
想用英文表達「我也沒辦法」的固定句型，
大家記下來吧。

all-you-can-eat
吃到飽
也可以説 buffet。

go on a diet
減肥
這個時候用的動詞是 go。

和朋友去泰國節
Thai Festival with my friends

今天我去了代代木公園的泰國節。

有好多賣泰式料理的攤販。

我呀,超喜歡泰式料理的!

雖然我不敢吃香菜⋯⋯

Today I went to the Thai   in Yoyogi Park.
今天我去了代代木公園的泰國節。

There were many   selling Thai foods.
有好多賣泰式料理的攤販。

You   what, I love Thai food!
我呀,超喜歡泰式料理的!

Even   I cannot eat coriander…
雖然我不敢吃香菜⋯⋯

Today I went to the Thai Festival in Yoyogi Park.

There were many stalls selling Thai foods.

You know what, I love Thai food!

Even though I cannot eat coriander…

- - - - - - - - - - - - 常用單字片語集 - - - - - - - - - - - -

festival
祭典、節日

stall
攤販
可以用這個單字表達常見的小吃攤或攤販。

you know what
我呀、你知道的
口語對話中常常用來當連接詞的片語。

even though
雖然~
注意不要和 even if(就算~)搞混。

五月 20

天氣不錯，走一走！

Let's take a walk

中文日記

今天天氣真好！

我要提早一站下車，走一走！

最近都沒運動，

這樣還可以消耗卡路里呢！

英文填空日記

＿＿＿＿ nice weather today!
今天天氣真好！

I'll get off one station ＿＿＿＿ and take a walk!
我要提早一站下車，走一走！

I haven't been doing any ＿＿＿＿ recently,
最近都沒運動，

and it's good to ＿＿＿＿ calories!
這樣還可以消耗卡路里呢！

英文日記

Such nice weather today!

I'll get off one station before and take a walk!

I haven't been doing any exercise recently,

and it's good to burn calories!

- - - - - - - - - - - - **常用單字片語集** - - - - - - - - - - - -

such ～
真～
無論後面的名詞是單數或複數都可以套用這個片語。

one station before
提早一站
before 也有「前一站」的意思。

do exercise
運動
exercise 也可以單獨做為動詞來使用。

burn calories
消耗卡路里
burn（燃燒）這個單字用在卡路里或能量的時候就是「消耗」的意思。

家裡出現蟑螂！

Cockroaches!!

中文日記

天啊，又是蟑螂！

我已經連續三天都看到牠們了！

我不喜歡用殺蟲劑，

所以都用打的。

英文填空日記

Oh no, _____, again!
天啊，又是蟑螂！

I've seen them three days in a _____!
我已經連續三天都看到牠們了！

I don't like _____ the spray,
我不喜歡用殺蟲劑，

so I always _____ them.
所以都用打的。

英文日記

Oh no, cockroaches, again!

I've seen them three days in a row!

I don't like using the spray,

so I always smash them.

- - - - - - - - - - - - - - 常用單字片語集 - - - - - - - - - - - - -

cockroach
蟑螂
注意不要拼錯字囉。

in a row
連續
row 是「排、列」的意思。

like -ing
喜歡～
也可以用 to do 代替 -ing。

smash
打死
也有「打碎、痛毆」的意思。

衛生紙用光了

No more toilet paper

中文日記

衛生紙用光了！

可是我家附近的店都關了……

便利商店有賣嗎？

總之，先去看看吧！

英文填空日記

I ran　　　　　of toilet paper!
衛生紙用光了！

But the shops　　　　　my house are all closed...
可是我家附近的店都關了……

Do they　　　　　it at the convenience store?
便利商店有賣嗎？

I'll go and check,　　　　　!
總之，先去看看吧！

英文日記

I ran out of toilet paper!

But the shops near my house are all closed...

Do they have it at the convenience store?

I'll go and check, anyways!

常用單字片語集

run out of ～
～用光了
run 的過去式是 ran，屬於不規則變化，要特別留意。

near ～
～附近
也可以說 nearby（附近的）。

They have ～
他們有賣～。
想表示店裡（有賣～）的時候，可以用 They 來代指店家。

anyways
總之
口語化的說法，也可以不要加 s，直接說 anyway。

好想泡澡，可是……

Wanna relax in the bath

中文日記

今天回到家很晚了。

雖然我想放洗澡水，

但又想早點睡。

不然今天淋浴就好了……

英文填空日記

I came back home _____ today.
今天回到家很晚了。

I wanna _____ a bath,
雖然我想放洗澡水，

but I wanna sleep as _____ as possible.
但又想早點睡。

Just take a shower _____ today...
不然今天淋浴就好了……

英文日記

I came back home late today.

I wanna run a bath,

but I wanna sleep as soon as possible.

Just take a shower for today...

常用單字片語集

late
晚的
可以做為形容詞和副詞。

run a bath
放洗澡水
也可以說 fill up a bathtub。

as soon as possible
早點、盡快
電子郵件裡經常會省略成 ASAP。

for today
今天暫且
想強調「今天」的時候就不會加介系詞。

熱門影片
A video gone viral

中文日記

聽説我朋友上傳的影片爆紅。

點閱率已經破兩萬了。

好厲害喔！

有點好奇是什麼樣的影片呢。

英文填空日記

The video my friend uploaded has gone _____ .
聽説我朋友上傳的影片爆紅。

It's already got 20000 _____ .
點閱率已經破兩萬了。

That's _____ !
好厲害喔！

I wanna know what _____ of video it is.
有點好奇是什麼樣的影片呢。

英文日記

The video my friend uploaded has gone viral.

It's already got 20000 views.

That's incredible!

I wanna know what kind of video it is.

常用單字片語集

go viral
爆紅
viral 是「病毒性的」的意思，形容快速傳播和擴散的樣子。

view(s)
點閱率、觀看次數
大多是做為網站點閱率或影片觀看次數後面的量詞。

incredible
厲害的、難以置信的
語感有點像是 amazing 的用法。

what kind of ～
什麼樣的～
類似「什麼類型的～」、「什麼樣的～」的意思。

和老家的朋友碰面了

Wow, everybody is married…

中文日記

今天和高中同學碰面了，

好多人都已經結婚了。

爸媽也會問我：「有沒有不錯的對象？」

好像差不多該找個對象了……

英文填空日記

I saw my friends   high school today,

今天和高中同學碰面了，

and many of them were already   .

好多人都已經結婚了。

My parents also asked me if I have anyone   .

爸媽也會問我：「有沒有不錯的對象？」

I think I gotta find   now…

好像差不多該找個對象了……

英文日記

I saw my friends from high school today,

and many of them were already married.

My parents also asked me if I have anyone special.

I think I gotta find someone now…

------------------------------ 常用單字片語集 ------------------------------

my friend from high school
高中同學
from high school 是指「從高中到現在的交情」的意思。

anyone/someone special
不錯的對象
通常在問對方有沒有交往的人時，會像這樣說成「不錯的對象」。

be married
已婚、結婚了
也可以說 be married to ～，就是「嫁給誰／娶了誰」的意思。

find someone
找個人（對象）
原文中省略了「不錯的對象」，但可以從前後文推理出來，所以省略也沒關係。

五月 26 和朋友去演唱會

Concert with my friend

中文日記

今天我和朋友一起去演唱會。

我們玩得超嗨的！

我是這個團體的忠實粉絲，

光是他們一站上舞台，我就激動到不行！

英文填空日記

I went to a _____ with my friend today.
今天我和朋友一起去演唱會。

We had a _____ there!
我們玩得超嗨的！

I've been a _____ fan of this group,
我是這個團體的忠實粉絲，

so I got so excited when they showed _____ on stage!
光是他們一站上舞台，我就激動到不行！

英文日記

I went to a concert with my friend today.

We had a blast there!

I've been a big fan of this group,

so I got so excited when they showed up on stage!

常用單字片語集

go to a concert
去演唱會
演唱會不用 live 而是用 concert。

have a blast
盡情狂歡、玩得愉快
在形容派對或演唱會「氣氛高漲」的時候會
使用這個片語。

be a big fan of ～
～的忠實粉絲
很實用的片語，可以整句一起記下來。

show up
登場、現身
表示「露面」的意思時，經常會使用 show
這個單字。

喊得太賣力，嗓子都啞了

My voice is gone

中文日記

我在演唱會上喊得太賣力，嗓子都啞了。

同事還問我：「怎麼了？是不是感冒了？」

好羞於開口啊，

我只好回答：「不是，只是因為喊得太賣力了。」

英文填空日記

I　　　　 my voice because I screamed a lot at the concert.
我在演唱會上喊得太賣力，嗓子都啞了。

My colleagues said "　　　　 happened? Do you have a cold?"
同事還問我：「怎麼了？是不是感冒了？」

It was kinda　　　　 to say,
好羞於開口啊，

"No, this is　　　　 because I screamed too much."
我只好回答：「不是，只是因為喊得太賣力了。」

英文日記

I lost my voice because I screamed a lot at the concert.

My colleagues said "What happened? Do you have a cold?"

It was kinda embarrassing to say,

"No, this is just because I screamed too much."

常用單字片語集

lose one's voice
聲音沙啞
發不出聲音時，經常會用 lose（失去）這個單字來表示。

What happened?
怎麼了？
詢問對方發生什麼事時常用的句子。

embarrassing
羞恥
如果句子主詞是人的話，就要改成 I'm embarrassed.。

just because ～
只是因為～
通常會像這樣加上 just（只是），一起記下來吧。

襪子破洞啦

A hole in my sock

中文日記

我的襪子破洞啦！

偏偏我今天晚上要去朋友家啊！

我有針線包嗎……

總之，得先修補一下！

英文填空日記

I got a   in my sock!
我的襪子破洞啦！

I'm going to my friend's   tonight!
偏偏我今天晚上要去朋友家啊！

Do I have a   kit with me…?
我有針線包嗎……

I have to   it up for now!
總之，得先修補一下！

英文日記

I got a hole in my sock!

I'm going to my friend's house tonight!

Do I have a sewing kit with me…?

I have to patch it up for now!

常用單字片語集

get a hole
破洞
可以用來表示衣物破洞的片語。

house
家
home 也是「家」的意思，但這種情況會使用 house，要特別留意。

sewing kit
針線包
和動詞 sew（縫）一起記下來會更好記。

patch up
修補
當受詞是代名詞時，要擺在片語的中間，如 patch it up。

肚子有點餓……

A bit hungry...

我肚子有點餓。

我想找點東西來吃。

但這麼晚了還吃東西好像不太好……

會害我變胖的！

I'm a   hungry.
我肚子有點餓。

I wanna   something to eat.
我想找點東西來吃。

But eating this   at night is not good...
但這麼晚了還吃東西好像不太好……

It   me gain weight!
會害我變胖的！

I'm a bit hungry.

I wanna grab something to eat.

But eating this late at night is not good...

It makes me gain weight!

常用單字片語集

a bit hungry
肚子有點餓
a bit 是「有一點」的意思，也可以說 a little。

grab something to eat
找點東西來吃
grab 是「抓取」的意思，可以用在表示「稍微吃點東西」的時候。

this late at night
這麼的晚
this 的語感像是「這麼的」。

make me do ～
害我～
直譯或許會有點怪怪的，也可以想成「我會～」的意思。

社交軟體好煩

I'm tired of social media

中文日記

最近我的朋友都沉迷在社交軟體裡。

總是低頭滑手機！

每次吃飯的時候都要拍照。

我覺得很煩。

英文填空日記

Recently, many of my friends are   to social media.

最近我的朋友都沉迷在社交軟體裡。

They've been checking their phone   the time!

總是低頭滑手機！

Also they wanna take a photo   time they eat.

每次吃飯的時候都要拍照。

I'm   of it.

我覺得很煩。

英文日記

Recently, many of my friends are addicted to social media.

They've been checking their phone all the time!

Also they wanna take a photo every time they eat.

I'm tired of it.

常用單字片語集

be addicted to ～
沉迷於～
介系詞要用 to，要記下來喔。

all the time
總是
跟 always 的意思一樣，但擺在句尾的時候，通常會用 all the time。

every time
每次
可以單獨使用，但也可以像這樣擺在動詞之前，表示「每次都要～」。

be tired of ～
覺得～很煩
tired（疲憊）這個單字也有「厭倦、煩躁」的意思。

77

交友軟體是什麼？
Curious about dating apps

中文日記

最近好像很流行交友軟體。

我滿有興趣的，但沒有勇氣嘗試。

我好多朋友都有註冊，

她們還真的有交到男朋友！

英文填空日記

_____ apps are getting popular recently.
最近好像很流行交友軟體。

I'm very _____, but I don't have the courage to do it.
我滿有興趣的，但沒有勇氣嘗試。

Many of my friends _____,
我好多朋友都有註冊，

and _____ got boyfriends!
她們還真的有交到男朋友！

英文日記

Dating apps are getting popular recently.

I'm very curious, but I don't have the courage to do it.

Many of my friends registered,

and actually got boyfriends!

常用單字片語集

dating app
交友軟體
app 是 application 的縮寫。

be curious
有興趣
be curious about ～就是「對～有興趣」的意思。

many of ～
好多～
可以跟 some of ～（有些～）一起記下來。

actually
真的、實際上
很實用的連接詞。

有關「戀愛」的十大表現手法

第 1 名	He's so cool. 他好帥。	在描述關於其他人的事情時，經常會以 He's ～做為開頭。如果是想講「她」的事情的話，就可以改成 She's。
第 2 名	He asked me out. 他約我出去。	邀別人約會時的常見句型，如果是自己主動邀約的話，就會是 I asked him/her out.。
第 3 名	I'm in love with him. 我愛上他了。	除了 love 和 like 之外，還有許多表示「喜歡」的說法，例如 I'm into him. 或 I've been thinking about him. 也是同樣的意思。
第 4 名	I go on a date. 我要去約會了。	如果要說明對象是「誰」的話，就會變成 I go on a date with ～。
第 5 名	Will you go out with me? 你願意和我交往嗎？	也可以說 Will you be my girlfriend/boyfriend? 另外，求婚的時候則是說 Will you marry me? （你願意和我結婚嗎？）
第 6 名	He's my perfect type. 他是我的天菜。	也可以更簡略地說 He's my type. （他是我的菜），加上 perfect（完美的）就會多了一層強調，變成「完美天菜、超級天菜」。
第 7 名	I had a fight with my boyfriend. 我和男朋友吵架了。	「吵架」的英文是 have a fight。若要表示「口角」的話，可以用 quarrel 取代 fight，改成 I had a quarrel with ～。
第 8 名	I wonder if he's seeing anyone now. 不知道他現在有沒有交往對象。	I wonder ～是寫日記時經常會用到的手法。自言自語時，通常會加上 if（是否～）。
第 9 名	I went for a drink with Daisuke. 我和大介去喝酒了。	go for ～這個句型不只能用在情侶之間，和其他人出去吃飯也可以使用。我們也經常會說 I went for lunch with ～（我和～去吃午餐了）。
第 10 名	A guy just hit on me. 有個男的向我搭訕。	除了 hit on 之外，也可以用 try to pick up 來表現「搭訕」這個行為，或者也可以說 A guy talked to me.（有個男的向我搭話）。

Best 10

JUNE

6 月

Even though I'm thinking I wanna lose weight,
雖然我一直抱持著要減肥的想法，

it's so hard to keep the motivation up...
但動力老是維持不久……

If I had a boyfriend who can take me to the beach,
如果有個會帶我去海邊的男朋友的話，

I would work harder...
我搞不好會更努力呢……

一樹聯繫我了

Kazuki contacted me

中文日記

今天沙織傳簡訊給我，

她說：「你記得一個叫做一樹的男生嗎？

他想知道你的聯繫方式。」

慢著，難道是 BBQ 那時候的那個帥哥嗎？

英文填空日記

Today Saori ⎯⎯⎯⎯ me and said,
今天沙織傳簡訊給我，

"Do you remember the guy ⎯⎯⎯⎯ Kazuki?
她說：「你記得一個叫做一樹的男生嗎？

He said he wants to ⎯⎯⎯⎯ to you."
他想知道你的聯繫方式。」

What, that ⎯⎯⎯⎯ I saw at the barbecue!?
慢著，難道是 BBQ 那時候的那個帥哥嗎？

英文日記

Today Saori texted me and said,

"Do you remember the guy called Kazuki?

He said he wants to talk to you."

What, that hottie I saw at the barbecue!?

常用單字片語集

text
傳簡訊
text 可以做為名詞，也可以做為動詞。這個情境下的「傳簡訊」是做為動詞來使用的。

the guy called ～
叫做～的男生
如果是女生的話，就把 guy 改成 girl。

talk to you
取得聯繫
這個情境的 talk 不見得一定是「說話」，也有可能是傳訊息。

hottie
帥哥
口語化的說法，也可以說 good-looking guy。

發薪日前要省吃儉用

Gotta save some money

中文日記

這個月花太多錢啦！

再這樣下去，我就要窮困潦倒了。

得節儉一點才行。

這個月的午餐都不要吃外食了！

英文填空日記

I ____ a lot of money this month!
這個月花太多錢啦！

If I keep doing this, I'll be ____ .
再這樣下去，我就要窮困潦倒了。

I gotta ____ up some.
得節儉一點才行。

I won't go ____ for lunch anymore this month!
這個月的午餐都不要吃外食了！

英文日記

I wasted a lot of money this month!

If I keep doing this, I'll be broke.

I gotta save up some.

I won't go out for lunch anymore this month!

- - - - - - 常用單字片語集 - - - - - -

waste a lot of money
花太多錢
waste 有「開銷太大」、「浪費」的意思。

I'm broke.
窮困潦倒。
日常對話中經常會用到的句子，是很口語化的用法。

save up
節儉、存錢
save 也可以單獨使用。

go out for lunch
在外面吃午餐
為了吃午餐而出門，即「在外面吃午餐」的意思。

梅雨季，衣服老是晒不乾

It takes forever to dry!

中文日記

這幾天一直在下雨。

我不喜歡把衣服晒在房間裡。

因為根本晒不乾呀！

到底什麼時候才會放晴啊……

英文填空日記

It's been raining ____ days.
這幾天一直在下雨。

I don't like ____ the laundry inside,
我不喜歡把衣服晒在房間裡。

because it takes ____ to dry!
因為根本晒不乾呀！

Wonder when the sun is coming ____ ...
到底什麼時候才會放晴啊……

英文日記

It's been raining these days.

I don't like hanging the laundry inside,

because it takes forever to dry!

Wonder when the sun is coming out...

---------------- 常用單字片語集 ----------------

these days
這幾天
注意是用 these（這些）來表示。

hang the laundry inside
晒在室內
hang（吊掛）＋ inside（裡面），即「把衣服晒在室內」。

it takes forever
根本不會～
比起 It takes a long time.（要花很長一段時間）還要更花時間，甚至根本達不到目的時，可以這麼說。

The sun comes out.
放晴。
這裡是表示不久的將來，所以用現在進行式 is coming out。

工作又搞砸了

Mistake again…

中文日記

今天有點低落。

我在工作上又犯了同樣的錯誤。

還給同事們添麻煩……

明天我會努力不犯錯的！

英文填空日記

Today I was a little　　　　　　,
今天有點低落。

because I　　　　　　 the same mistake.
我在工作上又犯了同樣的錯誤。

I also　　　　　 my colleagues…
還給同事們添麻煩……

I'll try　　　　　 to make a mistake tomorrow!
明天我會努力不犯錯的！

英文日記

Today I was a little down,

because I repeated the same mistake.

I also bothered my colleagues…

I'll try not to make a mistake tomorrow!

常用單字片語集

be a little down
有點低落
和 depressed 是相同意思。

repeat the same mistake
犯同樣的錯誤
Don't repeat the same mistake! 意思就是
「不要再犯同樣的錯誤了！」

bother
添麻煩、造成困擾
Don't bother me! 意思就是「不要煩我！」

try not to ～
努力不要～
注意 not 的擺放位置。

和同學吃午餐
Lunch with my classmate

中文日記

今天我和麻衣一起去吃午餐了。

她還帶了兒子小健來,他超可愛的

看了都讓我也想要有個孩子了……

不過,我得先找到對象才行,哈哈……

英文填空日記

Today I ＿＿＿＿ lunch with Mai.
今天我和麻衣一起去吃午餐了。

And she ＿＿＿＿ her son, Ken. He was so adorable ♡
她還帶了兒子小健來,他超可愛的 ♡

That ＿＿＿＿ me feel like I wanna have kids…
看了都讓我也想要有個孩子了……

But ＿＿＿＿, I need to find a partner, haha…
不過,我得先找到對象才行,哈哈……

英文日記

Today I had lunch with Mai.

And she brought her son, Ken. He was so adorable ♡

That makes me feel like I wanna have kids…

But first, I need to find a partner, haha…

常用單字片語集

have lunch with ～
和～吃午餐
比起 eat,用 have 會更得體。

bring
帶
除了「帶東西」以外,「帶人」也是使用這個動詞。

adorable
非常可愛
形容小孩或動物「好可愛」的時候可以使用這個單字。

but first
在那之前
直譯的話是「但是,首先得……」,語感上更貼近「在那之前」。

六月

6

愛海的婚禮

Wedding of Manami

中文日記

我去參加愛海的婚禮了。

這對新人真的好登對呀！

我很慶幸自己可以在場，

見證他們最幸福的瞬間。

英文填空日記

I _____ the wedding ceremony of Manami.
我去參加愛海的婚禮了。

They were such a _____ match!
這對新人真的好登對呀！

I was happy to _____ there,
我很慶幸自己可以在場，

and see their _____ moment ever.
見證他們最幸福的瞬間。

英文日記

I attended the wedding ceremony of Manami.

They were such a perfect match!

I was happy to be there,

and see their happiest moment ever.

--------- 常用單字片語集 ---------

attend
參加、出席
參加或出席典禮時可以使用這個動詞。

a perfect match
登對的情侶
日常對話中經常用來表示「登對」的說法。

such ~
真的好～
such 有很多種用法，在這個情境裡，語感更接近「多麼～」，即「真的好～」。

happiest moment ever
最幸福的瞬間
加上 ever 在語感上會有強調「有史以來最……」的感覺。

87

減肥計畫不持久

I wanna lose weight

中文日記

雖然我一直抱持著要減肥的想法，

但動力老是維持不久……

如果有個會帶我去海邊的男朋友的話，

我搞不好會更努力呢……

英文填空日記

Even _____ I'm thinking I wanna lose weight,
雖然我一直抱持著要減肥的想法，

it's so hard to keep the motivation _____ …
但動力老是維持不久……

If I _____ a boyfriend who can take me to the beach,
如果有個會帶我去海邊的男朋友的話，

I would work _____ …
我搞不好會更努力呢……

英文日記

Even though I'm thinking I wanna lose weight,

it's so hard to keep the motivation up…

If I had a boyfriend who can take me to the beach,

I would work harder…

常用單字片語集

even though ～
雖然～、即使～
在學校也會學到的標準用法，非常實用，可以記下來。

keep the motivation up
維持動力
keep ～ up 是「保持、維持」的意思。

if ＋過去式
如果～
在描述現實中沒有發生的事情時，要使用過去式。

work harder
更努力
work 除了「工作」以外，還有「努力」的意思。

一個人看電影
Movie alone

中文日記

今天下班後，我去看電影了。

我選了一部現在最紅的作品，超好看的！

偶爾一個人出門也不錯呢。

以後我還想試著一個人去旅行呢……

英文填空日記

I went to _____ a movie after work today.
今天下班後，我去看電影了。

I chose one of the _____ popular movies, which was really good!
我選了一部現在最紅的作品，超好看的！

Sometimes it's nice to go out by _____.
偶爾一個人出門也不錯呢。

I wanna do _____ travel someday…
以後我還想試著一個人去旅行呢……

英文日記

I went to see a movie after work today.

I chose one of the most popular movies, which was really good!

Sometimes it's nice to go out by myself.

I wanna do solo travel someday…

常用單字片語集

go to see a movie
看電影
日常對話中可以省略 to。

the most ～
最～的
無法用「-est」來表示最高級的時候，可以使用這種表現手法。

by oneself
一個人
也可以用 alone。

solo travel
一個人旅行
也可以説 traveling alone。

六月 9 公司會議
Meeting day

在今天的會議中，

我的企劃頭一次通過了！

我辦到了！

主管也誇獎我「幹得好」呢。

In the _____ today,
在今天的會議中，

my proposal got _____ for the first time!!
我的企劃頭一次通過了！

I _____ it!!
我辦到了！

My boss also said "You _____ a good job!"
主管也誇獎我「幹得好」呢。

In the meeting today,

my proposal got approved for the first time!!

I did it!!

My boss also said "You did a good job!"

常用單字片語集

proposal
企劃
也有「提案」的意思。

get approved
（企劃、提案）通過
商業場合經常會出現的用法。

I did it!
我辦到了！
完成一件事時會用到的句子。

You did a good job!
幹得好！
You did a great job! 也是同樣的意思。

10 聽了朋友轉職的事

She's changing jobs

4 月
5 月
6 月
7 月
8 月
9 月
10 月
11 月
12 月
1 月
2 月
3 月

中文日記

聽説佳奈要換工作了。

她現在是個空服員，

但好像很辛苦。

希望她能找到好工作。

英文填空日記

I heard Kana is going to　　　　 jobs.
聽說佳奈要換工作了。

She is working as a flight　　　 ,
她現在是個空服員，

but it　　　　 to be very tough.
但好像很辛苦。

**　　　 she will find a good job.**
希望她能找到好工作。

英文日記

I heard Kana is going to change jobs.

She is working as a flight attendant,

but it seems to be very tough.

Hope she will find a good job.

- - - - - - - - - - - 常用單字片語集 - - - - - - - - - - -

change jobs
轉職、換工作
也可以用 switch 代替 change。

flight attendant
空服員
也可以用 cabin crew 或 cabin attendant。

It seems to be ～ .
好像～、聽說～。
也可以說 It seems that ～ . 。

Hope ～ .
希望～。
I hope ～ . 省略了主詞的用法。

91

11 工作搞砸了

Made a mistake!

中文日記

我今天工作的時候搞砸了。

我記錯會議的時間，

讓客人等了很長一段時間。

以後要多加留意。

英文填空日記

Today I _____ a mistake at work.
我今天工作的時候搞砸了。

I mistook the _____ of the meeting,
我記錯會議的時間，

and kept the guests _____ for a long time.
讓客人等了很長一段時間。

I'll be _____ next time.
以後要多加留意。

英文日記

Today I made a mistake at work.

I mistook the time of the meeting,

and kept the guests waiting for a long time.

I'll be careful next time.

常用單字片語集

make a mistake
搞砸、出錯
mistake 就是「錯誤、過失」的意思。

mistake the time of ～
記錯～的時間
這裡的 mistake 是動詞，要特別注意。

keep ～ waiting
讓～等待
make ～ wait 也是相同的意思，要留意 wait 的時態。

I'll be careful next time.
我以後要多加留意。
Please be careful next time.（以後要多加注意喔）也經常使用。

六月 12 一樹約我吃晚餐

Kazuki asked me out

在那之後，我和一樹偶爾會聯繫。

他約我今天一起吃晚餐，

有點期待呢。

我該穿什麼才好呢？

_____ then, I have talked to Kazuki sometimes,
在那之後，我和一樹偶爾會聯繫。

and he _____ me to dinner tonight.
他約我今天一起吃晚餐，

I'm _____ excited.
有點期待呢。

What _____ I wear…?
我該穿什麼才好呢？

Since then, I have talked to Kazuki sometimes,

and he invited me to dinner tonight.

I'm kinda excited.

What should I wear…?

常用單字片語集

since then
在那之後
since（自從～）和 then（那個時候）合在一起就是「在那之後」。

invite ~ to...
約～去……
邀請他人用餐時常用的説法。

kinda
有點
將 kind of 縮短後的口語用詞。

What should I wear?
我該穿什麼才好呢？
一邊思考一邊自言自語「該怎麼辦才好呢～」的時候，可以用 should 這個單字。

和一樹共進晚餐
Dinner with Kazuki

和一樹共進晚餐，開心是很開心啦，

但有件事讓我很介意⋯⋯

他跟我分帳分到個位數日圓⋯⋯

這是合理的嗎？

The dinner with Kazuki was really   ,
和一樹共進晚餐，開心是很開心啦，

but there's one   that bothered me...
但有件事讓我很介意⋯⋯

He   the bill to the last yen...
他跟我分帳分到個位數日圓⋯⋯

Is this   ? Or not   ...?
這是合理的嗎？

The dinner with Kazuki was really fun,

but there's one thing that bothered me...

He split the bill to the last yen...

Is this okay? Or not okay...?

常用單字片語集

fun
開心
另一個類似的單字 funny 是「有趣、好笑」
的意思，要學會區別喔。

There's one thing that bothers me.
有件事讓我很介意。
bother 是表示「令人煩惱、令人困擾」的
動詞。

split the bill
分帳、分攤費用
和別人一起吃飯的時候經常用到的片語，大
家學起來吧。

Is this okay? Or not okay?
這是合理的嗎？
雖然還有許多類似的說法，但這裡選擇使用
okay（可以）。

用英文交流好難……

Communication in English

4 月
5 月
6 月
7 月
8 月
9 月
10 月
11 月
12 月
1 月
2 月
3 月

中文日記

今天美國分公司的史密斯先生來我們公司了。

他完全不會日文，

溝通起來很辛苦。

要是我的英文更流利就好了。

英文填空日記

Today Mr. Smith from US　　　came to our office.
今天美國分公司的史密斯先生來我們公司了。

He doesn't speak　　　Japanese,
他完全不會日文，

so we kinda　　　to communicate with him.
溝通起來很辛苦。

I wish I　　　speak English better.
要是我的英文更流利就好了。

英文日記

Today Mr. Smith from US branch came to our office.

He doesn't speak any Japanese,

so we kinda struggled to communicate with him.

I wish I could speak English better.

常用單字片語集

~ branch
～分公司
「～分店」也是同樣的說法。

do not speak any Japanese
完全不會日文
雖然只有 do not speak Japanese 也能表示「不會日文」，但加上 any 就有強調「完全」的意思。

struggle to ~
～很艱難、很辛苦
struggle 是表示「辛苦、奮鬥」的動詞。

I wish I could ~ .
要是～就好了。
中文裡並不會有時態的分別，但這種情況要用 can 的過去式 could。

95

電車上人擠人，累死了

Rush-hour train

中文日記

今天早上電車超擠的！

因為我睡過頭，錯過平時搭的那班電車。

我人都還沒到公司，

卻已經累到不行……

英文填空日記

The train was so _____ this morning!
今天早上電車超擠的！

I overslept and _____ the one I always get on.
因為我睡過頭，錯過平時搭的那班電車。

I haven't _____ to the office yet,
我人都還沒到公司，

but I'm already _____ …
卻已經累到不行……

英文日記

The train was so crowded this morning!

I overslept and missed the one I always get on.

I haven't got to the office yet,

but I'm already exhausted…

- - - - - - - - - - 常用單字片語集 - - - - - - - - - -

crowded
人擠人
電車以外的各種場合也用得到。

get to～
抵達～
可以代替 arrive at（到達～）。

miss
錯過
可以用在錯過電車的時候。

exhausted
累壞了
也可以用 tired，但語感上 exhausted 的疲憊感更強烈。

16 零食吃太多了

Ate too many sweets

中文日記

我平時都會盡量少吃零食，

但同事們拿來的慰勞品我就不好意思拒絕了。

他們常常給我一些國外的零食，

明明知道這樣不好，但我就是忍不住啊……

英文填空日記

I always try to   **eating sweets,**
我平時都會盡量少吃零食，

but I can't   **the gifts from my colleagues.**
但同事們拿來的慰勞品我就不好意思拒絕了。

They always give me some sweets from   **.**
他們常常給我一些國外的零食，

I know this is no good, but I can't   **it…**
明明知道這樣不好，但我就是忍不住啊……

英文日記

I always try to avoid eating sweets,

but I can't refuse the gifts from my colleagues.

They always give me some sweets from overseas.

I know this is no good, but I can't help it…

常用單字片語集

avoid -ing
避免～
這種情境不能接 to do，要特別留意。

refuse
拒絕
decline 和 turn down 也是同樣意思。

overseas
國外
和 abroad 是同樣意思。

can't help it
沒有辦法、忍不住
help（幫助）的相關片語，非常實用，學起來吧。

17 豪雨打亂了電車時刻

Where is my train?

電車老是不來！

車站廣播說：

「受到豪雨影響，所有列車將延誤到站。」

什麼時候才會恢復正常呀⋯⋯

The train is not _____ !
電車老是不來！

There was an _____ saying,
車站廣播說：

"All the trains are delayed _____ to heavy rain."
「受到豪雨影響，所有列車將延誤到站。」

When is it gonna be back to _____ …
什麼時候才會恢復正常呀⋯⋯

The train is not coming!

There was an announcement saying,

"All the trains are delayed due to heavy rain."

When is it gonna be back to normal…

- - - - - - - - - - - - - 常用單字片語集 - - - - - - - - - - - - -

be not coming
不來
交通工具遲遲不來時可以使用的片語。

announcement
廣播
也有「發表、公告」的意思。

due to ～
由於～、因為～
比 because 更正式的說法。

back to normal
恢復原狀、恢復正常
也可以說 back to original。

18 因爲感冒去了醫院

I have a cold

中文日記

因為感冒，我去了醫院。

雖然我有流鼻涕和咳嗽，

但沒有發燒，

明天可以照常去上班。

英文填空日記

I went to the ___ because I had a cold.
因為感冒，我去了醫院。

I had a ___ nose and a cough,
雖然我有流鼻涕和咳嗽，

but I didn't have any ___ .
但沒有發燒，

I think I can go to ___ tomorrow.
明天可以照常去上班。

英文日記

I went to the doctor because I had a cold.

I had a runny nose and a cough,

but I didn't have any fever.

I think I can go to work tomorrow.

- - - - - - - - - - - 常用單字片語集 - - - - - - - - - - -

go to the doctor
去醫院
hospital 在日常對話中比較不常用到。

runny nose
流鼻涕
在描述感冒症狀時經常用到的説法。

have a fever
發燒
要改成否定句的話，大多會像這裡使用
any。

go to work
上班
日常對話裡要講「上班」最普通的説法。

身體還很不舒服
Still feeling sick

本來以為感冒已經好了，

但我又覺得不太舒服。

我是不是應該早退，再去看一次醫生呢？

不過我還有好多事要做啊……

I thought I got   my cold.
本來以為感冒已經好了，

I'm feeling   again.
但我又覺得不太舒服。

Should I leave early and go to the   again?
我是不是應該早退，再去看一次醫生呢？

But I still have many   to do…
不過我還有好多事要做啊……

I thought I got over my cold.

I'm feeling sick again.

Should I leave early and go to the clinic again?

But I still have many things to do…

常用單字片語集

get over ～
～復原、～治癒
也有「克服～」的意思。

feel sick
不舒服
除了感冒以外，身體不舒服的時候都可以用這個片語。

go to the clinic
去醫院
比起 hospital，clinic 這個單字比較常用。

things to do
要做的事
可以和 something to do（有事情要做）一起記下來。

20 送出父親節禮物

Father's Day gift

中文日記

今天是父親節，

所以我送了爸爸一個禮物。

他一直說想要一條新的領帶，

我就買了一條適合他的。

（註：日本的父親節是每年六月第三週的週日。）

英文填空日記

It's _____ Day today.
今天是父親節，

So I _____ a gift to my father.
所以我送了爸爸一個禮物。

He said he wanted a new _____,
他一直說想要一條新的領帶，

so I bought one which _____ him.
我就買了一條適合他的。

英文日記

It's Father's Day today.

So I sent a gift to my father.

He said he wanted a new tie,

so I bought one which suits him.

常用單字片語集

Father's Day 父親節 母親節是 Mother's Day。	**tie** 領帶 比起 necktie，更常使用這個單字。
send 送 send 的過去式是 sent，屬於不規則變化。	**suit** 適合 和 look good on ～是同樣意思。

煮菜調味失敗了

Messed up on cooking

中文日記

今天我本來打算做味噌湯的，

但我搞砸了！

味噌放太多了，

變得太鹹啦！

英文填空日記

Today I tried to make ＿＿＿＿ soup,
今天我本來打算做味噌湯的，

but I ＿＿＿＿ up!
但我搞砸了！

I put too ＿＿＿＿ miso,
味噌放太多了，

and it became ＿＿＿＿ !
變得太鹹啦！

英文日記

Today I tried to make miso soup,

but I messed up!

I put too much miso,

and it became salty!

常用單字片語集

miso soup
味噌湯
用 miso 就可以表達「味噌」的意思。

mess up
搞砸、失敗
screw up 也是同樣的意思。

too much
太多
如果是可數名詞的話，就把 much 改成 many。

salty
鹹的
由 salt（鹽）衍生出來的單字。

22 一個人去看電影

Movie alone

中文日記

今天本來和沙織約好十二點碰面，

但她身體不舒服，無法過來。

所以我決定自己一個人去看電影。

現在正在上映的有哪些電影呢？

英文填空日記

I was　　　　　　to meet Saori at 12 today,
今天本來和沙織約好十二點碰面，

but she couldn't come because she was　　　　　.
但她身體不舒服，無法過來。

So I decide to go to the movies　　　　　.
所以我決定自己一個人去看電影。

What movies are　　　　　now?
現在正在上映的有哪些電影呢？

英文日記

I was supposed to meet Saori at 12 today,

but she couldn't come because she was sick.

So I decide to go to the movies alone.

What movies are playing now?

------------------------------ 常用單字片語集 ------------------------------

be supposed to ～
本來要～
to 之後要接原形動詞或 be 動詞。

sick
生病、不舒服
日常對話中時常出現的單字，學起來吧。

alone
一個人
也可以說 by oneself。

be playing
上映中
play 不只有「玩耍」的意思，也有「播放、播映」的意思。

雨下了整整三天
Raining like forever

中文日記

東京已經下了整整三天的雨。

我真的很討厭梅雨季！

我想去慢跑也跑不成！

希望梅雨季快點結束……

英文填空日記

It's been raining　　　　　3 days in Tokyo.
東京已經下了整整三天的雨。

I really hate this　　　　season!
我真的很討厭梅雨季！

I wanted to go　　　　, but I can't!
我想去慢跑也跑不成！

Hope this will be　　　　soon…
希望梅雨季快點結束……

英文日記

It's been raining for 3 days in Tokyo.

I really hate this rainy season!

I wanted to go jogging, but I can't!

Hope this will be over soon…

常用單字片語集

for 3 days
整整三天
for 是經常用到的介系詞，有「～這段期間」的意思。

rainy season
梅雨季
雨的季節，即「梅雨季」的意思。

go jogging
去慢跑
也可以說 go for a jog。

be over
結束
over 這個單字有「結束、跨越」的意思。

24 電車坐過站了

Missed my stop

中文日記

今天搭電車的時候，不小心睡著了，

然後就坐過站了！

去公司的路上差點就遲到了。

呼，鬆了一口氣！

英文填空日記

Today I　　　　　asleep in the train,
今天搭電車的時候，不小心睡著了，

and I　　　　　my stop!
然後就坐過站了！

I was almost late　　　　　work.
去公司的路上差點就遲到了。

Phew,　　　　　a relief!
呼，鬆了一口氣！

英文日記

Today I fell asleep in the train,

and I missed my stop!

I was almost late for work.

Phew, what a relief!

------ 常用單字片語集 ------

fall asleep
睡著、打瞌睡
並非刻意入睡的時候就會用 fall 來表現。

miss
坐過站
miss 有「錯過」的意思。

be late for ～
～遲到
也可以用在「上學遲到」時，如 be late for school。

What a relief!
太好了、鬆了一口氣！
經常和 phew 這些感嘆詞一起使用。

初次見面的人對我說……
Someone you just met

中文日記

今天和咖啡店的店員聊了幾句，

結果他突然問了我的年紀！

問別人年紀有點沒禮貌吧？

而且還是第一次見面的人！

英文填空日記

When I was talking to the _____ of a café,
今天和咖啡店的店員聊了幾句，

he suddenly asked my _____ !
結果他突然問了我的年紀！

Isn't it kinda _____ to ask someone's age
問別人年紀有點沒禮貌吧？

when you meet this person _____ the first time!?
而且還是第一次見面的人！

英文日記

When I was talking to the staff of a café,

he suddenly asked my age!

Isn't it kinda rude to ask someone's age

when you meet this person for the first time!?

常用單字片語集

staff
店員
泛指店家的店員、公司的員工。

ask one's age
問某個人年紀
age（年齡）這個單字相當實用。

rude
失禮
也會說 You're so rude!（你太失禮了！）

for the first time
第一次
這種情況下的介系詞要用 for。

六月
26

怎麼做能提升英文能力？

What should I do?

中文日記

我真的很想精進自己的英文能力，

但我不知道要從哪一方面下手！

我想和各個國家的人溝通交流，

想必會很有意思。

英文填空日記

I really want to _____ **my English.**
我真的很想精進自己的英文能力，

But I don't know _____ **to start!**
但我不知道要從哪一方面下手！

I wanna communicate _____ **people from overseas.**
我想和各個國家的人溝通交流，

It _____ **be very fun.**
想必會很有意思。

英文日記

I really want to improve my English.

But I don't know where to start!

I wanna communicate with people from overseas.

It would be very fun.

常用單字片語集

improve
精進、提升
在表達提升英文能力或運動等技能時可以用
這個單字。

I don't know where to start.
不知道要從哪裡下手。
很實用的句子，可以整句記下來。

communicate with ～
和～溝通交流
別忘記介系詞 with。

It would be ～ .
想必會～。
和 It will be ～ . 相比，would 是沒那麼絕對
的説法。

平時常吃的吐司賣完了

My white bread!

中文日記

我每天早上會吃一片吐司，

但我今天去超市的時候，

發現我平時常買的吐司賣完了！

好失望啊！

英文填空日記

I eat a slice of _____ bread every morning.
我每天早上會吃一片吐司，

But when I went to the _____ today,
但我今天去超市的時候，

the one I always buy was _____ out!
發現我平時常買的吐司賣完了！

What a _____ !
好失望啊！

英文日記

I eat a slice of white bread every morning.

But when I went to the supermarket today,

the one I always buy was sold out!

What a bummer!

- - - - - - - - - - 常用單字片語集 - - - - - - - - - -

white bread
吐司
也可以説 sandwich bread。

supermarket
超市
單一個 super 是無法代表超市的，要特別留意。

sold out
售罄
有時候店家也會以 sold out 來標示東西賣完了。

What a bummer!
真失望！真掃興！
表示「低落、消沉」的俚語。

108

腳的水腫都不消

Swollen legs

中文日記

我的腳今天水腫好嚴重，

因為我一整天都坐在電腦前面！

回家以後我要拉拉筋才行！

我的眼睛也好疲勞。

英文填空日記

My legs are _____ today
我的腳今天水腫好嚴重，

because I _____ all day sitting in front of my computer!
因為我一整天都坐在電腦前面！

I should _____ some stretches when I get home!
回家以後我要拉拉筋才行！

My eyes are also _____.
我的眼睛也好疲勞。

英文日記

My legs are swollen today

because I spent all day sitting in front of my computer!

I should do some stretches when I get home!

My eyes are also tired.

常用單字片語集

swell
浮腫、水腫
過去式是 swelled，過去分詞是 swollen。

spend all day -ing
一整天都在～
spend 的過去式是 spent，要多加注意。

do some stretches
拉筋、伸展
可以和 do some exercises（運動）一起學起來。

be tired
疲勞
主詞也可以是人，例如 I'm tired.

指甲變長了

Long nails are annoying

我的指甲變長了，

得修剪一下才行。

我把指甲剪放到哪裡去了？

怎麼找不到啊……

My nails　　　　　so long.
我的指甲變長了，

I gotta　　　　　them.
得修剪一下才行。

Where did I put my nail　　　　　?
我把指甲剪放到哪裡去了？

I can't　　　　　them…
怎麼找不到啊……

My nails got so long.

I gotta clip them.

Where did I put my nail clippers?

I can't find them…

常用單字片語集

get long
變長
也可以用 become 代替 get。

clip
修剪
直覺會想用 cut 這個動詞，但在表示「剪指甲」時，最普遍使用的動詞是 clip。

nail clippers
指甲剪
clipper 是從 clip（修剪）衍生出來的名詞。

find
找
find 的過去式和過去分詞都是 found。

老是吃便利商店的便當

Lunch box at a convenience store

中文日記

我最近懶得煮飯，

所以常常買便利商店的便當來吃。

明明知道這樣很不健康，

但我實在是忙得沒時間煮飯啊。

英文填空日記

I've been too   to cook recently.
我最近懶得煮飯，

So I always buy a lunch   at a convenience store.
所以常常買便利商店的便當來吃。

I know it's not good for my   ,
明明知道這樣很不健康，

but I'm   busy to cook.
但我實在是忙得沒時間煮飯啊。

英文日記

I've been too lazy to cook recently.

So I always buy a lunch box at a convenience store.

I know it's not good for my body,

but I'm too busy to cook.

- - - - - - - - 常用單字片語集 - - - - - - - -

lazy to ～
懶得～
lazy 是「怠惰」的意思。

good for one's body
對身體好、健康
也可以用 health（健康）代替 body。

lunch box
便當
也可以說 bento box。

too ～ to...
太～以致於無法……
很實用的慣用句型，學起來吧。

JULY

It's getting hot recently.
最近慢慢變熱了，
I already hear the buzz of cicadas.
我都聽見蟬鳴聲了。
That means the summer is just around the corner!
這表示夏天即將來臨！
It's hot in summer, but I don't hate it.
雖然夏天總是很熱，但我並不討厭呢。

變熱了
Getting hot recently

最近慢慢變熱了，

我都聽見蟬鳴聲了。

這表示夏天即將來臨！

雖然夏天總是很熱，但我並不討厭呢。

It's   hot recently.
最近慢慢變熱了，

I already hear the   of cicadas.
我都聽見蟬鳴聲了。

That   the summer is just around the corner!
這表示夏天即將來臨！

It's hot in summer, but I don't   it.
雖然夏天總是很熱，但我並不討厭呢。

It's getting hot recently.

I already hear the buzz of cicadas.

That means the summer is just around the corner!

It's hot in summer, but I don't hate it.

常用單字片語集

It's getting hot.
慢慢變熱。
be getting 是「漸漸變得～」的意思。

buzz of cicada(s)
蟬鳴聲
buzz 是指昆蟲的叫聲。

just around the corner
即將來臨、近在眼前
提及季節轉變時經常用到的說法。

That means ～ .
表示～。
雖然直譯是「這就代表～」，但意思更貼近
「這表示～」。

瀏海剪太短了

My bangs!

中文日記

瀏海剪太短了！

我本來沒打算剪這麼短的。

這樣看起來好像小孩啊！

我不想讓別人看到我這副模樣……

英文填空日記

I cut my _____ too short!
瀏海剪太短了！

It wasn't _____ to be like this.
我本來沒打算剪這麼短的。

I _____ like a child!
這樣看起來好像小孩啊！

I don't want _____ to see this…
我不想讓別人看到我這副模樣……

英文日記

I cut my bangs too short!

It wasn't supposed to be like this.

I look like a child!

I don't want anyone to see this…

常用單字片語集

bangs
瀏海
英式英文會用 fringe。

be supposed to ～
本來應該～
日常對話中經常用到的句型，可以更換主詞，靈活運用。

look like ～
看起來好像～
like 後面要接名詞，「look ＋形容詞」也是常見用法。

don't want ～ to...
不想讓～做……
記得留意受詞擺放的位置。

遲到
I'm gonna be late!

糟糕,我睡過頭了!

我會趕不上和佳奈約好的午餐!

我得搭十一點的電車才行!

究竟趕不趕得上呢?

Oh my god, I　　　　　!
糟糕,我睡過頭了!

I'm　　　　be late for lunch with Kana!!
我會趕不上和佳奈約好的午餐!

I　　　　catch the train at 11!!
我得搭十一點的電車才行!

Am I gonna　　　　it or not…?
究竟趕不趕得上呢?

Oh my god, I overslept!

I'm gonna be late for lunch with Kana!!

I gotta catch the train at 11!!

Am I gonna make it or not…?

常用單字片語集

overslept
睡過頭
原形是 oversleep。

I'm gonna be late.
我會遲到。
已經確定會晚到的情況則用 I'm late.。

gotta ～
必須～
結合 got to 的口語用法。

make it
趕上
日常對話中經常用到的片語。

今天去名古屋出差

Business trip to Nagoya

4 月
5 月
6 月
7 月
8 月
9 月
10 月
11 月
12 月
1 月
2 月
3 月

中文日記

我現在要出發前往名古屋了！

我們要和名古屋分公司的人開會。

在那之後，我要去吃鰻魚飯、味噌豬排⋯⋯

我等不及了！

英文填空日記

Now I'm _____ to Nagoya!
我現在要出發前往名古屋了！

We _____ a meeting with the people at the Nagoya branch.
我們要和名古屋分公司的人開會。

_____ that, I'll meet Hitsu-mabushi, Miso-katsu, and...
在那之後，我要去吃鰻魚飯、味噌豬排⋯⋯

I can't _____ to get there!!
我等不及了！

英文日記

Now I'm off to Nagoya!

We have a meeting with the people at the Nagoya branch.

After that, I'll meet Hitsu-mabushi, Miso-katsu, and...

I can't wait to get there!!

常用單字片語集

be off to ～
出發、前往～
想表達「我出門了」的時候，經常會說 I'm off!。

have a meeting
開會
這種情境使用的動詞是 have，要記住喔。

after that
在那之後
有「在那之後」、「然後」的意思，可以做為連接詞使用。

I can't wait to ～.
我等不及要～。
就是「很期待要～」的意思。

獎金
Got a bonus!

耶！我領到獎金啦！

今年要買什麼好呢？

還是要存一些錢，用在下一趟旅行上呢？

總之，今晚我要吃一頓好料的！

Woo-hoo!! I've _____ a bonus!!
耶！我領到獎金啦！

What _____ I buy this year…?
今年要買什麼好呢？

Or maybe I'll _____ some for the next trip?
還是要存一些錢，用在下一趟旅行上呢？

_____, I'll eat something good tonight!!
總之，今晚我要吃一頓好料的！

Woo-hoo!! I've got a bonus!!

What should I buy this year…?

Or maybe I'll save some for the next trip?

Anyways, I'll eat something good tonight!!

常用單字片語集

get a bonus
領獎金
最簡單好用的說法。

save some
存一些錢
save 也有「存錢、節儉」的意思。

What should I buy?
我要買什麼好呢？
自言自語的時候經常使用的句子。

anyways
總之
和 anyway 意思相同，但在輕鬆的日常對話中也滿多人使用 anyways。

6 想邁向下一個階段

Time to move on

中文日記

我在這間公司已經工作四年了……

一直待在這裡真的好嗎？

這份工作真的是我想做的事嗎？

我是不是應該邁向下一個階段呢？

英文填空日記

It's been already 4 years since I　　　this company.
我在這間公司已經工作四年了……

Is it　　　for me to stay here forever?
一直待在這裡真的好嗎？

Is this really　　　I wanna do in my life?
這份工作真的是我想做的事嗎？

Should I move　　　to the next stage?
我是不是應該邁向下一個階段呢？

英文日記

It's been already 4 years since I joined this company.

Is it okay for me to stay here forever?

Is this really what I wanna do in my life?

Should I move on to the next stage?

------------------------------ 常用單字片語集 ------------------------------

join the company
進公司
也可以用 enter，但 join 是最常見的用法。

Is it okay for me to ～?
我～真的好嗎？
自問自答的時候經常使用的句型。

what I wanna do
我想做的事
wanna 是結合 want to 的口語用法。

move on to ～
邁向～
也可以用 move up 或 step up。

七月 7 很重要的報告

A big presentation today

中文日記

今天有個很重要的報告。

雖然很緊張,但我覺得自己表現得還不錯!

既然我現在都可以駕馭這麼重大的工作了,

我還想再嘗試看看不一樣的事!

英文填空日記

I _____ a big presentation today.
今天有個很重要的報告。

I got _____, but I think I did it well!
雖然很緊張,但我覺得自己表現得還不錯!

Now I can _____ this kind of big job.
既然我現在都可以駕馭這麼重大的工作了,

I wanna _____ something different!
我還想再嘗試看看不一樣的事!

英文日記

I had a big presentation today.

I got nervous, but I think I did it well!

Now I can handle this kind of big job.

I wanna try something different!

常用單字片語集

nervous
緊張
可以說 I'm a little nervous.(我有點緊張)。

do it well
表現不錯
well 是「好」的意思,如果想說「更好」的話,就要用比較級的 better。

handle
駕馭、處理
I can't handle this.(這個我應付不來)等句子也很實用。

try something different
嘗試不一樣的事
這裡如果用了 challenge 的話,就會是完全不一樣的意思,所以要特別留意。

七月 8 現在會和大介單獨吃飯了

Go out with Daisuke

中文日記

今天我和大介去喝酒了。

這已經是我第三次和他單獨出門了,

而且我們滿合得來的。

和他在一起,我覺得很放鬆也很開心。

英文填空日記

I went   a drink with Daisuke today.
今天我和大介去喝酒了。

This is the   time to go out with him actually,
這已經是我第三次和他單獨出門了,

and we have good   .
而且我們滿合得來的。

I feel relaxed and enjoy   with him.
和他在一起,我覺得很放鬆也很開心。

英文日記

I went for a drink with Daisuke today.

This is the third time to go out with him actually,

and we have good chemistry.

I feel relaxed and enjoy being with him.

常用單字片語集

go for a drink
去喝酒
或是 go for coffee(去喝咖啡)等,能做出很多變化。

This is the third time to ~ .
這是我第三次~。
third 的部分可以自由變化。

have good chemistry
合得來
chemistry 一般來說指的是「化學」,但也有這樣的用法。

enjoy being with him
和他在一起很開心
「享受和他在一起」,即「在一起很開心」的意思。

跟小瞳聊聊近況
Lunch with Hitomi

中文日記

今天我和小瞳去吃午餐了。

我很高興可以得知她的近況。

她說她養的兩隻小貓很可愛，

我下次也要去看看！

英文填空日記

Today I _____ lunch with Hitomi.
今天我和小瞳去吃午餐了。

I was glad to hear _____ she's been recently.
我很高興可以得知她的近況。

She got two _____ which are so cute!
她說她養的兩隻小貓很可愛，

I'll go _____ them sometime!
我下次也要去看看！

英文日記

Today I had lunch with Hitomi.

I was glad to hear how she's been recently.

She got two kittens which are so cute!

I'll go see them sometime!

- - - - - - - - - - - - - - 常用單字片語集 - - - - - - - - - - - - - -

be glad to hear ～
很高興能聽見～
也可以用 happy 代替 glad。

how she's been recently
聊聊近況
「她最近過得如何」，即「聊聊近況」。

kitten
小貓
可以和 puppy（小狗）一起記下來。

go see ～
去看～
省略了 go to see ～的 to，日常對話中經常用到。

122

在咖啡店讀書

Study at a café

中文日記

我決定從今天開始學英文！

我想講一口流利的英文，

這樣我就可以用英文跟各式各樣的人交流了！

我會努力的！

英文填空日記

I decided to study English   today!
我決定從今天開始學英文！

I want to be   ,
我想講一口流利的英文，

**   that I can communicate with many people in English!**
這樣我就可以用英文跟各式各樣的人交流了！

I'll try my   .
我會努力的！

英文日記

I decided to study English from today!

I want to be fluent,

so that I can communicate with many people in English!

I'll try my best!

常用單字片語集

from today
今天開始
如果想説「明天開始」的話，就是 from tomorrow。

fluent
流利的
也可以説 fluent in English（英文很流利）。

so that ～
這樣我就能～
日常生活中經常會聽見的句型，學起來吧。

I'll try my best.
我會努力。
和 I'll do my best. 的意思差不多，但在挑戰比較困難的事情時會用 try。

11

喜歡幾片裝的吐司？

How many slices do you want?

中文日記

噢，又來了！

為什麼東京沒有五片裝的呀？

不是六片裝就是八片裝！我從來沒在大阪看過八片裝的！

喔，我是在說吐司啦。

英文填空日記

Oh no,   !
噢，又來了！

Why don't they   any 5 slices in Tokyo!?
為什麼東京沒有五片裝的呀？

It's always 6 or 8! I've   seen 8 slices in Osaka!
不是六片裝就是八片裝！我從來沒在大阪看過八片裝的！

Well, I'm   about white bread.
喔，我是在說吐司啦。

英文日記

Oh no, again!

Why don't they have any 5 slices in Tokyo!?

It's always 6 or 8! I've never seen 8 slices in Osaka!

Well, I'm talking about white bread.

常用單字片語集

Again!
又來了！
想表示「又搞砸了！」或「又這樣！」的時候可以用。

they have ~ in...
……有~
提到「有」的時候，通常會想要用 there is 的句型，但這種情境大多會使用 they have ~。

I've never seen ~ .
從來沒有見過。
用現在完成式來表達「從來沒有~」。

I'm talking about ~ .
~的事。
直譯是「我是在說~」，即「~的事」。

七月
12

跌個狗吃屎
Fell down on the street

中文日記

今天早上我在路上跌倒了。

超丟臉的！

我常常在沒有東西的地方滑倒或絆倒⋯⋯

怎麼會這樣⋯⋯

英文填空日記

I   down on the street this morning.
今天早上我在路上跌倒了。

I was so   !
超丟臉的！

I often slip or   over nothing…
我常常在沒有東西的地方滑倒或絆倒⋯⋯

I   why…
怎麼會這樣⋯⋯

英文日記

I fell down on the street this morning.

I was so embarrassed!

I often slip or stumble over nothing…

I wonder why…

常用單字片語集

fall down
跌倒
最普遍的説法。fall over 也是相同意思。

be embarrassed
感到丟臉
因為犯錯或出糗，感到「好難為情」的時候就會這麼説。

slip/stumble
滑倒／絆倒
兩者都是在跌倒的情境中可以使用的單字。

I wonder why.
為什麼會這樣？
在自問自答時最常使用的句子。

125

一樹突然打電話來

Call from Kazuki

中文日記

一樹突然打電話來問我：

「為什麼你不回我訊息？

你很忙嗎？還是有其他事？」

唔，他這樣有點煩人……

英文填空日記

Kazuki just gave me a　　　　　　call and said,
一樹突然打電話來問我：

"Why don't you text me　　　　？
「為什麼你不回我訊息？

Are you busy or　　　　？"
你很忙嗎？還是有其他事？」

Ugh, this is　　　　annoying…
唔，他這樣有點煩人……

英文日記

Kazuki just gave me a sudden call and said,

"Why don't you text me back?

Are you busy or something?"

Ugh, this is kinda annoying…

常用單字片語集

give ~ a sudden call
突然打電話給~
give a call 是「打電話」的片語。

text back
回覆
想表示「回覆~」的時候，可以在 text ~ back 的中間擺上人名。

or something
還是~
中文裡的「還是~」就可以用這種說法。

be annoying
煩人
表現「厭煩、不爽」這類情緒時可以使用的片語。

去特賣會
Go to the sale

中文日記

今天我去了銀座的特賣會。

我本來只打算買洋裝和鞋子的,

結果還是買了一堆東西……

沒關係!我心滿意足!

英文填空日記

Today I went　　　　 the sale in Ginza.
今天我去了銀座的特賣會。

I was　　　　 to buy only a dress and shoes,
我本來只打算買洋裝和鞋子的,

but I　　　　 up buying some more stuff...
結果還是買了一堆東西……

It's okay!! I'm　　　　!!
沒關係!我心滿意足!

英文日記

Today I went to the sale in Ginza.

I was planning to buy only a dress and shoes,

but I ended up buying some more stuff...

It's okay!! I'm satisfied!!

常用單字片語集

go to the sale
去特賣會
和中文是一樣的說法。

plan to do ～
原本打算～
plan(計畫)的相關片語。

end up -ing
最後～
經常會用到「最後還是～」這樣的句型。

dress
洋裝
名詞表示一件式的洋裝、連衣裙。

大介約我去煙火大會

Daisuke asked me out

中文日記

大介問我：「要不要一起去看煙火？」

我也不知道怎麼回事，

心已經開始撲通撲通跳了！

這是不是代表我對他抱有特殊的感覺呢？

英文填空日記

Daisuke said, "Do you wanna go _____ firework?"
大介問我：「要不要一起去看煙火？」

I don't _____ why,
我也不知道怎麼回事，

but my heart is _____ now!!
心已經開始撲通撲通跳了！

This _____ I have a special feeling for him!?
這是不是代表我對他抱有特殊的感覺呢？

英文日記

Daisuke said, "Do you wanna go see firework?"

I don't know why,

but my heart is pounding now!!

This means I have a special feeling for him!?

常用單字片語集

go see ～
去看～
省略 go to see 的 to 的口語説法。

I don't know why, but ～
我也不知道怎麼回事，但～
這裡的 why 就是表示「怎麼一回事」。

My heart is pounding.
心撲通撲通的跳。
My heart is beating so fast.（心臟跳得好快）也是同樣的意思。

This means ～ .
這代表～。
means 是「意味、代表」的動詞，也可以用在這樣的表現手法上。

想吃炸物

Wanna eat something oily

中文日記

好想吃炸雞喔。

但是我最近好像吃太多炸物了。

啊,我昨天才剛吃過薯條。

那今天還是算了吧。

英文填空日記

I feel   eating fried chicken.
好想吃炸雞喔。

But I think I've been eating too much   food.
但是我最近好像吃太多炸物了。

Oh, I just had   fries yesterday.
啊,我昨天才剛吃過薯條。

I'll   today.
那今天還是算了吧。

英文日記

I feel like eating fried chicken.

But I think I've been eating too much oily food.

Oh, I just had French fries yesterday.

I'll pass today.

常用單字片語集

feel like -ing
想要～
大多用在自言自語的時候。

oily food
oily 是「油的」的意思。

French fries
薯條
fried potatoes 屬於和製英語,通用性較低,要特別留意。

I'll pass.
算了、不做了。
也會說 I'll pass this time.(這次先算了)。

今天穿什麼好呢？

What to wear today

中文日記

今天穿什麼好呢？

要穿這件洋裝還是那件裙子呢⋯⋯

好難抉擇呀！

我老是要花很多時間才能決定。

英文填空日記

What should I　　　　　 today?

今天穿什麼好呢？

This　　　　　 or that skirt...

要穿這件洋裝還是那件裙子呢⋯⋯

I can't　　　　 !

好難抉擇呀！

It always takes time to make up my　　　　 .

我老是要花很多時間才能決定。

英文日記

What should I wear today?

This dress or that skirt...

I can't decide!

It always takes time to make up my mind.

常用單字片語集

wear
穿
wear 的過去式是 wore，過去分詞是 worn。

This ~ or that...
這個～還是那個⋯⋯
經常用來表示買東西時的猶豫不決。

can't decide
難以抉擇
也可以用來表示「猶豫」。

make up one's mind
決定、下定決心
和 decide 的意思相近。

我有記得關掉冷氣嗎？

Did I turn off the AC?

中文日記

今天早上出門的時候，我有把冷氣關掉嗎？

我不記得了！

我怎麼這麼健忘呀！

我得振作一點才行。

英文填空日記

Did I turn ____ the AC when I left home this morning…?
今天早上出門的時候，我有把冷氣關掉嗎？

I can't ____!
我不記得了！

Why am I so ____!?
我怎麼這麼健忘呀！

I gotta ____ myself together.
我得振作一點才行。

英文日記

Did I turn off the AC when I left home this morning…?

I can't remember!

Why am I so forgetful!?

I gotta pull myself together.

常用單字片語集

turn off
關
在描述關掉電視、冷氣等家電的開關時經常用到的片語。

can't remember
不記得、想不起來
remember 有「記得」和「回想」兩種意思。

forgetful
健忘的
從動詞 forget（忘記）衍生而來。

pull oneself together
振作
pull（拉、拔）的相關慣用語。

131

媽媽打電話來了

Mom called me

今天媽媽打電話給我，

問我怎麼用智慧型手機。

她明明拿著最新型號的手機，

卻連怎麼上網都不知道……

Today my _____ **called me and,**

今天媽媽打電話給我，

asked me how _____ **use her smart phone.**

問我怎麼用智慧型手機。

Even _____ **she has the latest model,**

她明明拿著最新型號的手機，

she doesn't _____ **know how to use the Internet…**

卻連怎麼上網都不知道……

Today my mom called me and,

asked me how to use her smart phone.

Even though she has the latest model,

she doesn't even know how to use the Internet…

常用單字片語集

mom
媽媽
比 mother 更口語化的說法，日常對話經常用到。

how to ~
怎麼做~
to 的後面要接原形動詞，要特別留意。

even though ~
明明~、雖然~
注意不要和 even if（就算~）混用。

even ~
居然連~
在各種情境的日常對話都用得到的單字。

打錯電話了

Wrong number…

中文日記

我本來是要打電話給廣美的，

結果我打錯號碼了！

對方跟我說：「你打錯電話了。」

我覺得好丟臉啊！

英文填空日記

I _____ to call Hiromi,
我本來是要打電話給廣美的，

but I called someone else by _____!
結果我打錯號碼了！

She said, "I think you _____ the wrong number."
對方跟我說：「你打錯電話了。」

I was so _____!
我覺得好丟臉啊！

英文日記

I tried to call Hiromi,

but I called someone else by mistake!

She said, "I think you have the wrong number."

I was so embarrassed!

常用單字片語集

try to ～
打算～
另外，try -ing 有「試著～」的意思。

by mistake
弄錯
在 mistake（錯誤）前面加上介系詞 by 的
用法，經常會用到。

You have the wrong number.
你打錯電話了。
這種情況普遍會用的動詞是 have。

be embarrassed
丟臉
形容詞 embarrassing 也很常用到。

在咖啡店打發時間

Killing time at a café

在和 A 公司開會之前還有一點時間，

所以我在咖啡店打發時間。

好無聊呀……

早知道就帶本書了。

I still have   **time until the meeting with A Company,**

在和 A 公司開會之前還有一點時間，

I'm   **time at a café.**

所以我在咖啡店打發時間。

I'm   **now…**

好無聊呀……

I should   **brought a book.**

早知道就帶本書了。

I still have some time until the meeting with A Company,

I'm killing time at a café.

I'm bored now…

I should have brought a book.

常用單字片語集

have time
還有時間
提到「有」這個詞會馬上聯想到 there is～，但這個情境應該用 have。

kill time
打發時間
經常會說 kill some time（稍微打發時間）。

be bored
閒暇、無聊
日常對話中經常用到的表現手法，可以和 boring（無聊的）一起記下來。

should have ＋過去分詞
早知道就～
should 不能接過去式，所以改用「have ＋過去分詞」表示。

蟬鳴聲……

The buzz of cicadas

中文日記

今天早上醒來的時候，

我聽見蟬鳴聲，

讓我覺得夏天真的來了！

我超愛這個季節。

英文填空日記

When I   **up this morning,**
今天早上醒來的時候，

I heard the   **of cicadas.**
我聽見蟬鳴聲，

Now I feel summer has   **!**
讓我覺得夏天真的來了！

I like this season so   **.**
我超愛這個季節。

英文日記

When I woke up this morning,

I heard the buzz of cicadas.

Now I feel summer has come!

I like this season so much.

常用單字片語集

wake up
起床、醒來
get up 有「起床、下床」的意思，語感上
有點不同。

buzz
鳴叫聲
表示蟬等昆蟲的叫聲。

Summer has come.
夏天來了。
用現在完成式來表示，come 的過去分詞還
是 come，沒有變化。

so much
超級、非常
very much 也是同樣的用法。

連假三天要做什麼好呢？

3-day holiday!

中文日記

這個週末有三天連假！

我想隨便去個地方走走……

不然我約沙織好了！

希望她有空！

英文填空日記

It's going to be 3-day   **this weekend!**
這個週末有三天連假！

I wanna go   **…**
我想隨便去個地方走走……

Maybe I'll   **Saori!**
不然我約沙織好了！

Hope she'll be   **!**
希望她有空！

英文日記

It's going to be 3-day holiday this weekend!

I wanna go somewhere…

Maybe I'll ask Saori!

Hope she'll be free!

常用單字片語集

3-day holiday
三天連假
也可以說 3 days off。

somewhere
某個地方
很實用的單字，可以和 anywhere（任何地方）一起記下來。

ask
約、邀請
除了表示「問、詢問」以外，ask 也有這種用法。

free
有空閒的
「不忙、沒事」，即「有空閒的」，在日常對話中經常會用到。

我也想擁有小蠻腰

I wanna get curves

中文日記

我根本是個水桶腰。

我要開始健身,打造出小蠻腰!

先從仰臥起坐開始好了!

在達到目標以前,我不會輕言放棄的!

英文填空日記

I have no   .
我根本是個水桶腰。

I gotta work   to get curves!
我要開始健身,打造出小蠻腰!

Let's start with   !
先從仰臥起坐開始好了!

I won't give   on my goal!
在達到目標以前,我不會輕言放棄的!

英文日記

I have no waist.

I gotta work out to get curves!

Let's start with sit-ups!

I won't give up on my goal!

常用單字片語集

have no waist
水桶腰、沒有腰身
waist 就是「腰身、腰」的意思。

work out
健身、肌力訓練
泛指一般的健身或慢跑等讓身體更加緊實的運動。

sit-ups
仰臥起坐
單指腹肌的話是 ABS。

give up
放棄
常用片語,常見用法像是 Never give up!
(別放棄!)

在海邊被搭訕了

A guy hit on us

當我們在海邊的時候，

有個男的來向我們搭訕。

我不太擅長和陌生人說話，

所以我就沒理他了⋯⋯

**　　　　　we were at the beach,**
當我們在海邊的時候，

a guy just　　　　　on us.
有個男的來向我們搭訕。

I'm not　　　　at talking to strangers,
我不太擅長和陌生人說話，

so I just　　　　　him...
所以我就沒理他了⋯⋯

When we were at the beach,

a guy just hit on us.

I'm not good at talking to strangers,

so I just ignored him...

- - - - - - - - - - 常用單字片語集 - - - - - - - - - -

when ～
當～
除了疑問句之外，when 也可以像這樣活用在各種句型中。

hit on ～
搭訕～
也可以用 pick up。

be good at ～
擅長～
改成否定句則會變成「不擅長～」。

ignore
不理睬
日常生活中會頻繁用到的單字，學起來吧。

口好渴

I'm thirsty

中文日記

我口好渴。

因為今天一整天都在室外，

我想喝點東西！

不然吃刨冰也不錯。

英文填空日記

I'm   .
我口好渴。

I've been   all day today,
因為今天一整天都在室外，

so I wanna get something   drink!
我想喝點東西！

Or   ice is good, too.
不然吃刨冰也不錯。

英文日記

I'm thirsty.

I've been outside all day today,

so I wanna get something to drink!

Or shaved ice is good, too.

--------- 常用單字片語集 ---------

thirsty
口渴
注意 th 的發音。這是很常用的單字。

outside
室外
和 out 的意思相似，但 outside 還有「外面」、「室外」的意思。

something to drink
喝點什麼
可以和 something to eat（吃點什麼）一起記下來。

shaved ice
刨冰
也可以說 snow cone。

牙科定期檢查
Checkup at a dentist

我去牙科做了定期檢查。

謝天謝地，我沒有蛀牙！

不過我的智齒還在⋯⋯

不曉得是不是總有一天必須拔掉它⋯⋯

I went to the ⟨⟨⟨⟩⟩⟩ for a checkup.
我去牙科做了定期檢查。

⟨⟨⟨⟩⟩⟩ god, I didn't have any cavity!
謝天謝地，我沒有蛀牙！

But I still have ⟨⟨⟨⟩⟩⟩ teeth…
不過我的智齒還在⋯⋯

I wonder it has to be ⟨⟨⟨⟩⟩⟩ out someday…
不曉得是不是總有一天必須拔掉它⋯⋯

I went to the dentist for a checkup.

Thank god, I didn't have any cavity!

But I still have wisdom teeth…

I wonder it has to be pulled out someday…

常用單字片語集

go to the dentist
去牙科
go to the doctor 是「去醫院」。

thank god
謝天謝地
鬆一口氣時會用到的感嘆句。

wisdom teeth
智齒
wisdom 是「智慧」的意思，據說由來是「擁有智慧時長出來的牙齒」。

pull out
拔掉
除了拔牙齒以外，也可以用在拔出其他東西。

七月 28

鞋子磨腳
My feet hurt!

中文日記

我的腳起水泡了。

這雙高跟鞋太緊了。

早知道就買大一號的。

不知道我的小包包裡有沒有 OK 繃呢？

英文填空日記

I got a _____ on my feet.
我的腳起水泡了。

These pumps are too _____ for me.
這雙高跟鞋太緊了。

I should have bought _____ ones.
早知道就買大一號的。

Do I have a bandage in my _____ ?
不知道我的小包包裡有沒有 OK 繃呢？

英文日記

I got a blister on my feet.

These pumps are too tight for me.

I should have bought bigger ones.

Do I have a bandage in my mini-bag?

- - - - - - - - - 常用單字片語集 - - - - - - - - -

blister
水泡
英文裡沒有單字可以表示「鞋子磨腳」，所以改用這樣的說法。

tight
緊
想表示鞋子或衣服「太緊」的時候可以用的單字。

bigger one
大一號
bigger 是 big 的比較級。

mini-bag
小包包
用來指化妝包等容量較小的包包。

要記得去買棉花棒

Gotta go get cotton swabs

今天我得去藥妝店一趟！

要買的東西太多了！

棉花棒、衛生棉、防蟲噴霧……

我得記下來，不然一定會忘記。

Today I gotta go to the _____ !
今天我得去藥妝店一趟！

I have so many _____ to buy!
要買的東西太多了！

_____ , sanitary pads, bug repellent…
棉花棒、衛生棉、防蟲噴霧……

I'll forget it if I don't make a _____ .
我得記下來，不然一定會忘記。

Today I gotta go to the drugstore!

I have so many things to buy!

Q-tips, sanitary pads, bug repellent…

I'll forget it if I don't make a note.

常用單字片語集

drugstore
藥妝店
也會説 pharmacy。

things to buy
要買的東西
這裡使用 thing（東西）的複數形。

Q-tip
棉花棒
Q-tip 是從商標直接變成通用名稱了。也可以説 cotton swab。

make a note
記下來
大多會用 note 來代替 memo。

30 綜藝節目笑死我了

The comedy show cracked me up!

中文日記

昨天我在電視上看了一個搞笑節目，

實在是太好笑了！

我本來想錄下來的，

結果空間不夠，沒能錄下來。

英文填空日記

I was watching a _____ show on TV last night.
昨天我在電視上看了一個搞笑節目，

It was so _____!
實在是太好笑了！

I wanted to _____ it,
我本來想錄下來的，

but I couldn't because the _____ was full.
結果空間不夠，沒能錄下來。

英文日記

I was watching a comedy show on TV last night.

It was so funny!

I wanted to record it,

but I couldn't because the storage was full.

常用單字片語集

comedy show
搞笑節目
comedy 是「搞笑、喜劇」的意思。

funny
有趣、好笑
fun 是「開心」，funny 是「有趣、好笑」
的意思，語感上有些不同，要注意。

want to ～
我想～
這裡的情境已經是過去式了，所以會用
wanted to ～。

storage
空間、容量
指資料數據的存放空間。

去了眼科診所

Eye clinic

中文日記

我去眼科診所買隱形眼鏡。

我明明就有預約，

但他們卻讓我等了三十分鐘！

搞什麼鬼啊！

英文填空日記

I went to the eye _____ to buy contact lenses.
我去眼科診所買隱形眼鏡。

I made an _____,
我明明就有預約，

but they _____ me waiting for 30 minutes!
但他們卻讓我等了三十分鐘！

_____ crap!
搞什麼鬼啊！

英文日記

I went to the eye clinic to buy contact lenses.

I made an appointment,

but they kept me waiting for 30 minutes!

Holy crap!

- - - - - - - - - - **常用單字片語集** - - - - - - - - -

eye clinic
眼科診所
這個情況不會用 hospital，要特別留意。

make an appointment
預約
醫院或診所的預約不會用 reservation（通常用於餐廳預約）。

keep ～ waiting
讓～等待
keep 除了「維持」以外，還有「讓～做什麼事」的意思。

Holy crap!
糟糕透頂！
發生令人厭惡或意料之外的事情時，可以這麼說。

有關「工作」的十大表現手法

第 1 名	I go to work. 我去上班。	想表示「去公司」的時候，通常會用 I go to my work place. 或 I go to my office.。一般會用 company 來表示「公司」，但基本上在這種情況下不會用到。
第 2 名	I'm busy. 我好忙。	也常常會用現在完成式 have，像是 I've been busy.（我一直都很忙），這個 have 有「持續」的意思，也可以在句尾補充上 today（今天）。
第 3 名	I have a meeting. 我有個會議。	和工作相關的話題經常會用到 I have ～，把 meeting（會議）、interview（面試）這些單字學起來的話，就可以搭配 I have 句型一起使用了。
第 4 名	I'm off today. 我今天休假。	這是用來描述「休假」時最簡單的說法。除此之外，也可以說 Today's my day off. 或 I'm not working today.。
第 5 名	I got a call from A Company. A 公司打電話來了。	行政工作常常需要接聽電話，想表達「接到電話」的情況，get a call 是最簡單的說法。其他像是～ called me（～打給我）也是簡單實用的句型。
第 6 名	I have a lot of things to do. 我有好多事要做。	to do 句型相當實用，一定要學起來。比方說，把 things 改成 something，就是 I have something to do.（我有點事情要做）。
第 7 名	I have to work overtime today. 我今天要加班。	要表示「加班」的時候，小心不要用錯成 overwork。work overtime 才是「加班」的正確說法，整個片語一起記下來吧。
第 8 名	I wanna quit. 我想辭職了。	比 I wanna quit my job. 更簡短的句子。resign 這個單字雖然也是辭職的意思，但語感上更貼近「請辭」，所以這種情境還是用 quit 較好。
第 9 名	I'm tired with work. 工作累死我了。	I'm tired 的句型不僅限於工作上，更是日常生活中經常用到的表現手法。也可以把其他像是 I'm exhausted.（筋疲力盡）的說法一起記下來，都很實用。
第 10 名	This document is due today. 這份文件的繳交期限是今天。	due ～是「期限是～」的意思。除此之外，也可以用 deadline 代替 due，像是 the deadline for submission（繳交期限）。

Best 10

AUGUST

8 月

I went to the beach with my friends,
我和朋友一起去海邊玩，
but accidentally, I stepped on a sea urchin...
但不小心踩到海膽了……
And I got a barb in the sole of my foot!
刺還扎到我的腳底板！
That was horrible...
好衰啊……

1 好姊妹聚餐
Girls' night out

中文日記

今晚是女孩之夜！

我們在惠比壽集合，

一起為小瞳慶生！

她看起來超開心的！

英文填空日記

It's a _____ night out tonight!
今晚是女孩之夜！

We all _____ in Ebisu,
我們在惠比壽集合，

and _____ Hitomi's birthday!
一起為小瞳慶生！

She _____ so happy!
她看起來超開心的！

英文日記

It's a *girls'* night out tonight!

We all *gathered* in Ebisu,

and *celebrated* Hitomi's birthday!

She *looked* so happy!

常用單字片語集

a girls' night out
好姊妹聚餐
因為是複數形的 girls 變化成所有格，所以要注意「'」的位置。

gather
聚集、集合
gather 同時具有「聚集」和「集合」兩種意思。

celebrate
慶祝
celebration 是「慶祝」的名詞。

look happy
看起來很開心
look ＋形容詞是「看起來很～、好像很～」的意思。

2 美髮店

Hair salon

中文日記

我去美髮店剪頭髮了。

雖然我一直想嘗試留短髮，

但我還是沒有勇氣……

到頭來還是維持一樣的長度。

英文填空日記

I went to the hair salon to _____ a haircut.
我去美髮店剪頭髮了。

I've been thinking I wanna _____ a short haircut,
雖然我一直想嘗試留短髮，

but I don't have enough _____ to do it…
但我還是沒有勇氣……

After _____, it's the same length as usual.
到頭來還是維持一樣的長度。

英文日記

I went to the hair salon to get a haircut.

I've been thinking I wanna try a short haircut,

butI don't have enough courage to do it…

After all, it's the same length as usual.

常用單字片語集

get a haircut
剪頭髮
問別人「你剪頭髮了嗎？」可以説 Did you
get a haircut?。

try
嘗試、挑戰
注意不要和 challenge 搞混了。

don't have courage to do ～
沒有勇氣去～
加上 enough，語感會更貼近「沒有足夠的
勇氣」。

after all
到頭來
語感更接近「果然還是」的説法。

一樹又約我了……

Kazuki asked me out again…

中文日記

一樹又約我出去喝酒了，

但我沒那個興致……

他人很好，

但我已經心有所屬了。

英文填空日記

Kazuki asked me to go ⬚⬚⬚ **a drink again,**
一樹又約我出去喝酒了，

but I don't feel ⬚⬚⬚ **it…**
但我沒那個興致……

He's a nice ⬚⬚⬚ **,**
他人很好，

but there's someone else I have a ⬚⬚⬚ **on.**
但我已經心有所屬了。

英文日記

Kazuki asked me to go for a drink again,

but I don't feel like it…

He's a nice person,

but there's someone else I have a crush on.

常用單字片語集

go for a drink
去喝酒
其他也有像是 go for dinner（去吃晚餐）
的用法。

don't feel like it
沒有興致
feel like ～是「想做～」的意思，可以一併
學起來。

nice person
好人
person 是「人」的意思，複數形是
people，但一般會使用 person。

have a crush on ～
喜歡～
日常對話中會出現的説法。

八月 4 在海邊被海膽的刺扎到了
Barbs of a sea urchin

中文日記

我和朋友一起去海邊玩，

但不小心踩到海膽了……

刺還扎到我的腳底板！

好衰啊……

英文填空日記

I went to the _____ with my friends,
我和朋友一起去海邊玩，

but accidentally, I stepped _____ a sea urchin...
但不小心踩到海膽了……

And I got a barb in the _____ of my foot!
刺還扎到我的腳底板！

That was _____ ...
好衰啊……

英文日記

I went to the beach with my friends,

but accidentally, I stepped on a sea urchin...

And I got a barb in the sole of my foot!

That was horrible...

- - - - - - - - - - - - - 常用單字片語集 - - - - - - - - - - - - -

beach
海、海邊
容易錯用成 sea（海、海洋），但一般指可以游泳的「海」會用 beach。

step on ～
踩到～
和介系詞 on 一起記下來吧。

sole
腳底板
foot（腳踝以下）、leg（大腿以下）等，關於「腳」的單字有很多。

horrible
糟糕的
terrible 也是相近的意思。

151

珍珠奶茶

Bubble tea is gone viral

這間珍珠奶茶店生意超好的。

好多人在排隊。

我應該沒辦法排這麼長的隊伍。

我太小看珍珠奶茶的人氣了……

This　　　　　tea shop is really popular.
這間珍珠奶茶店生意超好的。

Many people are　　　　up.
好多人在排隊。

I don't think I can wait in this long　　　　.
我應該沒辦法排這麼長的隊伍。

I　　　　the popularity of tapioca…
我太小看珍珠奶茶的人氣了……

This bubble tea shop is really popular.

Many people are lining up.

I don't think I can wait in this long line.

I underestimated the popularity of tapioca…

常用單字片語集

bubble tea
珍珠奶茶
也可以說 boba tea。

lining up
排隊
也有另一種說法 wait in line，要留意拼字。

line
隊伍
queue 也可以用來指「隊伍」。

underestimate
小看、低估
從動詞 estimate（估計、估價）衍生而來的單字。

八月 6 在超市結帳時被插隊了

A lady cut in my line!

中文日記

我在超市排隊結帳的時候，

突然有個女的插隊！

她在想什麼呀！

守規矩一點好不好。

英文填空日記

I was waiting   line for the cashier at the supermarket,
我在超市排隊結帳的時候，

and suddenly a lady   in!
突然有個女的插隊！

What the   was she thinking!?
她在想什麼呀！

Let's keep   manners.
守規矩一點好不好。

英文日記

I was waiting in line for the cashier at the supermarket,

and suddenly a lady cut in!

What the hell was she thinking!?

Let's keep good manners.

- - - - - - - - - - - - - 常用單字片語集 - - - - - - - - - - - - -

wait in line
排隊
這個片語的介系詞要用 in，學起來吧。

cut in
中斷
cut in line 就是「插隊」的意思。

the hell
到底
可以說 What the hell are you doing!?（你到底在搞什麼 !?），有很多種用法。

keep good manners
遵守規矩
此外，也經常使用 Mind your manners!（注意你的行為舉止！）

153

回大阪老家
Went back to Osaka

中文日記

我回大阪老家了。

大家知道的，我爸媽每次都會問：

「你現在沒有交往的對象嗎？」

好煩呀！

英文填空日記

I went back to my _____ in Osaka.
我回大阪老家了。

You _____ what, every time my parents ask me,
大家知道的，我爸媽每次都會問：

"Are you _____ anyone right now?"
「你現在沒有交往的對象嗎？」

I'm _____ up!
好煩呀！

英文日記

I went back to my hometown in Osaka.

You know what, every time my parents ask me,

"Are you seeing anyone right now?"

I'm fed up!

常用單字片語集

go back to one's hometown
返鄉
回去 hometown（故鄉），就是「返鄉」的意思。

you know what
你知道的
朋友間的日常對話經常使用的說法，整句話一起記下來吧。

see anyone/someone
和某個人交往
使用動詞 see（看、見面）可以表示「交往」的意思。

be fed up
煩躁
I'm fed up with ～.（～讓我覺得好煩）也是常用句型。

八月 **8** 一樹跟我告白了

Kazuki confessed to me

中文日記

最後我還是跟一樹去吃飯了。

他説：「你願意跟我交往嗎？」

雖然感到很抱歉，但我還是告訴他：

「我們之間沒有辦法超越朋友的關係。」

英文填空日記

_____, I went for dinner with Kazuki,
最後我還是跟一樹去吃飯了。

and he said, "Will you _____ out with me?"
他説：「你願意跟我交往嗎？」

I felt _____ but I said,
雖然感到很抱歉，但我還是告訴他：

"I don't think we can become _____ than friends."
「我們之間沒有辦法超越朋友的關係。」

英文日記

Eventually, I went for dinner with Kazuki,

and he said, "Will you go out with me?"

I felt sorry but I said,

"I don't think we can become more than friends."

常用單字片語集

eventually
最後
可以用來表現「雖然有所遲疑，但最後還是……」的語感。

go out with ～
和～交往
其他還有像 dating、seeing 都可以表示「交往」的意思。

feel sorry
感到抱歉
這個情況不用 think，而是用 feel。

become more than friends
發展超越朋友的關係
此處要使用比較級 more than。

下班途中去了趟書店

Drop by a bookstore

下班後我繞去了書店，

發現我喜歡的作家出了新書！

我今天就要開始看！

今晚搞不好會熬夜……

I　　　　 by a bookstore after work,
下班後我繞去了書店，

and I found the new book of my favorite　　　　 !
發現我喜歡的作家出了新書！

I'll start　　　　 it today!
我今天就要開始看！

I might be staying　　　　 late tonight...
今晚搞不好會熬夜……

I dropped by a bookstore after work,

and I found the new book of my favorite author!

I'll start reading it today!

I might be staying up late tonight...

常用單字片語集

drop by ~
繞去~
前往預定行程外的地點時所使用的片語。

author
作者、作家
可以用在像是 Who is the author of this book?（這本書的作者是誰？）的情況。

start -ing
開始~
學校也會教的常用片語。

stay up late
熬夜
stay up 就是「醒著」的意思。

八月 10 熱到要融化了！

Melting hot!!

中文日記

熱到要融化了！

我完全沒有食慾。

唯一吃得下的食物就只有冰淇淋了。

不過我應該沒辦法出門去買。

英文填空日記

It's _____ hot!!
熱到要融化了！

I don't have any _____.
我完全沒有食慾。

The _____ thing I can eat now is ice cream.
唯一吃得下的食物就只有冰淇淋了。

But I don't _____ I can go out to buy it.
不過我應該沒辦法出門去買。

英文日記

It's melting hot!!

I don't have any appetite.

The only thing I can eat now is ice cream.

But I don't think I can go out to buy it.

- - - - - - - - - - - - - - - 常用單字片語集 - - - - - - - - - - - - - - -

It's melting hot.
熱到要融化了。
比一般的「炎熱」更加誇飾的說法。

appetite
食慾
想表示「有食慾」會說 have a good appetite。

the only thing ～
唯一～的是
thing 後面要接帶有主詞的完整句子。

I don't think I can ～ .
我應該沒辦法～。
注意不要把 I can ～的部分寫成否定形了。

157

把廣美介紹給我的朋友

Introduced Hiromi to Kenji

中文日記

今天我把廣美介紹給我的朋友健司認識。

我覺得他們兩個很登對。

而且健司肯定是廣美的菜！

希望他們兩個可以順利發展。

英文填空日記

Today I introduced Hiromi ⎯⎯⎯⎯ my other friend, Kenji.
今天我把廣美介紹給我的朋友健司認識。

I think they are a perfect ⎯⎯⎯⎯.
我覺得他們兩個很登對。

I'm sure Kenji is just Hiromi's ⎯⎯⎯⎯!
而且健司肯定是廣美的菜！

Hope it will ⎯⎯⎯⎯ well.
希望他們兩個可以順利發展。

英文日記

Today I introduced Hiromi to my other friend, Kenji.

I think they are a perfect match.

I'm sure Kenji is just Hiromi's type!

Hope it will go well.

常用單字片語集

introduce ～ to...
把～介紹給……
把 introduce 和 to 一起記下來吧。

be a perfect match
很登對
也可以說 They look good together.。

just ～'s type
是～的菜
加不加 just 都可以。

go well
順利發展
經常用在 Everything is going well.（一切都很順利）。

去百貨公司買鞋

Go to a department store

中文日記

我去了百貨公司買鞋子。

我每次買東西總是會花很多時間。

光是買一雙鞋子，

就花了一個小時！

英文填空日記

I went to a   **store to buy shoes.**
我去了百貨公司買鞋子。

It always   **me a long time to do shopping.**
我每次買東西總是會花很多時間。

I just bought one   **of shoes,**
光是買一雙鞋子，

and it   **an hour!!**
就花了一個小時！

英文日記

I went to a department store to buy shoes.

It always takes me a long time to do shopping.

I just bought one pair of shoes,

and it took an hour!!

常用單字片語集

department store
百貨公司
單獨使用 depart 是無法清楚表達的，要特別注意。

It takes ~ a long time to...
～花很多時間做……
應用了 it takes time（花時間）的句型。

one pair of shoes
一雙鞋子
兩雙就會變成 two pairs of shoes。

It took ~ .
花費了～。
take 的過去式是 took，過去分詞是 taken。

13 超市的雞蛋超級便宜

OMG, only 138 yen!?

中文日記

我在採買食材的時候，

發現雞蛋在特價！

只要一百三十八日圓！

太便宜了吧！

英文填空日記

When I was doing　　　　shopping,
我在採買食材的時候，

I found some eggs　　　　sale!
發現雞蛋在特價！

They were　　　　138 yen!!
只要一百三十八日圓！

**　　　　cheap!!**
太便宜了吧！

英文日記

When I was doing grocery shopping,

I found some eggs on sale!

They were only 138 yen!!

How cheap!!

常用單字片語集

do grocery shopping
採買食材
grocery store 就是「市場、超市」。

on sale
特價
也可以單純表示「販售中」，語意會根據前後文而截然不同，要特別留意。

only ～
只要～
在提及價格時，經常會說「只要～元」。

How ～！
多麼～呀！
原文是 How cheap it is!，但可以省略掉 it is 的部分。

14

終於要和大介去煙火大會

Fireworks with Daisuke

4 月
5 月
6 月
7 月
8 月
9 月
10 月
11 月
12 月
1 月
2 月
3 月

中文日記

就是今天了！

我要和大介去看煙火！

我期待到睡不著覺呢！

希望他會喜歡我的浴衣……

英文填空日記

Today's the _____ !
就是今天了！

I'm going to see _____ with Daisuke!
我要和大介去看煙火！

I was _____ excited to sleep!
我期待到睡不著覺呢！

_____ he likes my yukata…
希望他會喜歡我的浴衣……

英文日記

Today's the day!

I'm going to see fireworks with Daisuke!

I was too excited to sleep!

Hope he likes my yukata…

常用單字片語集

Today's the day.
就是今天了。
常用的表現手法，整句學起來吧。

fireworks
煙火
別忘了加上複數形的 s。

too ~ to...
太過～而無法……
中文會使用否定形，但英文不會。

Hope ~ .
希望～。
I hope ~ . 省略掉主詞的 I。

15 大介跟我告白了

Daisuke asked me out!

中文日記

天呀，好開心喔！

你知道發生什麼事了嗎？

大介跟我告白了！

這是我至今為止最幸福的瞬間！

英文填空日記

Oh my god, it was really　　　　!
天呀，好開心喔！

And you　　　　 what happened?
你知道發生什麼事了嗎？

Daisuke asked me　　　!
大介跟我告白了！

It was my happiest moment　　　　!
這是我至今為止最幸福的瞬間！

英文日記

Oh my god, it was really fun!

And you know what happened?

Daisuke asked me out!

It was my happiest moment ever!

- - - - - - - - - - - 常用單字片語集 - - - - - - - - - - -

fun
開心
have fun 就是「享受」的意思。

You know what happened?
你知道發生什麼事了嗎？
應用 you know 的表現手法，相當實用，整句一起記下來吧。

ask ～ out
告白
也可以用在「約會邀約」上。

ever
至今為止
常和最高級搭配使用的單字。

挑戰咖啡店的新飲品

New flavor of the café

中文日記

我經過那間常去的咖啡店時，

發現他們開始賣季節限定的新口味了！

我忍不住想喝喝看。

果然很好喝，不辜負我的期待。

英文填空日記

When I _____ by the café I often go to,
我經過那間常去的咖啡店時，

I found they started the new _____ flavor!
發現他們開始賣季節限定的新口味了！

I couldn't _____ but try it.
我忍不住想喝喝看。

It was so good _____ expected!
果然很好喝，不辜負我的期待。

英文日記

When I passed by the café I often go to,

I found they started the new seasonal flavor!

I couldn't help but try it.

It was so good as expected!

--- 常用單字片語集 ---

pass by ～
經過～
pass 有「通過、經過」的意思。

seasonal
季節性的、季節限定
經常用於店家的菜單標示上。

cannot help but do
忍不住想～
過去式則要將 cannot 改為 couldn't。

as expected
符合期望
想表達「果然！跟我想的一樣！」時經常用
到的片語。

163

做了奇怪的夢
Had a nightmare…

中文日記

我做了一個惡夢。

夢見我的牙齒一顆一顆掉了！

超恐怖的，對吧？

這種夢會不會有什麼特殊含義啊……

英文填空日記

I had a _____ **.**
我做了一個惡夢。

My teeth were _____ **out one after another!**
夢見我的牙齒一顆一顆掉了！

It's so scary, _____ **it!?**
超恐怖的，對吧？

Does this _____ **of dream mean something…?**
這種夢會不會有什麼特殊含義啊……

英文日記

I had a nightmare.

My teeth were falling out one after another!

It's so scary, isn't it!?

Does this kind of dream mean something…?

常用單字片語集

nightmare
惡夢
也可以說 bad dream 或 scary dream。

fall out
掉落
長牙齒則是 come in。

~ , isn't it?
～，對吧？
根據前文的主詞和時態會有變化。

this kind of ~
這種～
想表達「這種～」的時候經常用到的片語。

冰箱裡空空如也

The fridge is empty!

中文日記

我今天不想去採買食材，

所以打算用冰箱裡的東西做點簡單的料理。

唔……這個嘛……

冰箱裡面什麼都沒有！空空如也！

英文填空日記

I don't feel like going ___ shopping today,
我今天不想去採買食材，

so I'll make something simple with the things in the ___ .
所以打算用冰箱裡的東西做點簡單的料理。

Well... ___ ...
唔……這個嘛……

There's ___ left! It's empty!
冰箱裡面什麼都沒有！空空如也！

英文日記

I don't feel like going grocery shopping today,

so I'll make something simple with the things in the fridge.

Well... actually...

There's nothing left! It's empty!

常用單字片語集

go grocery shopping
採買食材
grocery 是「食材」的意思。

fridge
冰箱
冰箱的正式名稱為 refrigerator，但幾乎都會簡略成 fridge。

actually
其實、這個嘛
平時常用來接續對話的片語。

There's nothing left.
什麼都沒有。
結合 nothing（沒有東西）和 left（留下來）的句型。

去奶奶家
Go to grandma's house

中文日記

今天我去了奶奶家。

我的表弟妹也在。

他們長大好多！

時間過得真快。

英文填空日記

Today I visited my   place.
今天我去了奶奶家。

And my   were also there.
我的表弟妹也在。

They've grown a   !
他們長大好多！

**   flies.**
時間過得真快。

英文日記

Today I visited my grandma's place.

And my cousins were also there.

They've grown a lot!

Time flies.

常用單字片語集

grandma
奶奶
grandmother 簡化後的口語用法。

cousin
表兄弟姊妹

have grown a lot
長大了
grow（成長）是原形，過去式是 grew，過去分詞是 grown。

Time flies.
時光飛逝。
即成語「光陰似箭」的常見英譯。

八月 20 這是騷擾吧？

Isn't this harassment!?

中文日記

主管有時候會問我：「你有男朋友嗎？」

他這樣真的很煩！

關你什麼事呀！

每次他問這個問題都讓我好煩躁。

英文填空日記

My _____ sometimes asks me, "Have you got a boyfriend?",

主管有時候會問我：「你有男朋友嗎？」

_____ is so annoying!!

他這樣真的很煩！

It's none of your _____!

關你什麼事呀！

I get _____ every time he asks me this.

每次他問這個問題都讓我好煩躁。

英文日記

My boss sometimes asks me, "Have you got a boyfriend?",

which is so annoying!!

It's none of your business!

I get irritated every time he asks me this.

常用單字片語集

boss
主管
也可以說 manager 或 supervisor。

which is ～
這樣～
用逗號連接前面的子句。

none of one's business
不關某個人的事
慣用句，直接記下來吧。

get irritated
感到煩躁
be irritated 是用來表示「很煩躁」的狀態。

167

下雨了，該不該買傘呢？

Raining outside…

外面下雨了！

我該不該買傘呢……？

其實從這裡走回家也只要五分鐘而已。

算了，我用跑的吧！

It's　　　　　　outside!
外面下雨了！

**　　　　　I buy an umbrella or not…?**
我該不該買傘呢……？

Actually, it's only a 5-minute　　　　　from here to my place.
其實從這裡走回家也只要五分鐘而已。

Maybe　　　　. I can run!
算了，我用跑的吧！

It's raining outside!

Should I buy an umbrella or not…?

Actually, it's only a 5-minute walk from here to my place.

Maybe not. I can run!

常用單字片語集

It's raining.
下雨了。
使用片語 be -ing 的句子。

Should I ~ or not?
我該不該～呢？
語感是從「應該～呢？還是不應該～呢？」，變成「該不該～呢？」屬於常用的表現手法。

~ -minute walk.
走路～分鐘
以單數形式呈現，記得前面要加個 a。

Maybe not.
算了。
根據情境會有不一樣的解釋。

八月 22 看見超美的夕陽

What a beautiful sunset!

中文日記

今天回家的路上，

我看見超美的夕陽。

好感動呀！

我原本很疲憊的，整個人精神都來了！

英文填空日記

On my　　　　　home today,
今天回家的路上，

I saw a very beautiful　　　　.
我看見超美的夕陽。

That made me　　　　!
好感動呀！

I was a bit tired today, but that made me feel　　　　!
我原本很疲憊的，整個人精神都來了！

英文日記

On my way home today,

I saw a very beautiful sunset.

That made me moved!

I was a bit tired today, but that made me feel better!

- - - - - - - - - - - - - - 常用單字片語集 - - - - - - - - - - - - -

on one's way home
回家途中
one's 的部分會隨著主詞變化。

sunset
夕陽
可以和 sunrise（日出）一起記下來。

be moved
感動
動詞 move（移動）同時也有「令人感動」
的意思。

feel better
有精神
使用 well 和 good 的比較級 better。

鄰居好吵

Noisy people…

中文日記

鄰居好像在開趴。

他們好吵呀！

現在都已經凌晨了耶！

有沒有常識啊。

英文填空日記

My ⎯⎯⎯⎯⎯ seems to be having a party.
鄰居好像在開趴。

They are so ⎯⎯⎯⎯⎯!!
他們好吵呀！

It's already ⎯⎯⎯⎯⎯!?
現在都已經凌晨了耶！

They don't have any ⎯⎯⎯⎯⎯ sense.
有沒有常識啊。

英文日記

My neighbor seems to be having a party.

They are so noisy!!

It's already midnight!?

They don't have any common sense.

常用單字片語集

neighbor
鄰居
和 neighborhood（鄰里、街坊）一起記下來吧。

noisy
吵鬧的
從 noise（噪音、雜音）衍生的形容詞。

midnight
凌晨
at midnight 是指「午夜十二點」。

common sense
常識
common 有「一般的、共同的」的意思。

八月 24 我忘記帶手機出門了

Forgot my phone!

中文日記

我今天忘記帶手機出門了！

我現在才發現！

我怎麼這麼粗心呀！

沒有手機會很不方便的！

英文填空日記

I _____ to bring my phone today!
我今天忘記帶手機出門了！

I just _____ now!
我現在才發現！

_____ careless I am!
我怎麼這麼粗心呀！

It's so _____ without my phone!
沒有手機會很不方便的！

英文日記

I forgot to bring my phone today!

I just realized now!

How careless I am!

It's so inconvenient without my phone!

常用單字片語集

forget to ～
忘記～
to 的後面要接動詞或原形 be 動詞。

realize
發現
I just realized now. 是很常用到的句子，整句一起記下來吧。

How ～ !
多麼～呀！
這種情境下想表現的不是疑問句，而是肯定句。要特別留意語序。

inconvenient without ～
沒有～會很不方便
使用 without（沒有～）的表現手法。

妹妹突然來借住

She just came to my place

中文日記

妹妹突然打電話給我,

說:「我想借住你那邊,來接我。」

說是和男朋友吵架了。

這也太突然了吧。

英文填空日記

My sister called me　　　　　　of the blue,
妹妹突然打電話給我,

and said, "I wanna stay at your place, so　　　　pick me up."
說:「我想借住你那邊,來接我。」

She had a　　　　　with her boyfriend.
說是和男朋友吵架了。

That's　　　　too sudden.
這也太突然了吧。

英文日記

My sister called me out of the blue,

and said, "I wanna stay at your place, so come pick me up."

She had a fight with her boyfriend.

That's way too sudden.

常用單字片語集

out of the blue
突然、猝不及防
電視劇或電影也經常出現的慣用語。

have a fight with ～
和～吵架
使用了 fight（吵架)的片語。

come pick me up
來接我
省略了 come and pick me up 的 and,或 come to pick me up 的 to。

way too ～
太～
在 way 的後面加上形容詞便可以加深強調。

26

吵架的原因超無言

The reason they had a fight is…

中文日記

我問了妹妹他們吵架的原因，

結果她告訴我：

「他沒經過我的同意就轉台了！」

超無言！

英文填空日記

I asked my sister the　　　　　why they had a fight.
我問了妹妹他們吵架的原因，

And　　　　　she said is,
結果她告訴我：

"He changed the channel　　　　　my permission!"
「他沒經過我的同意就轉台了！」

That's so　　　　　!
超無言！

英文日記

I asked my sister the reason why they had a fight.

And what she said is,

"He changed the channel without my permission!"

That's so dumb!

- - - - - - - - - - - - - - - - **常用單字片語集** - - - - - - - - - - - - - - -

the reason why ～
～的原因
回答的時候大多會以 because 開頭。

what she said is ～
她跟我說～
這種情況的 what 指的不是「什麼」而是「某件事」。

without permission
擅自、未經允許
使用 without（沒有～）的片語。

dumb
無言、愚蠢
日常對話中經常用到的口語表現。

27 酒吧的價位根本是暴利

What a rip-off!!

昨天我們去酒吧喝酒，

看見菜單的時候，嚇了我們一跳！

所有飲料都超過兩千日圓！

根本是暴利吧！

We went to a ⬚ to have a drink yesterday,
昨天我們去酒吧喝酒，

and we were ⬚ when we saw the menu!
看見菜單的時候，嚇了我們一跳！

⬚ the drinks were over 2000 yen!!
所有飲料都超過兩千日圓！

What a ⬚ -off!!
根本是暴利吧！

We went to a bar to have a drink yesterday,

and we were surprised when we saw the menu!

All the drinks were over 2000 yen!!

What a rip-off!!

常用單字片語集

bar
酒吧
英文發音就和「吧」一樣。

be surprised
嚇一跳
surprise 是「使對方驚奇」的意思，所以通常會使用被動式。

all the ～
所有的～
除此之外還有許多使用 all 的片語。

rip-off
暴利
指「暴利店家」的時候也可以直接用 rip-off來表示。

香織沒男人緣的原因
The reason Kaori hasn't been dating anyone

中文日記

香織已經很長一段時間沒有交往對象了，

她總是説：「我就不受歡迎呀。」

但我覺得她並不是不受歡迎，

只是太挑而已。

英文填空日記

Kaori hasn't been   anyone for a long time,
香織已經很長一段時間沒有交往對象了，

and she always says, "I'm not   ."
她總是説：「我就不受歡迎呀。」

But I think that's   because she's not popular,
但我覺得她並不是不受歡迎，

but because she's just   .
只是太挑而已。

英文日記

Kaori hasn't been dating anyone for a long time,

and she always says, "I'm not popular."

But I think that's not because she's not popular,

but because she's just picky.

------------------- 常用單字片語集 -------------------

date
交往
也可以用 see 或 go out 來表示。

popular
受歡迎的
也會説 popular with girls/boys（受到女生／男生歡迎）。

not because ～ but because...
不是因為～只是因為……
活用 not ～ but... 的句型。

picky
標準太高
語感更接近「太挑剔」。

咖啡店的店員態度超差
The attitude of the staff

中文日記

我和朋友去了一間咖啡店，

他們店員的服務態度超差的。

她甚至連句「歡迎光臨」都沒說！

從來沒見過那樣子的人！

英文填空日記

I went to a café with my friend,
我和朋友去了一間咖啡店，

the staff there treated us so　　　　　.
他們店員的服務態度超差的。

She didn't even　　　　　"hello"!
她甚至連句「歡迎光臨」都沒說！

I've never met anyone　　　　　that before!
從來沒見過那樣子的人！

英文日記

When I went to a café with my friend,

the staff there treated us so badly.

She didn't even say "hello"!

I've never met anyone like that before!

常用單字片語集

when ～
～的時候
when 的後面可以接一般的句子。

treat ～ badly
（對～）態度很差
使用 treat（對待）、badly（差勁地）的表現手法。

say "hello"
打招呼
英文並沒有「歡迎光臨」的固定說法，所以這裡用了 hello。

like that
那樣的
跟 like this（這樣的）一起學起來吧。

八月 30

主管請我吃午餐

My boss treated me lunch

中文日記

今天主管帶我去吃午餐，

他還說：「這頓我請客！」

我真幸運！

下次回請他喝咖啡吧。

英文填空日記

Today my boss ＿＿＿ me out for lunch,
今天主管帶我去吃午餐，

and he said, "It's ＿＿＿ me!"
他還說：「這頓我請客！」

Lucky ＿＿＿ !
我真幸運！

I'll buy him a coffee in ＿＿＿ .
下次回請他喝咖啡吧。

英文日記

Today my boss took me out for lunch,

and he said, "It's on me!"

Lucky me!

I'll buy him a coffee in return.

常用單字片語集

take ～ out for lunch
帶～去吃午餐
take 除了「拿取」之外，還有「帶去」的意思。

It's on me.
我請客。
請他人吃飯時的固定句型。

Lucky me!
我真幸運！
說別人很幸運的時候要改成 Lucky you!。

in return
回請
可以和 in return for ～（做為～的回禮）一起記下來。

177

熱到沒幹勁……

Too hot…

中文日記

我今天好沒幹勁。

最近實在是太熱了，我覺得很累，

而且沒什麼食慾。

今晚我想吃點清爽的東西。

英文填空日記

I feel　　　　today.
我今天好沒幹勁。

It's been too hot recently, so I feel　　　　,
最近實在是太熱了，我覺得很累，

and have no　　　　.
而且沒什麼食慾。

I want something　　　　tonight.
今晚我想吃點清爽的東西。

英文日記

I feel dull today.

It's been too hot recently, so I feel tired,

and have no appetite.

I want something light tonight.

- - - - - - - - - - 常用單字片語集 - - - - - - - - - -

feel dull
倦怠
使用了 dull（遲鈍、倦怠）的片語。

feel tired
疲憊
也可以說 be tired。

have no appetite
沒有食慾
和 have an appetite（有食慾）一起記下來吧。

something light
清爽的東西
使用了 light（輕的）的表現手法。

有關「生活用品」的十大表現手法

第1名	I gotta go buy a laundry detergent. 我得去買洗衣精才行。	gotta 是 have got to 的簡化，主要用於日常生活的對話中。因為不是正統的用法，所以不會出現在教科書上，但會很頻繁地出現在一般會話中，一定要學起來喔。
第2名	I'll clean my room. 我要來打掃房間。	寫日記時常常會用到 I'll～和未來式所組成的句型。教科書通常會出現比較生硬的「我打算～」，但在寫日記的時候，通常會用「我要～」、「不然我～」來表現未來的行為。
第3名	I forgot to take out the trash. 我忘記丟垃圾了。	使用 forget 的過去式 forgot 的句型。I forgot to～就會變成「我忘記做～」，也可以用更簡短的方式說 I forgot!（我忘了）。
第4名	I ran out of toilet paper! 衛生紙用完了！	除了衛生紙以外，生活用品用完的時候都可以使用 I ran out of～的句型。動詞「run」的過去式是 ran，屬於不規則變化，拼字時要特別留意。
第5名	I do grocery shopping. 我去採買食材。	也可以用 go（去）代替 do（做）。如果只有 do shopping 的話，就是「買東西」的意思，加上一個 grocery 就可以用來表示採買食材。
第6名	I'll cook for myself. 我要自己煮。	「煮飯給自己吃」，即「自己煮」的意思，也可以說 cook my own food。此外，在問對方的時候，只要說 Do you cook? 就能表示「你會煮飯嗎？」
第7名	Where did I put my nail clippers? 我把指甲剪放到哪裡了？	自言自語時會使用的句型。不光是寫日語，自言自語也能有效提升口語能力，訓練自己可以大量說出、寫出這種句型吧。
第8名	The remote of the TV is broken. 電視搖控器壞掉了。	電視搖控器的正式名稱為 TV remote controller，但也可以用 remote of the TV 或只用 remote 來表示。
第9名	I put a bandage on my finger. 在手指上貼 OK 繃。	除了「放置」以外，put 還有「放入」、「貼上」、「裝飾」等各式各樣的意思。根據後面接續的介系詞會產生不同的意思和用法，把各種 put 的片語都學起來吧。
第10名	I'll brush my teeth and go to bed. 我要刷牙睡覺了。	brush my teeth（刷牙）所使用的 teeth（牙齒）是複數形，單數形為 tooth，但一般不會只描述「一顆」牙齒，所以更常使用 teeth。

Best 10

SEPTEMBER

9 月

I've been eating out recently,
我最近老是吃外食，
so I should cook for myself sometimes.
偶爾也該自己煮吧。
I'm getting rough skin,
我最近膚況很差，
because I've been eating too many sweets.
都是因為我吃太多甜食啦。

1

睡過頭了！

I overslept!

中文日記

今天我睡過頭了！

我醒來的時候已經八點了。

我在十五分鐘內準備好了。

所以我還是有趕上！

英文填空日記

I　　　　　today!
今天我睡過頭了！

When I　　　　up, it was already 8.
我醒來的時候已經八點了。

I got myself　　　　in 15 minutes.
我在十五分鐘內準備好了。

So I　　　　it to work!
所以我還是有趕上！

英文日記

I overslept today!

When I woke up, it was already 8.

I got myself ready in 15 minutes.

So I made it to work!

常用單字片語集

oversleep
睡過頭
過去式為 overslept，要多加留意。

wake up
醒來
get up 則是「起床、下床」的意思，小心不要混用了。

get oneself ready
準備
也可以單用 get ready。

make it
趕上
日常對話中頻繁出現的表現手法。I made it! 是「我趕上了！」的意思。

2 在咖啡店讀書
Study at a café

中文日記

在咖啡店讀英文是我每天的例行事項，

今天有個店員招待我吃餅乾，

還對我說：「加油！」

我會再努力一個小時的！

英文填空日記

It's my daily ＿＿＿＿ to study English at a café,
在咖啡店讀英文是我每天的例行事項，

and today one staff member gave me a ＿＿＿＿ cookie,
今天有個店員招待我吃餅乾，

saying, "＿＿＿＿ it up!"
還對我說：「加油！」

I'll work ＿＿＿＿ for another hour!
我會再努力一個小時的！

英文日記

It's my daily routine to study English at a café,

and today one staff member gave me a free cookie,

saying, "Keep it up!"

I'll work hard for another hour!

- - - - - - - - - - - - 常用單字片語集 - - - - - - - - - - - -

daily routine
日常例行公事
routine 有「常規、例行公事」的意思。

give free ～
招待～
這種情況不能使用 service 這個單字，要特別注意。

Keep it up!
繼續加油！
「雖然很辛苦但要加油喔」的意思。日常對話中經常會用到的句子。

work hard
努力
work 除了「工作」之外，還有「專注於某件事」的意思。

最近老是吃外食

I gotta cook sometimes

我最近老是吃外食，

偶爾也該自己煮吧。

我最近膚況很差，

都是因為我吃太多甜食啦。

I've been eating　　　　　recently,
我最近老是吃外食，

so I should cook for　　　　sometimes.
偶爾也該自己煮吧。

I'm getting　　　　　skin,
我最近膚況很差，

because I've been eating too many　　　　　.
都是因為我吃太多甜食啦。

I've been eating out recently,

so I should cook for myself sometimes.

I'm getting rough skin,

because I've been eating too many sweets.

常用單字片語集

eat out
吃外食
使用表示持續性的句型 I've been 就會變成「最近都吃外食」的意思。

cook for oneself
自己煮
「煮飯給自己吃」，即「自己煮」的意思。

rough skin
膚況差
也可以用 have rough skin 來表示「膚況很差」的意思。

sweets
甜食
也可以說 something sweet。

去看朋友的貓

Go to see cute kittens

中文日記

今天我去小瞳家了。

她養了兩隻小貓，超可愛的！

雖然我是個愛狗人士，

但我覺得貓也滿可愛的。

英文填空日記

I went to Hitomi's ＿＿＿＿ today.
今天我去小瞳家了。

She had two ＿＿＿＿, which were so cute!
她養了兩隻小貓，超可愛的！

I'm a dog ＿＿＿＿,
雖然我是個愛狗人士，

but I thought cats are so lovely, ＿＿＿.
但我覺得貓也滿可愛的。

英文日記

I went to Hitomi's place today.

She had two kittens, which were so cute!

I'm a dog person,

but I thought cats are so lovely, too.

常用單字片語集

～'s place
～的住處
和～'s house 是同樣的用法，但 place 不光指一般住家，還能表示租屋處，是個很方便的單字。

kittens
小貓們
單數是 kitten，也可以說 kitty。

a dog person
愛狗人士
a cat person 就是「愛貓人士」。

～ , too.
也～
使用時會接在句尾，同樣意思的單字還有 also。

肩膀好僵硬

A stiff neck is killing me

中文日記

一直處理文書作業讓我肩膀好僵硬。

累死我了。

我的腳還水腫了！

一定是因為我坐了一整天啊。

英文填空日記

I got a _____ neck from doing deskwork.
一直處理文書作業讓我肩膀好僵硬。

It's _____ me.
累死我了。

And my legs are _____, too!
我的腳還水腫了！

That's _____ I've been sitting all day long.
一定是因為我坐了一整天啊。

英文日記

I got a stiff neck from doing deskwork.

It's killing me.

And my legs are swollen, too!

That's because I've been sitting all day long.

常用單字片語集

stiff neck
肩膀僵硬
也可以用 stiff shoulder，但 neck 也經常用來指「肩膀僵硬」。

swollen
水腫、腫脹
原形為 swell。「水腫」的名詞為 swelling。

That's because ～.
那是因為～。
是將 ...because ～（……都是因為～）這個句型拆成兩句。

和大介去水族館約會

Aquarium with Daisuke

中文日記

今天我和大介去約會了。

我好緊張，昨晚都沒睡好呢。

我們去了千葉的水族館，

玩得很開心！

英文填空日記

Today I went　　　　　a date with Daisuke.
今天我和大介去約會了。

I was so nervous　　　　　I couldn't sleep well last night.
我好緊張，昨晚都沒睡好呢。

We went to the　　　　　in Chiba,
我們去了千葉的水族館，

and　　　　　a really good time!
玩得很開心！

英文日記

Today I went for a date with Daisuke.

I was so nervous that I couldn't sleep well last night.

We went to the aquarium in Chiba,

and had a really good time!

常用單字片語集

go for a date
去約會
和 go for dinner 一樣，介系詞要使用 for。

so... that ～
太過……導致～
教科書裡也會教的句型，在日常對話中可以省略掉 that。

aquarium
水族館、水族箱

have a good time
玩得很開心
「度過愉快的時光」，即「玩得很開心」的意思。

整理資料
A lot of paperwork

中文日記

今天要整理的資料有好多。

我們小組現在正在進行大型專案，

最近變得比較忙。

大家一起完成吧！

英文填空日記

I had a lot of   today.
今天要整理的資料有好多。

Our team is now working   a big project,
我們小組現在正在進行大型專案，

so it's been   busy recently.
最近變得比較忙。

Let's get   this together!
大家一起完成吧！

英文日記

I had a lot of paperwork today.

Our team is now working on a big project,

so it's been kinda busy recently.

Let's get through this together!

------------------------------ 常用單字片語集 ------------------------------

paperwork
資料整理、文書工作
指一般的資料整理或文書事務。

work on ～
進行～
經常用來表示「致力於」工作或專案上。

kinda
有點
將 kind of 縮短後的口語用詞。

get through ～
一起完成～
也有「克服、通過」的意思。

存錢

I gotta save!

中文日記

最近我開始思考，

應該要為了將來開始存錢。

我們誰都沒把握到底可以領到多少退休金。

我不想要上了年紀後變窮呀！

英文填空日記

Recently, I've started　　　　　 that
最近我開始思考，

I have to　　　　 some money for my future.
應該要為了將來開始存錢。

We　　　　 know how much pension we can receive.
我們誰都沒把握到底可以領到多少退休金。

I don't wanna be poor when I get　　　　 !
我不想要上了年紀後變窮呀！

英文日記

Recently, I've started thinking that

I have to save some money for my future.

We never know how much pension we can receive.

I don't wanna be poor when I get old!

- - - - - - - - - - - - - - - 常用單字片語集 - - - - - - - - - - - - - - -

start -ing
開始～
用 start thinking 時，通常會在後面接一個 that，然後說明自己在思考什麼。

save some money
存錢
加不加 some 都無所謂，也可以用來表示「節約」。

never know ～
～說不準
You never know.（這還說不準。）也是常用句。

get old
上年紀
也可以使用比較級 get older。

189

煩惱保險

Worried about insurance

中文日記

我還有另一件擔心的事，

那就是生重病的時候該怎麼辦？

如果沒辦法工作了該怎麼辦？

我現在身上有哪些保險呢⋯⋯

英文填空日記

Another＿＿＿＿＿I've been worrying about is
我還有另一件擔心的事，

what's going to happen＿＿＿＿＿I become very sick.
那就是生重病的時候該怎麼辦？

What＿＿＿＿＿I become unable to work?
如果沒辦法工作了該怎麼辦？

I wonder what kind of＿＿＿＿＿do I hold now?
我現在身上有哪些保險呢⋯⋯

英文日記

Another thing I've been worrying about is

what's going to happen when I become very sick.

What if I become unable to work?

I wonder what kind of insurance do I hold now?

常用單字片語集

Another thing ～
另一件事～
another thing that bothers me... 也是相同意思。

What's going to happen when ～ ?
～的時候該怎麼辦？
根據情況不同，會用 if 來代替 when。

What if ～ ?
如果～該怎麼辦？
教科書也會教的句型。和 What's going to happen if ～？是同樣意思。

insurance
保險
也會說 insurance policy（保單）。

10

註冊轉職網

To get a new job…

中文日記

我在轉職網站上註冊了。

我目前在找新工作，

但我還沒看到不錯的。

轉職感覺也很不容易呀……

英文填空日記

I　　　　　on a recruitment website.
我在轉職網站上註冊了。

Now I'm　　　　　for jobs,
我目前在找新工作，

but I haven't found a good one　　　　　.
但我還沒看到不錯的。

Changing　　　　　seems to be difficult.
轉職感覺也很不容易呀……

英文日記

I registered on a recruitment website.

Now I'm searching for jobs,

but I haven't found a good one yet.

Changing jobs seems to be difficult.

常用單字片語集

register
註冊
註冊會員時經常會用到的單字，也可以做為名詞使用。

search for ～
搜尋～
也有「尋找」的意思。

haven't ～ yet
還沒～
經常用來表示「還沒～」的現在完成式句型，和 already（已經）一起學起來吧。

changing jobs
轉職
change jobs（換工作）也可以做為動詞。

弄丟耳環

Lost my earrings!

糟了，我弄丟耳環了！

我放到哪裡了？

我想不起來！

那可是媽媽送我的生日禮物呀！

Oh my god, I lost my _____ !!
糟了，我弄丟耳環了！

Where did I _____ them!?
我放到哪裡了？

Can't _____ !!
我想不起來！

My mom gave them to me _____ a birthday present!
那可是媽媽送我的生日禮物呀！

Oh my god, I lost my earrings!!

Where did I put them!?

Can't remember!!

My mom gave them to me as a birthday present!

- - - - - - - - - - 常用單字片語集 - - - - - - - - - -

earrings
耳環
pierce 是「穿耳洞」的動詞。

put
放置
put 的過去式和過去分詞都一樣是 put，記下來吧。

Can't remember.
想不起來。
I can't remember. 省略掉主詞的 I，是常見的用法。

as ～
做為～
翻譯並不會直譯出來，但 as 在這裡是「做為生日禮物」的意思。

九月 12 和客戶開會

Meeting with our business partner

中文日記

今天我和一個客戶開會。

我們的專案目前進行得很順利。

如果我們可以獲取大筆利潤的話，

我搞不好有機會加薪！

英文填空日記

I had a meeting with one of our business   today.
今天我和一個客戶開會。

Our project seems to be going well so   .
我們的專案目前進行得很順利。

If we can make a big   ,
如果我們可以獲取大筆利潤的話，

I might get a   !?
我搞不好有機會加薪！

英文日記

I had a meeting with one of our business partners today.

Our project seems to be going well so far.

If we can make a big profit,

I might get a raise!?

常用單字片語集

business partner
客戶、生意夥伴
也會說 client。

so far
目前
有個慣用句是 So far, so good.（目前一切順遂）可以一起記下來。

make a big profit
獲取大筆利潤
profit 是「利益」的意思，這個情境的動詞會使用 make。

get a raise
加薪
會說 I got a raise!（我加薪了！）

發現一間好吃的麵包店

Found a nice bakery

中文日記

今天我去了一間麵包店，

我老早就想去看看了。

我吃了最受歡迎的可頌。

果然和預期中一樣好吃！

英文填空日記

Today I went to the　　　　　　

今天我去了一間麵包店，

I had always　　　　　　**to go to.**

我老早就想去看看了。

I tried a croissant which is the　　　　　　**popular.**

我吃了最受歡迎的可頌。

That was so good as　　　　　**!**

果然和預期中一樣好吃！

英文日記

Today I went to the bakery

I had always wanted to go to.

I tried a croissant which is the most popular.

That was so good as expected!

- - - - - - - - - - - - - - 常用單字片語集 - - - - - - - - - - - - - -

bakery
麵包店
複數形為 bakeries。

I have always wanted to go
一直很想去看看
雖然這裡是使用過去完成式的 had，但根據情況不同，也會使用現在完成式。

the most popular
最受歡迎的
使用最高級 the most 的表現手法。

as expected
和預期中一樣
常用片語，日常對話中也能使用。

一整天在家耍廢

Chilling at home

中文日記

今天沒事做！

好閒啊……

我該出門還是待在家裡好呢？

好，今天就在家裡耍廢吧。

英文填空日記

Today I have _____ to do!!
今天沒事做！

I'm _____ …
好閒啊……

Should I go out or _____ home?
我該出門還是待在家裡好呢？

…Okay, I'll just _____ at home.
好，今天就在家裡耍廢吧。

英文日記

Today I have nothing to do!!

I'm bored…

Should I go out or stay home?

…Okay, I'll just chill at home.

常用單字片語集

have nothing to do
沒事做
若改成 have something to do 就會變成「有事要做」。

bored
閒暇、感到無聊
如果用成 boring 就會變成「我是一個無聊的人」，要多加留意。

stay home
待在家裡
stay at home 也是同樣意思。

chill at home
在家耍廢
chill 還有「玩樂」、「休息」的意思。

15 散步了一個車站的距離

Let's take a walk!

中文日記

早上我比平時早一個小時起床，

所以我走路到離公司最近的車站。

偶爾散散步，感受一下外面的空氣也不錯。

雖然我應該沒辦法天天這樣……

英文填空日記

I got up an hour _____ **this morning,**
早上我比平時早一個小時起床，

so I'm walking to the _____ **station from the office.**
所以我走路到離公司最近的車站。

It's good to _____ **a walk and feel fresh air sometimes.**
偶爾散散步，感受一下外面的空氣也不錯。

I don't think I can do this every morning, _____ **…**
雖然我應該沒辦法天天這樣……

英文日記

I got up an hour earlier this morning,

so I'm walking to the nearest station from the office.

It's good to take a walk and feel fresh air sometimes.

I don't think I can do this every morning, though…

常用單字片語集

get up an hour earlier
早一個小時起床
使用 early 的比較級 earlier，要注意拼字。

the nearest station from ～
離～最近的車站
這裡使用最高級來表示「最近的車站」。

take a walk
散步
也可以說 go for a walk。

～ ,though
雖然～
放在句尾，日常對話中經常用到。

九月 16 我又衝動購物了

An impulse buy again

中文日記

我又衝動購物了……

我在愛店看見的洋裝實在是太可愛了。

我現在有幾件洋裝了呀？

真是壞習慣。

英文填空日記

I made an ＿＿＿＿＿ buy again…
我又衝動購物了……

The ＿＿＿＿＿ I found at my favorite shop was really cute.
我在愛店看見的洋裝實在是太可愛了。

✏ **How ＿＿＿＿＿ dresses do I have now?**
我現在有幾件洋裝了呀？

This is my bad ＿＿＿＿＿.
真是壞習慣。

英文日記

I made an impulse buy again…

The dress I found at my favorite shop was really cute.

How many dresses do I have now?

This is my bad habit.

常用單字片語集

make an impulse buy
衝動購物
使用 impulse（衝動、趨勢）的片語。

dress
洋裝
要用這個單字，而非 one piece。

how many
幾個、幾件
如果是不可數名詞的話，就改成 how much。

bad habit
壞習慣
habit 有「習性、習慣」的意思。

手機沒電了
My phone died

中
文
日
記

糟糕，我手機沒電了！

我沒有帶充電器在身上。

怎麼辦……？

我還得打電話跟廣美說我會晚到呀！

英
文
填
空
日
記

Oh no, my phone !
糟糕，我手機沒電了！

I don't have a now.
我沒有帶充電器在身上。

to do…?
怎麼辦……？

I gotta call Hiromi and say I'm late!
我還得打電話跟廣美說我會晚到呀！

英
文
日
記

Oh no, my phone died!

I don't have a charger now.

What to do…?

I gotta call Hiromi and say I'm running late!

- - - - - - - - - - 常用單字片語集 - - - - - - - - - -

my phone died
手機沒電
也可以説 battery died。

my charger
充電器
可以和動詞 charge（充電）一起學起來。

What to do?
怎麼辦？
日常對話中會使用的固定句型。

be running late
晚到
想表示現在要遲到的時候，可以用這種表現手法。

迷路了
I got lost

中文日記

我迷路了！

我現在人在哪？

我還是第一次來這個地方，

我真是路痴呀！

英文填空日記

I'm _____ !
我迷路了！

_____ am I now?
我現在人在哪？

It's my first _____ to come here,
我還是第一次來這個地方，

and I have no sense of _____ !
我真是路痴呀！

英文日記

I'm lost!

Where am I now?

It's my first time to come here,

and I have no sense of direction!

常用單字片語集
---

be lost
迷路
和 be lost（迷路中）一起記下來吧。

Where am I?
我現在人在哪？
雖然也可以用 I wonder ～，但用這種簡單的句型也可以。

It's my first time to ～ .
這是我第一次～。
first time（第一次）是很常用的單字，學起來吧。

have no sense of direction
路痴
即「沒有方向感」的意思。sense of direction 是「方向感」。

19

壓力好大
So stressed!

中文日記

我最近壓力好大！

我老是在加班。

好想去國外旅遊充電一下！

但我現在也請不了長假……

英文填空日記

I've been so   lately!
我最近壓力好大！

I have too much   at work.
我老是在加班。

I wanna   myself by traveling abroad!!
好想去國外旅遊充電一下！

But I cannot   a long vacation now…
但我現在也請不了長假……

英文日記

I've been so stressed lately!

I have too much overtime at work.

I wanna refresh myself by traveling abroad!!

But I cannot afford a long vacation now…

------------- 常用單字片語集 -------------

be stressed
壓力大
用 stress 這個單字來表示壓力。

refresh oneself
放鬆、充電
通常會補上 by -ing（做什麼事來～）。

have overtime
加班
work overtime 也是同樣意思。

afford
有能力、有餘裕
常搭配 can 或 cannot 一起使用的單字。

電視搖控器壞了

The remote is broken

中文日記

電視搖控器壞了。

我換過電池，但還是不能用。

我得去電器行了。

對了，我還要買燈泡！

英文填空日記

The _____ **of the TV is broken.**
電視搖控器壞了。

I changed the _____ **but it still doesn't work.**
我換過電池，但還是不能用。

I gotta go to an _____ **store.**
我得去電器行了。

Oh, and I gotta buy light _____ **, too!**
對了，我還要買燈泡！

英文日記

The remote of the TV is broken.

I changed the battery but it still doesn't work.

I gotta go to an electronics store.

Oh, and I gotta buy light bulbs, too!

------------------------ 常用單字片語集 ------------------------

remote
搖控器
正式名稱為 remote controller，但通常會這樣簡化。

battery
電池
複數形為 batteries。

electronics store
電器行
一般有販賣家電的店都可以用這個單字。

light bulb
燈泡
可以說 This light bulb is burned out.（燈泡壞了）。

去買朋友的生日禮物

Bought a present for my friend

我去百貨公司挑選朋友的生日禮物。

好猶豫要買什麼喔！

我自己覺得這個香水不錯，

但不知道她喜不喜歡呀……

I came to the _____ store to buy a birthday present for my friend.

我去百貨公司挑選朋友的生日禮物。

I can't _____ what to buy!

好猶豫要買什麼喔！

I think this _____ is good,

我自己覺得這個香水不錯，

but I don't know _____ she likes it or not...

但不知道她喜不喜歡呀……

I came to the *department* store to buy a birthday present for my friend.

I can't *decide* what to buy!

I think this *perfume* is good,

but I don't know *if* she likes it or not...

常用單字片語集

department store
百貨公司
單獨一個 depart 是「出發」的意思，要特別留意。

can't decide
難以抉擇、猶豫
can't choose 也是同樣意思。

perfume
香水
「噴香水」的片語是 wear perfume。

if ～ or not
不知道是否～
對一件事沒有把握的時候所使用的句型。

更新駕照
Renewal of my license

中文日記

我去更新我的駕照了！

其實一個月前就收到通知了，

但我完全忘了這回事！

我得請半天假才行。

英文填空日記

I have to renew my ___ license!!
我去更新我的駕照了！

Actually, I got a ___ from the police about a month ago,
其實一個月前就收到通知了，

but I ___ forgot about it!
但我完全忘了這回事！

I have to take a ___ day off.
我得請半天假才行。

英文日記

I have to renew my driver's license!!

Actually, I got a notice from the police about a month ago,

but I totally forgot about it!

I have to take a half day off.

常用單字片語集

driver's license
駕照
也可以說 driving license。

notice
通知
也可以說 notification。

totally
完全地、澈底地
常常搭配 forget 一起使用。

a half day off
半天假
a half day 是「半天」的意思。

中文日記

我去郵局要寄包裹，

結果他們說我的包裹太大不能寄！

我以為他們會受理的……

得想辦法弄小一點才行。

英文填空日記

I went to a post ⬚⬚⬚ to send a package,
我去郵局要寄包裹，

but they said it was ⬚⬚⬚ big to send!
結果他們說我的包裹太大不能寄！

I thought they would ⬚⬚⬚ it…
我以為他們會受理的……

I have to ⬚⬚⬚ it smaller now.
得想辦法弄小一點才行。

英文日記

I went to a post office to send a package,

but they said it was too big to send!

I thought they would accept it…

I have to make it smaller now.

常用單字片語集

post office
郵局
日常生活中的實用單字，學起來吧。

too ~ to...
太~以致於無法……
日常對話會頻繁出現的句型。

accept
受理、接受
想表示「受理」文件或申請時，可以用這個單字。

make ~ smaller
使~變小
使用 small 的比較級 smaller 的片語。

同事太會講場面話了

I don't like this person...

中文日記

老實説，我不太喜歡這個人。

她老是在講場面話。

我摸不透她真正的想法。

我跟她合不來吧。

英文填空日記

**　　　　 be honest, I don't like this person.**
老實說，我不太喜歡這個人。

She's always　　　　 too much.
她老是在講場面話。

I don't know　　　　 she's really thinking.
我摸不透她真正的想法。

I don't really get　　　　 with her.
我跟她合不來吧。

英文日記

To be honest, I don't like this person.

She's always flattering too much.

I don't know what she's really thinking.

I don't really get along with her.

------------------------------ 常用單字片語集 ------------------------------

to be honest
老實說
使用 honest（誠實的、率直的）的慣用語。

flatter
說場面話
會說 You flatter me!（你真會講場面話！）

I don't know what ～ think.
我不知道～在想什麼。
很實用的表現手法，可以整句記下來。

get along with ～
和～感情好、合得來
這個情況是用 don't 來表示「合不來」。

銀行到了月底都大排長龍

The bank is so crowded

我來銀行存錢,

結果人超多的!

居然要「等候六十分鐘」!

畢竟是月底嘛,這也是沒辦法的事。

I'm at the bank to _____ money now,
我來銀行存錢,

but it's so _____!
結果人超多的!

It says " _____ time 60 minutes"!
居然要「等候六十分鐘」!

It's the _____ of the month. Cannot be helped.
畢竟是月底嘛,這也是沒辦法的事。

I'm at the bank to deposit money now,

but it's so crowded!

It says "Wait time 60 minutes"!

It's the end of the month. Cannot be helped.

------------------------------ 常用單字片語集 ------------------------------

deposit
存款
與錢相關的實用單字。

be crowded
人潮多
表示人擠人、人潮多的場面。

wait time
等候時間
也可以說 waiting time。

the end of the month
月底
the end of the year 就是「年末」。

我買了清潔劑，可是……

The price of detergent

4 月
5 月
6 月
7 月
8 月
9 月
10 月
11 月
12 月
1 月
2 月
3 月

中文日記

今天我在藥妝店買了清潔劑。

可是後來我在網路上看到一樣的商品，

居然比我買的價格還要便宜！

太虧了。

英文填空日記

I bought   **at a drugstore today.**
今天我在藥妝店買了清潔劑。

But after that, I found the   **product online,**
可是後來我在網路上看到一樣的商品，

and it was   **cheaper than this!!**
居然比我買的價格還要便宜！

I feel   **off.**
太虧了。

英文日記

I bought detergent at a drugstore today.

But after that, I found the same product online,

and it was much cheaper than this!!

I feel ripped off.

常用單字片語集

detergent
清潔劑
laundry detergent 則是「洗衣精」。

the same ～
一樣的～
別忘了要加上 the。

much... er than ～
比～還要……
結合 much（很、非常）和比較級的句型。

feel ripped off
覺得吃虧
口語對話中常出現的表現手法。

27 網購又踩雷了
Never do online shopping again!

中文日記

看看我買的這件廉價襯衫！

我根本就被騙了！

我在網站上看到的時候還覺得很不錯！

我再也不會在網路上買東西了！

英文填空日記

Looking at this _____ shirt!
看看我買的這件廉價襯衫！

I was totally _____!
我根本就被騙了！

When I saw this _____, it looks really nice!
我在網站上看到的時候還覺得很不錯！

I'll never do online shopping _____!!
我再也不會在網路上買東西了！

英文日記

Looking at this cheesy shirt!

I was totally cheated!

When I saw this online, it looks really nice!

I'll never do online shopping again!!

常用單字片語集
---

cheesy
廉價的
口語對話中常用的單字。

online
在網站上
這個情境會使用這個單字而非 net。

be cheated
被騙
cheat 還有「作弊」、「出軌」等意思。

never ～ again
再也不會～
never 已經是否定詞了，注意前面不要再用否定形。

羨慕食量小又苗條的愛海

I'm jealous of Manami

中文日記

我一直很納悶，

愛海根本就是小鳥胃！

所以才會這麼瘦的吧。

我好羨慕她呀。

英文填空日記

I've been   **for a long time.**
我一直很納悶，

Manami eats like a   **!**
愛海根本就是小鳥胃！

That's why she is so   .
所以才會這麼瘦的吧。

I'm   .
我好羨慕她呀。

英文日記

I've been wondering for a long time.

Manami eats like a bird!

That's why she is so slim.

I'm jealous.

常用單字片語集

wonder
好奇、納悶
也會說 I wonder ～ .，表示「是因為～嗎？」的意思。

eat like a bird
食量小
「食量和鳥差不多」，即「小鳥胃」的意思。

slim
瘦、苗條
也可以用 skinny 或 thin。

jealous
羨慕
envy 也是相同意思，但觀感上比較負面，要特別留意。

討論理想型

What's your type?

中文日記

同事突然問我：「你喜歡什麼樣的類型？」

我說：「我喜歡高個子，至少要有一七五公分……」

結果她跟我說：「你認清現實吧。」

我的要求也沒有很離譜吧？

英文填空日記

My colleague suddenly asked me, "   your type?",
同事突然問我：「你喜歡什麼樣的類型？」

so I said, "I want a tall guy.   least 175 cm…"
我說：「我喜歡高個子，至少要有一七五公分……」

Then she said, "Hey, be   ."
結果她跟我說：「你認清現實吧。」

I'm not   too high, am I!?
我的要求也沒有很離譜吧？

英文日記

My colleague suddenly asked me, "What's your type?",

so I said, "I want a tall guy. At least 175 cm…"

Then she said, "Hey, be realistic."

I'm not aiming too high, am I!?

常用單字片語集

What's your type?
你喜歡什麼類型？
直接使用 type 就可以了。

at least
至少
可以和 at most（最多）一起學起來。

Be realistic.
認清現實吧。
語感上是「實際一點」，即「認清現實」的意思。

aim too high
目標太高
使用 aim（瞄準、目標）這個單字的片語。

有點餓

Just wanna grab a bite

中文日記

今天我比較晚吃午餐，

所以還沒有很餓……

但又想吃點東西，

我繞去超商看看好了。

英文填空日記

I had a _____ lunch today,
今天我比較晚吃午餐，

so I'm not _____ hungry…
所以還沒有很餓……

But I just wanna _____ a bite.
但又想吃點東西，

I'll _____ by a convenience store.
我繞去超商看看好了。

英文日記

I had a late lunch today,

so I'm not that hungry…

But I just wanna grab a bite.

I'll drop by a convenience store.

常用單字片語集

have a late lunch
晚吃午餐
early lunch 就是「早吃午餐」。

not that ～
沒那麼～
that 有各式各樣的用法，像這樣表示「那麼
地」也是其中一種用法。

grab a bite
吃點東西
使用 grab（抓取）的片語。

drop by
繞去
也可以用 stop by。

211

OCTOBER

10 月

We had a birthday party for my best friend today!
今天我們為好朋友辦了生日派對！

This is like our annual event.
這已經是我們每年的慣例活動了。

It's been already 5 years since we had the first one.
從第一次辦到現在都過了五年。

Time flies!
時光飛逝呀！

廣美和健司感覺有戲

They get along with each other

中文日記

我問廣美：「你和健司處得怎麼樣了？」

她回答我：「還算不錯吧。」

我覺得兩個人交往是遲早的事了！

我越來越期待了！

英文填空日記

I asked Hiromi, "How are you getting　　　　with Kenji?",

我問廣美：「你和健司處得怎麼樣了？」

and she said, "I think it's going　　　　　."

她回答我：「還算不錯吧。」

I think they will get　　　　very soon!!

我覺得兩個人交往是遲早的事了！

I'm　　　　excited!

我越來越期待了！

英文日記

I asked Hiromi, "How are you getting along with Kenji?",

and she said, "I think it's going well."

I think they will get together very soon!!

I'm getting excited!

常用單字片語集

get along with ～
和～相處
除了戀人，也可以用來描述朋友或家人。

go well
進展順利
It's going well. 表示「進展得很順利」，也就是「還不錯」的意思。

get together
交往
「在一起」，即「交往」的意思。

be getting excited
越來越期待
be getting＋形容詞是「越來越～」的意思。

第一次和大介起口角

Had a quarrel with Daisuke

中文日記

我和大介發生了一點無聊的小口角。

他一直在滑手機，

而且我們難得見一次面！

我很火大！

英文填空日記

I had a silly ⎽⎽⎽⎽⎽ with Daisuke.
我和大介發生了一點無聊的小口角。

He was ⎽⎽⎽⎽⎽ with his phone all the time.
他一直在滑手機，

⎽⎽⎽⎽⎽, we saw each other after so long!
而且我們難得見一次面！

I got ⎽⎽⎽⎽⎽!!
我很火大！

英文日記

I had a silly fight with Daisuke.

He was playing with his phone all the time.

Besides, we saw each other after so long!

I got irritated!!

常用單字片語集

have a silly fight with ～
和～發生了無聊的小口角
silly 是形容詞，意思是「愚蠢的、不重要」。

play with one's phone
滑手機
手機有很多種説法，像是 smartphone、cellphone、mobile phone 等。

besides
而且
也可以用 what's more。

get irritated
被惹火、被激怒
也可以説 It irritates me. 代表「這件事激怒我」，即「我很火大」的意思。

死黨三人組的生日派對

Birthday party for 3 of us

中文日記

今天我們為好朋友辦了生日派對！

這已經是我們每年的慣例活動了。

從第一次辦到現在都過了五年。

時光飛逝呀！

英文填空日記

We had a birthday party for my   friend today!

今天我們為好朋友辦了生日派對！

This is like our   event.

這已經是我們每年的慣例活動了。

It's been already 5 years   we had the first one.

從第一次辦到現在都過了五年。

Time   !

時光飛逝呀！

英文日記

We had a birthday party for my best friend today!

This is like our annual event.

It's been already 5 years since we had the first one.

Time flies!

--------- 常用單字片語集 ---------

best friend
好朋友、死黨
意思是「最要好的朋友」。

annual event
每年的慣例活動
annual 有「每年的、年度的」的意思，而
monthly 是「每個月」，一起學起來吧。

It's been... since ～ .
從～到現在過了……。
在 ... 裡填入時間。這是很實用的說法，在
日常對話中也用得到。

Time flies.
時光飛逝。
即成語「光陰似箭」的常見英譯。

今天有點冷

A bit chilly today

中文日記

今天有點冷，

風也很大。

樹葉也漸漸轉紅了。

秋天來了呢……

英文填空日記

It was a　　　　cold today,
今天有點冷，

and the wind was　　　　.
風也很大。

The leaves started turning red　　　　well.
樹葉也漸漸轉紅了。

Fall is　　　…
秋天來了呢……

英文日記

It was a bit cold today,

and the wind was strong.

The leaves started turning red as well.

Fall is here...

常用單字片語集

a bit
有點、稍微
和 a little 是相同意思。

the wind is strong
風大
也可以說 It's windy.（今天風很強）。

〜 as well
也〜
英式英文經常使用的片語，必須擺在句尾。

Fall is here.
秋天來了。
意思是「秋天來到這裡了」，即「現在是秋天、秋天來了」。

工作沒進展
Totally stuck

中文日記

我現在束手無策了！

這個專案讓我好頭痛。

我已經沒辦法好好思考了，

今天就到這裡吧！

英文填空日記

I'm totally　　　　　now!
我現在束手無策了！

This project is giving me a　　　　　.
這個專案讓我好頭痛。

I can't think　　　　　anymore,
我已經沒辦法好好思考了，

so that's　　　　　for today!!
今天就到這裡吧！

英文日記

I'm totally stuck now!

This project is giving me a headache.

I can't think straight anymore,

so that's all for today!!

常用單字片語集

be stuck
束手無策
也可以說 be stuck on ～來表示「對～束手無策」。

give me a headache
讓我很頭痛、苦惱的源頭
經常用來表示對一件事情很煩惱、很煩躁。

think straight
好好思考、清楚思考
也可以用 correctly 代替 straight。

That's all for today.
今天到這裡。
課堂結束時也會用這個句子來表示「今天就到這裡」。

6 朋友說她懷孕了！

Good news from my friend!

中文日記

昨天亞彌告訴我一個好消息！

那就是她懷孕了！

亞彌，恭喜你！

但聽說她現在孕吐得很厲害……

英文填空日記

Yesterday I got good　　　　　 from Aya.
昨天亞彌告訴我一個好消息！

She got　　　　　!!
那就是她懷孕了！

**　　　　　, Aya!!**
亞彌，恭喜你！

Now she has terrible　　　　 sickness, she said…
但聽說她現在孕吐得很厲害……

英文日記

Yesterday I got good news from Aya.

She got pregnant!!

Congratulations, Aya!!

Now she has terrible morning sickness, she said…

常用單字片語集

news
通知、新聞
除了電視上看到的新聞以外，從他人得知消息也可以用這個單字。

get pregnant
懷孕
be pregnant 則是表示「懷孕中」的狀態。

Congratulations
恭喜
經常省略成 Congrats。

morning sickness
孕吐、害喜
要表達「有孕吐情況」時，動詞會使用 have。

開始讀多益

Start studying for TOEIC

我覺得如果有一張證照，

找起工作來會更有優勢，

所以我開始讀多益了。

我的目標分數是八百分！

I thought having   is
我覺得如果有一張證照，

**   to get a job,**
找起工作來會更有優勢，

so I started   for TOEIC.
所以我開始讀多益了。

My   score is 800!
我的目標分數是八百分！

I thought having qualifications is

beneficial to get a job,

so I started studying for TOEIC.

My target score is 800!

常用單字片語集

qualification
證照、證書
也可以說 certification。

beneficial
有利的、有優勢的
beneficial for ＋人（對某人來說是有利的）
也是常見的用法。

start -ing
開始～
這個 -ing 是「做～」的意思。

target score
目標分數
target 是「目標」的意思。

我哪知道主管的喜好啊！

Who cares!!

中文日記

我主管超煩的！

端咖啡給他的時候，

他居然說：「怎麼沒加奶精和糖呀？」

我哪知道啊！

英文填空日記

My boss is so ＿＿＿＿!!
我主管超煩的！

When I ＿＿＿ him a coffee,
端咖啡給他的時候，

he said, "Why didn't you ＿＿＿ milk and sugar?"...
他居然說：「怎麼沒加奶精和糖呀？」

＿＿＿ cares!!
我哪知道啊！

英文日記

My boss is so annoying!!

When I served him a coffee,

he said, "Why didn't you put milk and sugar?"...

Who cares!!

常用單字片語集

annoying
煩人的、惱人的
無論是對人或對事都可以使用。

serve
端出（食物或飲品）
也有「招待、服務」的意思。

put
放入、加入
也有「擺放」的意思。

Who cares!
誰知道！
感到煩躁、暴躁，想表達「誰知道這種事啊」的時候可以使用的句子。

221

一不小心就吃了太多零食

Can't help it!!

上班時間要是沒有事情做的話，

我就會忍不住吃零食。

要怎麼做才能克制自己呀？

我真的該減肥了……

When I have nothing to do　　　　 work,
上班時間要是沒有事情做的話，

I can't 　　　　 eating sweets.
我就會忍不住吃零食。

How can I 　　　　 this!?
要怎麼做才能克制自己呀？

I really have to 　　　　 on a diet…
我真的該減肥了……

When I have nothing to do at work,

I can't help eating sweets.

How can I stop this!?

I really have to go on a diet…

常用單字片語集

at work
上班時間、在公司裡
也可以説 while working 或 during work。

can't help -ing
忍不住～
語感類似 end up -ing（結果還是～）。

stop
停止、克制
也經常説 stop -ing（停止做～）。

go on a diet
減肥
也可以搭配 be 動詞，改成 I'm on a diet.
（我現在在減肥）。

老是來炫耀的朋友

Sick of my friend's brag

中文日記

她老是來跟我炫耀她的男朋友！

我覺得好煩，

誰想知道你男朋友喜歡吃什麼呀！

我受夠了……

英文填空日記

She is _____ **about her boyfriend all the time!!**
她老是來跟我炫耀她的男朋友！

I'm _____ **of it now!**
我覺得好煩，

Who _____ **to know your boyfriend's favorite food!?**
誰想知道你男朋友喜歡吃什麼呀！

_____ **already…**
我受夠了……

英文日記

She is bragging about her boyfriend all the time!!

I'm sick of it now!

Who wants to know your boyfriend's favorite food!?

Enough already…

常用單字片語集

brag about ～
炫耀～
這是帶有負面意味的詞，要多加留意使用的情境。

sick of ～
對～感到厭煩
sick 也有「生病的」的意思，但在日常對話中也經常用到這個句型。

Who wants to do ～ ?
誰想～呀？
經常用於挖苦或諷刺他人的情境。

Enough already.
我受夠了。
也會說 Enough!（夠了）。

大介放我鴿子

He cancels again!!

中文日記

大介又放我鴿子了！

今天本來約好要一起去逛街的。

我也知道他最近比較忙，

但這次已經是第三次了耶！

英文填空日記

Daisuke canceled our date　　　　　　the last minute again!!
大介又放我鴿子了！

We were　　　　　to go shopping today.
今天本來約好要一起去逛街的。

I know he's　　　　busy recently,
我也知道他最近比較忙，

but this is the third　　　　　!?
但這次已經是第三次了耶！

英文日記

Daisuke canceled our date at the last minute again!!

We were going to go shopping today.

I know he's been busy recently,

but this is the third time!?

───── 常用單字片語集 ─────

cancel at the last minute
放鴿子
指在最後一刻取消約定或告知不赴約。

were/was going to do ～
原本預計要～
與 were/was supposed to do ～（原本應該要～）用法相近。

have been busy recently
最近很忙
使用完成式 have 可以強調「最近總是」的狀態。

this is the ～ time
這次是第～次
～中的數字要填入序數，像是 first、second 等。

十月

12

開始思考保養皮膚

Thinking about skin care

中文日記

我最近感受到肌膚在老化。

黑斑、皺紋、鬆弛……

明明二十出頭的時候還沒有這些狀況的。

我得更用心保養自己的皮膚了。

英文填空日記

I feel my skin is _____ recently.
我最近感受到肌膚在老化。

_____, wrinkles, sag…
黑斑、皺紋、鬆弛……

I had none of them in my _____ twenties.
明明二十出頭的時候還沒有這些狀況的。

I gotta take _____ care of my skin.
我得更用心保養自己的皮膚了。

英文日記

I feel my skin is aging recently.

Spots, wrinkles, sag…

I had none of them in my early twenties.

I gotta take better care of my skin.

- - - - - - - - - - - - **常用單字片語集** - - - - - - - - - - - -

be aging
老化
age 不只可以做為名詞「年齡」，也可以做為動詞「衰老」。

spot
黑斑
皮膚的黑斑是 spot，髒汙或汙漬則使用 stain。

in one's early twenties
二十出頭
想表示「後半」的話，就把 early 改為 late。

take better care of ～
更用心照顧～
從 take care of（關心、照顧）延伸的表現手法。

臨時變更企劃害我忙翻了

Being busy with the project

客戶突然要求我們

更改企劃摘要。

這不太妙啊……

我根本不確定能不能在期限前完成啊。

Our client _____ requested

客戶突然要求我們

to change the project _____.

更改企劃摘要。

This is not _____ …

這不太妙啊……

I don't know if we can finish it _____ the deadline.

我根本不確定能不能在期限前完成啊。

Our client suddenly requested

to change the project summary.

This is not good…

I don't know if we can finish it by the deadline.

常用單字片語集

suddenly
突然地
all of a sudden 也是同樣意思,學起來吧。

summary
摘要
商業英語會話中經常會出現的單字。

This is not good.
糟糕、不妙
自言自語的說法,經常用在遇到危機,想表達「糟糕、不妙」的時候。

by the deadline
交期、期限之前
by 是能表示「在～之前」的介系詞。

昨天吃太多了

Ate too much yesterday

中文日記

我昨天吃太多了！

現在好像有點消化不良……

早知道就不要吃那麼多了。

我今天完全沒有食慾……

英文填空日記

I ate too _____ yesterday!
我昨天吃太多了！

Feeling _____ in the stomach…
現在好像有點消化不良……

I shouldn't _____ eaten that much.
早知道就不要吃那麼多了。

No _____ today…
我今天完全沒有食慾……

英文日記

I ate too much yesterday!

Feeling heavy in the stomach…

I shouldn't have eaten that much.

No appetite today…

------------------------- 常用單字片語集 -------------------------

eat too much
吃太多
too much 可以運用在各式各樣的情境裡，把這個片語學起來吧。

feel heavy in the stomach
消化不良、胃脹氣
和 have a heavy stomach 是相同意思。

shouldn't have ＋過去分詞
早知道就不要～
要特別留意 have 之後的動詞形態。

appetite
食慾
也可以說 I don't have an appetite.（我沒胃口）。

廣美和健司開始交往了

They started dating!!

聽我説！

廣美和健司開始交往了！

當廣美告訴我的時候，

我跟她一樣開心到不行呀！

You　　　　　what,
聽我說！

Hiromi and Kenji started　　　　　!!
廣美和健司開始交往了！

I　　　　　that from Hiromi,
當廣美告訴我的時候，

and I was so happy　　　　　if it happened to me!!
我跟她一樣開心到不行呀！

You know what,

Hiromi and Kenji started dating!!

I heard that from Hiromi,

and I was so happy as if it happened to me!!

常用單字片語集

you know what
欸，聽我說
朋友的日常對話中經常用來接續話題的開頭語。

start dating
開始交往
date 有「交往、約會」的意思。

hear... from ～
聽～說……
hear 的過去式是 heard，要特別留意。

as if it happened to me
跟對方一樣
應用 as if（宛如～一樣）的表現手法。

跟客戶喝得爛醉

Dead drunk

中文日記

我和客戶一起去喝一杯。

我整個人醉死了，

我的客戶也都爛醉如泥。

有點擔心他們有沒有平安回到家……

英文填空日記

I went for drinks with my ,
我和客戶一起去喝一杯。

and I was **drunk.**
我整個人醉死了，

But my clients were also totally .
我的客戶也都爛醉如泥。

I wonder if they got home .
有點擔心他們有沒有平安回到家……

英文日記

I went for drinks with my clients,

and I was dead drunk.

But my clients were also totally wasted.

I wonder if they got home safely.

常用單字片語集

clients
客戶
可以用來指商業客戶或顧客。

be dead drunk
酩酊大醉、爛醉
活用 dead（死亡的）的表現手法。

be wasted
爛醉如泥
意思近 be dead drunk。

get home safely
平安回家
使用 safely（平安地、安全地）的慣用句型，學起來吧。

229

田中小姐都不接電話

She never answers the call

我經常需要打電話給 A 公司的田中小姐，

但她總是不在座位上！

就算我請她回頭再聯繫我，

她也完全不回撥！

I ⎯⎯⎯⎯ call Ms. Tanaka from A Company,
我經常需要打電話給 A 公司的田中小姐，

but she's always not ⎯⎯⎯⎯!
但她總是不在座位上！

Even ⎯⎯⎯⎯ I ask her to call me back,
就算我請她回頭再聯繫我，

she ⎯⎯⎯⎯ does!!
她也完全不回撥！

I often call Ms. Tanaka from A Company,

but she's always not available!

Even though I ask her to call me back,

she never does!!

常用單字片語集

often
經常、頻繁
必學的常用單字。

not available
沒空、無法使用
在餐廳或飯店也經常用到 available 這個單字，學起來吧。

even though ～
就算～、即便～
可以活用在各種情境的句型，學會這個表達方式可以豐富會話內容。

never
絕對、完全不～
使用 never 這個單字就不需要再加上 not 等否定形，要特別留意。

18 搭飛機去長崎出差

Flight to Nagasaki

4 月
5 月
6 月
7 月
8 月
9 月
10 月
11 月
12 月
1 月
2 月
3 月

中文日記

我現在正在出差。

從東京搭飛機飛往長崎,

機上服務非常周到!

我終於知道這間航空公司的評價為什麼會這麼好了。

英文填空日記

I'm _____ a business trip now.
我現在正在出差。

I _____ a flight from Tokyo to Nagasaki.
從東京搭飛機飛往長崎,

They _____ me really good service!
機上服務非常周到!

Now I know the reason why this airline has a good _____ .
我終於知道這間航空公司的評價為什麼會這麼好了。

英文日記

I'm on a business trip now.

I took a flight from Tokyo to Nagasaki.

They gave me really good service!

Now I know the reason why this airline has a good reputation.

常用單字片語集

be on a business trip
出差中
介系詞要用 on。

take a flight
搭飛機
也可以說 be on a flight,表示「正在飛機上」的意思。

give good service
服務周到
「提供良好的服務」,就是「服務很好」的意思。

have a good reputation
評價優良
將 reputation(評價)和動詞 have 組合使用的表現手法。

231

想請假但被退件

I need days off!!

中文日記

今天我申請了一個星期的休假，

但被退回來了。

我也知道可能會給其他人添麻煩，

但我也有請假的權利吧？

英文填空日記

Today I ＿＿＿＿＿ **for a week off,**
今天我申請了一個星期的休假，

but it was ＿＿＿＿＿**.**
但被退回來了。

I know it would ＿＿＿＿＿ **others,**
我也知道可能會給其他人添麻煩，

but don't I have a ＿＿＿＿＿ **to take holidays!?**
但我也有請假的權利吧？

英文日記

Today I requested for a week off,

but it was rejected.

I know it would bother others,

but don't I have a right to take holidays!?

常用單字片語集

request for ～
申請～
把單字和介系詞 for 一起記下來吧。

be rejected
被退件
reject 也有「駁回、拒絕」的意思。

bother others
給其他人添麻煩
使用 bother（添麻煩、造成困擾）的表現手法。

have a right to ～
有～的權利
right 除了「右邊」以外，還有「權利、正確」的意思。

十月 20

早起吃了一頓豐盛的早餐

A big breakfast

中文日記

今天太早醒來了，

所以我吃了一頓豐盛的早餐。

吐司、滑蛋、優格……

超飽的！

英文填空日記

I _____ up too early this morning,
今天太早醒來了，

so I had a _____ breakfast.
所以我吃了一頓豐盛的早餐。

Some toast, _____ eggs, yogurt, and so on…
吐司、滑蛋、優格……

I'm _____!
超飽的！

英文日記

I woke up too early this morning,

so I had a big breakfast.

Some toast, scrambled eggs, yogurt, and so on…

I'm stuffed!

常用單字片語集

wake up
醒來
get up 是「下床、起床」的意思，要注意區別。

have a big breakfast
吃一頓豐盛的早餐
這種情境用 big 才是主流，學起來吧。

scrambled eggs
滑蛋
小心不要忘記 scrambled 的「d」喔。

be stuffed
吃飽的、吃撐的
和 be full 同樣意思。

233

有個同事要離職了

Someone leaving the company

中文日記

有個同事要離職了，

所以我們舉辦了歡送會。

她是一個很好的人，

我會想她的……

英文填空日記

One of my colleagues is _____ **the company,**
有個同事要離職了，

so we had a _____ **party.**
所以我們舉辦了歡送會。

She is _____ **a good person.**
她是一個很好的人，

I'm going to _____ **her…**
我會想她的……

英文日記

One of my colleagues is leaving the company,

so we had a farewell party.

She is such a good person.

I'm going to miss her…

常用單字片語集

leave the company
離職
leave（離開）這個單字有許多用法。

farewell party
歡送會
也可以説 leaving party。

such a ～
很～
～的部分通常會接續像 good person 這樣「形容詞＋名詞」的組合。

miss
感到寂寞
miss ～是「～不在，會感到寂寞」的意思。

22 被迫加班

Overtime work

中文日記

我今天被迫加班了。

還沒有半個人幫我！

都已經八點了。

我肚子開始餓了……

英文填空日記

I was _____ to do some extra work today.
我今天被迫加班了。

No one gave me a _____!!
還沒有半個人幫我！

It's _____ 8.
都已經八點了。

I'm _____ hungry…
我肚子開始餓了……

英文日記

I was forced to do some extra work today.

No one gave me a hand!!

It's already 8.

I'm getting hungry…

常用單字片語集

be forced to do ～
被迫～
force 有「促使、強迫」的意思。

give ～ a hand
幫忙
和 help 是同樣的意思。

It's already ～ .
已經～點了。
使用 already（已經）的表現手法，日常對話很常用。

be getting ～
開始～
如 I'm getting full.（我肚子開始飽了）等，可以做許多運用。

235

朋友問我美國人的個性

Something about American

中文日記

我朋友問我美國人怎麼樣，我告訴他：

「我覺得美國人都很直率。

他們很健談又溫和。

對了，他們都穿夾腳拖。」

英文填空日記

My friend asked me　　　　American people, so I said,
我朋友問我美國人怎麼樣，我告訴他：

"I think American people are very　　　　　　.
「我覺得美國人都很直率。

They are　　　　to talk to and so kind.
他們很健談又溫和。

Oh, and they wear　　　　　."
對了，他們都穿夾腳拖。」

英文日記

My friend asked me about American people, so I said,

"I think American people are very straightforward.

They are easy to talk to and so kind.

Oh, and they wear flip-flops."

常用單字片語集

ask... about ～
詢問……關於～的事
活用 about（關於）的表現手法，相當實用。

straightforward
坦率的、直爽的
straight（筆直的）＋ forward（向前）的組合詞。

easy to talk to
健談的、好交際的
easy（容易的）可以和許多單字結合成各種片語。

flip-flops
夾腳拖
在美國當地可以看見店家的看板上寫著這個單字。

24

一翻開漫畫就停不下來

Can't stop reading manga!!

中文日記

我一翻開漫畫開始看，

就怎麼樣也停不下來了！

我知道自己看上癮了，

但我也束手無策⋯⋯

英文填空日記

      I start reading comic books,
我一翻開漫畫開始看，

I can never   it!
就怎麼樣也停不下來了！

I know I'm already   .
我知道自己看上癮了，

But I don't know   to do...
但我也束手無策⋯⋯

英文日記

Once I start reading comic books,

I can never stop it!

I know I'm already addicted.

But I don't know what to do...

常用單字片語集

once ～
一旦開始～
這種情況的 once 是當連接詞使用。

I can never stop it.
怎麼樣也停不下來。
比起一般的否定句，用 never 可以有更強烈的感覺。

be addicted
上癮、沉迷
也可以說 be addicted to ～（沉迷於～）。

I don't know what to do.
不知道該怎麼辦才好。
可以原封不動使用，整句一起記下來吧。

一照鏡子就看見黑斑……

A spot on my face

中文日記

今天早上我照了鏡子，

發現臉上有黑斑！

打擊好大呀……

我平時明明很注重防晒的呀！

英文填空日記

When I looked _____ the mirror this morning,
今天早上我照了鏡子，

I found a _____ on my face!
發現臉上有黑斑！

I'm so _____ …
打擊好大呀……

I've always been careful not to get _____ !
我平時明明很注重防晒的呀！

英文日記

When I looked in the mirror this morning,

I found a spot on my face!

I'm so shocked…

I've always been careful not to get tanned!

常用單字片語集

look in the mirror
照鏡子
要表示照鏡子這個動作，比起 look at 更常使用 look in。

spot
黑斑
衣物上的汙點要用 stain。

be shocked
大受打擊
不要忘了 shocked 後面要加上 ed。

get tanned
晒黑
tan 是「晒成褐色」的意思。

這種季節居然還有颱風

Typhoon is coming!

中文日記

有個大型颱風正往日本靠近！

而且還有可能直撲東京！

如果是早上登陸的話，電車有可能全部停駛，

那我可能就沒辦法去上班了！

英文填空日記

The big typhoon is　　　　　Japan!
有個大型颱風正往日本靠近！

And it might　　　　　Tokyo!
而且還有可能直撲東京！

If it comes in the morning, all the trains　　　　　stop.
如果是早上登陸的話，電車有可能全部停駛，

I might not　　　　　able to go to work!
那我可能就沒辦法去上班了！

英文日記

The big typhoon is approaching Japan!

And it might hit Tokyo!

If it comes in the morning, all the trains might stop.

I might not be able to go to work!

---------------- 常用單字片語集 ----------------

approach
接近、靠近
不管是人或物，都可以運用在各種情境。

hit ～
直撲～
雖然 hit 也有「敲打、打擊」的意思，但在這個情境裡是「直撲」的意思。

might ～
有可能～
might 之後一定要接原形動詞。

might not be able to ～
可能沒辦法～
might 之後不能接 can/cannot，所以改用 be able to。

爸爸很愛棒球

My dad loves baseball

中文日記

一提起棒球，我爸的話匣子就停不下來了。

只要聊到他喜歡的球隊和選手，

他都瞭若指掌！

可惜的是我沒有很喜歡棒球……

英文填空日記

When it ＿＿＿＿＿ to baseball, my father can't stop talking.
一提起棒球，我爸的話匣子就停不下來了。

He ＿＿＿＿＿ about his favorite team, player.
只要聊到他喜歡的球隊和選手，

He knows a ＿＿＿＿＿ !
他都瞭若指掌！

But I'm not a big ＿＿＿＿＿ of baseball, unfortunately…
可惜的是我沒有很喜歡棒球……

英文日記

When it comes to baseball, my father can't stop talking.

He talks about his favorite team, player.

He knows a lot!

But I'm not a big fan of baseball, unfortunately…

常用單字片語集

when it comes to ～
一提起～
懂得活用就會很方便的慣用句型。

know a lot
瞭若指掌
「知道很多」，即「瞭若指掌」的意思。

talk about ～
聊到～
注意不要和 talk to ～ / talk with ～（和～聊天）搞混了。

not a big fan of ～
沒有很喜歡
和 a big fan of ～（非常喜歡～）一起記下來吧。

家門前發生車禍

Car accident in front of my place

中文日記

昨天我住的公寓門口發生車禍。

我聽見很大的撞擊聲，

嚇了我一大跳！

還好沒有人身亡，謝天謝地。

英文填空日記

There was a car   in front of my apartment yesterday.
昨天我住的公寓門口發生車禍。

I heard a big   sound last night,
我聽見很大的撞擊聲，

and I was so   !
嚇了我一大跳！

**   god, there was no one killed.**
還好沒有人身亡，謝天謝地。

英文日記

There was a car accident in front of my apartment yesterday.

I heard a big crash sound last night,

and I was so surprised!

Thank god, there was no one killed.

常用單字片語集

car accident
車禍
accident（事故）是日常對話中也經常出現的單字。

crash sound
撞擊聲
描述車輛撞擊時，經常用 crash 這個單字。

be surprised
嚇一跳
只有 surprise 的話，是「嚇對方」的動詞。

thank god
謝天謝地
鬆一口氣時會使用的說法。

低頭族很危險

It's really dangerous!

邊走邊滑手機真的很危險！

那個男的差點就要撞上我了，

因為他整個人都專注在他的手機上。

有可能會發生很嚴重的意外耶！

Texting　　　　　walking is so dangerous!
邊走邊滑手機真的很危險！

A guy almost　　　　　into me,
那個男的差點就要撞上我了，

because he was　　　　　on his phone too much.
因為他整個人都專注在他的手機上。

It　　　　be a big accident!
有可能會發生很嚴重的意外耶！

Texting while walking is so dangerous!

A guy almost bumped into me,

because he was concentrating on his phone too much.

It could be a big accident!

- - - - - - - - - - - - - - - - 常用單字片語集 - - - - - - - - - - - - - -

texting while walking
邊走邊滑手機
「邊走邊傳訊息」，即「低頭族」的意思。

concentrate on ～
專注於～
注意介系詞要使用 on。

bump into ～
撞上～
也有「巧遇」的意思。

It could be ～
可能會～
could 可以用來表示「可能發生的事」。

十月 30 和大介出門逛街

Shopping with Daisuke

中文日記

今天我和大介出門逛街了。

他這個人穿衣服沒什麼品味，

所以我叫他讓我幫他挑衣服！

來吧，我看看哪件適合他……

英文填空日記

Today I　　　　shopping with Daisuke.
今天我和大介出門逛街了。

He doesn't have good　　　　in fashion,
他這個人穿衣服沒什麼品味，

so I asked him to　　　　me choose his clothes!
所以我叫他讓我幫他挑衣服！

Well, which one looks　　　　on him…?
來吧，我看看哪件適合他……

英文日記

Today I went shopping with Daisuke.

He doesn't have good taste in fashion,

so I asked him to let me choose his clothes!

Well, which one looks good on him…?

常用單字片語集

go shopping
逛街
注意中間不需要加介系詞。

have good taste in fashion
擁有穿衣品味
也可以說 have a good sense of fashion，
意思是相同的。

let... ～
讓……做～
～裡擺的動詞一定要是原形動詞。

look good on ～
適合～
look good（好看）加上介系詞 on。

楓葉季

Season of autumn leaves

樹葉都轉紅了。

我想去京都看楓葉。

但實在是太遠了……

東京有沒有什麼不錯的地方可以賞楓呢？

The _____ are changing colors.
樹葉都轉紅了。

I wanna go to Kyoto to see _____ leaves.
我想去京都看楓葉。

But it's too _____ from here…
但實在是太遠了……

Is there any nice _____ to see in Tokyo?
東京有沒有什麼不錯的地方可以賞楓呢？

The leaves are changing colors.

I wanna go to Kyoto to see autumn leaves.

But it's too far from here…

Is there any nice place to see in Tokyo?

常用單字片語集

leaves
葉子
單數是 leaf，但基本上用的都是複數形。

autumn leaves
楓葉
多加留意 autumn（秋天）的拼字。

far
遠的
和反義詞 near（近的）一起記下來吧。

place
地方
any nice place（不錯的地方）也是常用表現手法。

有關「健康、節食」的十大表現手法

第 1 名	**I'm feeling sick.** 我病了。	feel〜是在描述身體狀況時，經常使用的單字。除此之外，I'm not feeling well.（我身體不舒服）也可以用在同樣情境，一起學起來吧。
第 2 名	**I have a cold.** 我感冒了。	除了 have a cold（感冒）以外，have a runny nose（流鼻水）、have a cough（咳嗽）等，各式各樣身體的症狀都可以用 have 來表示。
第 3 名	**I go on a diet.** 我要減肥。	如果要表示正在減肥的狀態，可以說 I'm on a diet.（現在正在肥減中）。記住除了減肥以外，只要想表達「狀態」，都可以使用 be 動詞。
第 4 名	**I ate too much.** 我吃太撐了。	too much 是用來表示事情做過頭時，經常使用的片語。That's too much.（做過頭了）則常用來形容對方的行為或情況，一起學起來吧。
第 5 名	**I lost 2 kg!** 我瘦了兩公斤！	相反的，「胖了兩公斤！」可以説 I gained 2 kg! 或 I put on 2 kg!。put 這個單字無論是現在式、過去式、過去分詞的動詞形態都沒有變化，要特別留意。
第 6 名	**I got fat!** 我變胖了！	此外，I gained weight.、I put on some weight. 這些句子也有相同的意思。反之，「我瘦了」則可以説 I lost weight.。
第 7 名	**I'll start working out.** 我要開始健身。	無論是「肌力訓練」或「運動」，都可以用 work out 表示。想具體說明健身內容的話，可以說 do push-ups（伏地挺身）、do sit-ups（仰臥起坐）等等。
第 8 名	**I got pimples!** 我長痘痘了！	「痘痘」除了 pimple 之外，也可以用 zit。可以和片語 pop a zit/pimple（擠痘痘）一起記下來，非常實用。
第 9 名	**I have rough skin.** 我的膚況很糟。	rough 是描述「乾燥、粗糙」的形容詞。have 除了「有」這個意思之外，還有許多用法，學著活用到各種情境中吧。
第 10 名	**I went to do yoga.** 我去做了瑜伽。	瑜伽和運動一樣，會讓人誤用 play 做為動詞，但其實普遍是用 do。除此之外，像是 judo（柔道）、boxing（拳擊）等格鬥技也是使用 do 做為動詞居多。

Best 10

NOVEMBER

It feels like autumn is setting in.
感覺秋天真的來了。

It's getting chilly in the morning and at night.
現在早晚都有些涼意。

I gotta take out my winter clothes this weekend.
這個週末我該把冬裝翻出來了。

What a pain!
麻煩死了！

換季

Taking out my winter clothes

中文日記

感覺秋天真的來了。

現在早晚都有些涼意。

這個週末我該把冬裝翻出來了。

麻煩死了！

英文填空日記

It feels like autumn is _____ in.
感覺秋天真的來了。

It's getting _____ in the morning and at night.
現在早晚都有些涼意。

I gotta _____ out my winter clothes this weekend.
這個週末我該把冬裝翻出來了。

_____ a pain!
麻煩死了！

英文日記

It feels like autumn is setting in.

It's getting chilly in the morning and at night.

I gotta take out my winter clothes this weekend.

What a pain!

常用單字片語集

set in
季節到來
也可以用 coming 代替 set in。

chilly
微冷的
cold 就是單純的「冷」，如果不到寒冷的程度，可以用 chilly 這個單字來表示「微冷的、涼的」。

take out
拿出來
「外帶」經常誤用 take out，但其實應該說 take away。

What a pain!
麻煩死了！
也可以說 I can't be bothered.。

十一月 2

要找什麼工作好呢？

Job searching

中文日記

今天我上網找了找工作，

但選擇實在是太多了！

得花點時間好好思考才行。

我想找一份有挑戰性的工作。

英文填空日記

I was searching　　　　　a job online today,
今天我上網找了找工作，

but there were　　　　　many choices!
但選擇實在是太多了！

I have to　　　　　my time and think about it.
得花點時間好好思考才行。

I want to find one which is　　　　　challenging.
我想找一份有挑戰性的工作。

英文日記

I was searching for a job online today,

but there were too many choices!

I have to take my time and think about it.

I want to find one which is worth challenging.

- - - - - - - - - - - - - - 常用單字片語集 - - - - - - - - - - - - - -

search for ～
找～
look for ～也是「找」的意思，但要指網路
搜尋的話，通常會使用 search。

There are too many ～ .
～實在是太多了。
如果～裡是不可數名詞的話，就要用 much
取代 many。

take one's time
花費某人的時間
Take your time.（慢慢來）也是實用短句。

be worth -ing
值得～
worth challenging 直譯是「值得挑戰的」，
但通常會翻譯成「有挑戰性的」。

249

和大介去一日遊

A day trip with Daisuke

中文日記

我和大介去了鎌倉一日遊。

天氣超好的！

我們搭了遊覽船，還看見了富士山。

真的很開心。

英文填空日記

I went for a _____ trip to Kamakura with Daisuke.
我和大介去了鎌倉一日遊。

It was _____ nice weather!
天氣超好的！

We took a _____ and saw Mt. Fuji.
我們搭了遊覽船，還看見了富士山。

I really _____ a good time.
真的很開心。

英文日記

I went for a day trip to Kamakura with Daisuke.

It was such nice weather!

We took a riverboat and saw Mt. Fuji.

I really had a good time.

- - - - - - - - - - 常用單字片語集 - - - - - - - - - -

a day trip
一日遊
也可以說 one-day trip。

nice weather
好天氣
weather（天氣）是實用單字，學起來吧。

riverboat
遊覽船
river（河）和 boat（船）組合而成的單字。

have a good time
過得很開心
和 enjoy、have fun 是相同意思。

十一月 4

目睹健司的劈腿現場

Kenji cheating with someone!?

中文日記

天啊，我撞見不該看見的東西了。

廣美的男朋友健司和別的女生走在一起！

我該不該告訴廣美呀……？

怎麼辦？

英文填空日記

On my god, I saw something I was not　　　　　 to see.
天啊，我撞見不該看見的東西了。

Kenji, Hiromi's boyfriend,　　　　 walking with a girl!
廣美的男朋友健司和別的女生走在一起！

**　　　　 I tell this to Hiromi or not…!?**
我該不該告訴廣美呀……？

**　　　　 should I do!?**
怎麼辦？

英文日記

On my god, I saw something I was not supposed to see.

Kenji, Hiromi's boyfriend, was walking with a girl!

Should I tell this to Hiromi or not…!?

What should I do!?

常用單字片語集

be supposed to ～
應該～
加上 not 就會變成「不應該～」的意思。

walk with ～
和～走在一起
with 大多用於「和～在一起」的意思。

Should I ～ or not?
我該不該～？
句尾加上 not 後，語感就會更接近「該不該？怎麼辦？」

What should I do?
怎麼辦？
直譯的話是「我該做什麼才好呢？」，這句話經常用在不知道該如何是好的情境。

在咖啡店讀書

Studying at a café, but…

我現在在咖啡店裡讀英文。

我在家裡無法專注，

換個地方讀書比較適合我。

不過我開始有點睏了……

I'm studying English at a _____ now.
我現在在咖啡店裡讀英文。

I can't _____ at home,
我在家裡無法專注，

so it's better for me to go _____ else to study.
換個地方讀書比較適合我。

But I'm getting _____ now…
不過我開始有點睏了……

I'm studying English at a café now.

I can't concentrate at home,

so it's better for me to go somewhere else to study.

But I'm getting sleepy now…

常用單字片語集

café
咖啡店
也可以說 coffee shop。

concentrate
專注、集中
concentrate on ～就是「專注於～」的意思。

somewhere else
別的地方、其他地方
其他像是 something else（別的東西）也是常用片語。

be getting sleepy
越來越睏
be getting ＋形容詞是「越來越～」的意思，是常見用法。

6

牙齒好痛，難道蛀牙了？

My tooth hurts…

中文日記

我的天呀，

我的牙齒好痛！

難道是蛀牙了……？

我不想去看牙醫呀！

英文填空日記

Oh　　　　　gosh,
我的天呀，

my tooth　　　　　!
我的牙齒好痛！

Is this a　　　　　…?
難道是蛀牙了……？

I don't wanna go to the　　　　　!!
我不想去看牙醫呀！

英文日記

Oh my gosh,

my tooth hurts!

Is this a cavity…?

I don't wanna go to the dentist!!

常用單字片語集

oh my gosh
我的天呀
和 oh my god 同義，多用於口語會話。

hurt
疼痛
It hurts!（很痛）也很常用，一起記下來吧。

cavity
蛀牙
一般會說 I have a cavity.（我有蛀牙）。

go to the dentist
去看牙醫
也可以說 dental clinic（牙醫診所）。

咖啡灑到白色毛衣上了！

My sweater got a stain!

糟了，我把咖啡灑到毛衣上了！

我很喜歡這一件的！

毛衣會留下咖啡漬的。

怎麼辦啊……？

Oh no, I ＿＿＿＿＿ coffee on my sweater!!
糟了，我把咖啡灑到毛衣上了！

This is my ＿＿＿＿＿!!
我很喜歡這一件的！

It's getting a ＿＿＿＿＿.
毛衣會留下咖啡漬的。

What ＿＿＿＿＿ do…?
怎麼辦啊……？

Oh no, I spilled coffee on my sweater!!

This is my favorite!!

It's getting a stain.

What to do…?

常用單字片語集

spill
灑
會說 spill...on ～（把……灑到～上）。

favorite
很喜歡的
在詢問別人的喜好時，會說 What's your favorite?（你喜歡哪一種？）

stain
汙漬
「汙漬」還有其他說法，像是 mark、spot 等等。

What to do?
怎麼辦？
自言自語、煩惱著該如何是好時，可以用的短句。

8 送洗毛衣

Take it to the dry cleaners

中文日記

果不其然，毛衣上留下汙漬了。

我得拿去送洗才行。

對了，我還要記得帶上我的裙子。

好麻煩呀！

英文填空日記

I thought, I got a stain on my sweater.
果不其然，毛衣上留下汙漬了。

I gotta take this to the dry　　　　　.
我得拿去送洗才行。

Oh, I remembered　　　　　take my skirt, too.
對了，我還要記得帶上我的裙子。

**　　　　　a drag!**
好麻煩呀！

英文日記

As I thought, I got a stain on my sweater.

I gotta take this to the dry cleaners.

Oh, I remembered to take my skirt, too.

What a drag!

常用單字片語集

as I thought
果不其然
I knew that!（我就知道！果然是這樣！）
也可以用於相同的情境。

take ～ to the dry cleaners
拿～去送洗
日常生活很實用的片語，趁機學起來吧。

remember to do
記得要～
小心不要寫成 doing 了。

What a drag!
好麻煩！
和 What a pain! 是同樣意思。

我到底想做什麼工作？

What do I want to do?

中文日記

最近我一直在思考一件事。

我這一輩子究竟想做什麼呢？

至今為止，我工作的時候有想過什麼目標嗎？

我想做一份能讓我有動力的工作。

英文填空日記

Recently I've _____ thinking.
最近我一直在思考一件事。

What do I want to do _____ my life?
我這一輩子究竟想做什麼呢？

I wonder if I've ever thought about a _____ when I've been working.
至今為止，我工作的時候有想過什麼目標嗎？

I want a job which _____ me a lot.
我想做一份能讓我有動力的工作。

英文日記

Recently I've been thinking.

What do I want to do with my life?

I wonder if I've ever thought about a goal when I've been working.

I want a job which motivates me a lot.

常用單字片語集

I've been thinking.
我一直在思考。
使用現在完成式代表狀態的持續性。

with my life
人生中
what to do with one's life 也會翻譯成「人生目標」。

goal
目標、目的
目標還有其他說法，但 goal 是最常用到的單字之一。

motivate ～
讓～有動力
I got motivated. 就是「我有幹勁了」的意思。

膚況好差

Rough skin

中文日記

最近我的膚況好差。

會不會是因為太乾燥了呢？

我還長痘痘了。

還是我應該換一款保養品呢？

英文填空日記

My skin has become　　　　　recently.
最近我的膚況好差。

Is it because of the　　　　air?
會不會是因為太乾燥了呢？

I also got　　　　.
我還長痘痘了。

Should I change my skin　　　　products?
還是我應該換一款保養品呢？

英文日記

My skin has become rougher recently.

Is it because of the dry air?

I also got pimples.

Should I change my skin care products?

常用單字片語集

become rougher
（肌膚）變得粗糙
使用單字 rough（粗糙）的比較級來表示。

dry air
乾燥
指空氣乾燥。

pimple
痘痘
醫學用語會說 acne，但一般對話比較常用 pimple。

skin care products
保養品

11

宿醉

Hangover…

嗯，宿醉好嚴重……

昨天我到底喝了多少呀？

喝完兩杯啤酒以後，

我什麼也不記得了……

Ugh, terrible **…**
嗯，宿醉好嚴重……

How **did I drink yesterday?**
昨天我到底喝了多少呀？

I finished the second beer,
喝完兩杯啤酒以後，

I don't remember **…**
我什麼也不記得了……

Ugh, terrible hangover…

How much did I drink yesterday?

After I finished the second beer,

I don't remember anything…

常用單字片語集

hangover
宿醉
I have a hangover. 就是「我宿醉了」的意思。

how much
多少
當描述的單字屬於可數名詞時，要將 much 改為 many。

after ～
在～之後
日常對話中經常用到的單字。

I don't remember anything.
我什麼也不記得了。
也可以用 at all（完全）來代替 anything。

12 打掃的時候發現耳環
Found the earrings

中文日記

今天我在打掃房間的時候，

發現了之前弄丟的耳環！

它們掉在床和牆壁中間！

它們是怎麼掉進那麼小的縫隙的呀？

英文填空日記

Today when I was ⎽⎽⎽⎽⎽ my room,
今天我在打掃房間的時候，

I found the ⎽⎽⎽⎽⎽ I lost before!
發現了之前弄丟的耳環！

They were in the space ⎽⎽⎽⎽⎽ the bed and wall!
它們掉在床和牆壁中間！

How did they go in this small ⎽⎽⎽⎽⎽…?
它們是怎麼掉進那麼小的縫隙的呀？

英文日記

Today when I was cleaning my room,

I found the earrings I lost before!

They were in the space between the bed and wall!

How did they go in this small gap…?

常用單字片語集

clean one's room
打掃房間
也經常使用 vacuum the floor（吸地板）。

earrings
耳環
無論是貼耳式耳環或垂掛式耳環，英文都一樣是 earrings。

between... and ～
在……和～中間
會出現在教科書裡的常用片語，學起來吧。

gap
縫隙
也有裂痕的意思。

13 親手做飯給大介吃

Nikujaga I made

中文日記

大介跟我說：「我想吃你做的料理。」

所以我試著做了馬鈴薯燉肉。

但完全搞砸了，

吃起來有股焦味……

英文填空日記

Daisuke said, "I wanna eat the food you　　　　　　 ,"
大介跟我說：「我想吃你做的料理。」

so I tried　　　　　 make Nikujaga.
所以我試著做了馬鈴薯燉肉。

But I totally　　　　　 up.
但完全搞砸了，

It tastes　　　　　 …
吃起來有股焦味……

英文日記

Daisuke said, "I wanna eat the food you made,"

so I tried to make Nikujaga.

But I totally screwed up.

It tastes burned...

常用單字片語集

the food you made
你親手做的料理
「你製作的料理」，即「你親手做的料理」
的意思。

try to ～
嘗試～
不要和 try doing（試試看～）混淆意思了。

screw up
失敗、搞砸
口語對話中經常出現的表現手法。

taste burned
有焦味
運用 burned（燒焦）的片語。

14 多益取得好成績！
Got a good score on TOEIC

中文日記

太好了！我多益考了個好成績！

本來我還很擔心自己表現得好不好，

希望這樣能有助於我找到好工作。

現在該認真開始找新工作啦！

英文填空日記

Yes!! I got a ⎵ score on TOEIC!
太好了！我多益考了個好成績！

I was worried if I did it ⎵ .
本來我還很擔心自己表現得好不好，

I hope this score will help me ⎵ get a good job.
希望這樣能有助於我找到好工作。

Now I gotta be ⎵ about hunting for a new job!
現在該認真開始找新工作啦！

英文日記

Yes!! I got a good score on TOEIC!

I was worried if I did it well.

I hope this score will help me to get a good job.

Now I gotta be serious about hunting for a new job!

常用單字片語集

get a good score on ～
～考得好成績
這個情況的介系詞要用 on，一起記下來吧。

do well
表現好
會像 do it well 一樣在中間插入代名詞。

help... to do ～
幫助……去做～
也有派上用場的意思。

be serious about ～
認真做～
about 後面可以接名詞，若要接動詞的話，動詞形態要改為 -ing。

客戶說沒收到商品

Got a call from A Company

中文日記

A 公司聯繫我說：

「我們訂的商品還沒有送到。」

這到底是怎麼回事？

我得馬上確認才行！

英文填空日記

I got a _____ from A Company and they said

A 公司聯繫我說：

the goods we ordered have not been _____ yet.

「我們訂的商品還沒有送到。」

What the hell is _____ on!?

這到底是怎麼回事？

I have to check it _____ away!

我得馬上確認才行！

英文日記

I got a call from A Company and they said

the goods we ordered have not been delivered yet.

What the hell is going on!?

I have to check it right away!

常用單字片語集

get a call from ～
～聯繫我
call 可以做為名詞，也可以做為動詞。

deliver
送達、寄送
表示下訂的商品送達時經常使用的單字。

What (the hell) is going on?
這到底是怎麼回事？
在 What is going on?（發生了什麼事？）
加上 the hell（到底）的表現手法。

right away
馬上
近同 now（立刻）的片語。

16 錯過史密斯先生的電話

Bad timing!

中文日記

我同事剛剛接到史密斯先生的電話，

我馬上回撥了，但對方沒有接。

所以我就去了一趟廁所，途中對方又打回來了！

怎麼一直錯過呀！

英文填空日記

My colleague   a call from Mr. Smith earlier.
我同事剛剛接到史密斯先生的電話，

I called him   right away, but he didn't answer.
我馬上回撥了，但對方沒有接。

So I went to the   , then he called me again!!
所以我就去了一趟廁所，途中對方又打回來了！

Bad   !
怎麼一直錯過呀！

英文日記

My colleague got a call from Mr. Smith earlier.

I called him back right away, but he didn't answer.

So I went to the bathroom, then he called me again!!

Bad timing!

常用單字片語集

get a call
接到電話
大多會加上 from ～（來自～）。

call back
回撥
Call me back 就是「回撥給我」的意思。
注意 me 擺放的位置。

go to the bathroom
去廁所
除了 bathroom 之外，廁所還有許多種說法，像是 restroom、toilet 等。

Bad timing!
錯過了！
時機點的英文用 timing 就可以了。

不擅長和剛認識的人聊天

What should I do?

中文日記

我不是很擅長和剛認識的人聊天，

我總是會因為太緊張而語無倫次。

該怎麼辦才好呀？

有沒有什麼方法可以克服呢……？

英文填空日記

I'm　　　　　 at talking with someone I just met.
我不是很擅長和剛認識的人聊天，

I always get nervous and　　　　　 .
我總是會因為太緊張而語無倫次。

**　　　　　 should I do?**
該怎麼辦才好呀？

Is there any good way to get　　　　　 it…?
有沒有什麼方法可以克服呢……？

英文日記

I'm bad at talking with someone I just met.

I always get nervous and awkward.

What should I do?

Is there any good way to get over it…?

---------- **常用單字片語集** ----------

be bad at ～
不擅長～
和 be good at ～（擅長）一起記下來吧。

get awkward
變得語無倫次、不自然
把 get ＋形容詞（變得很～）這個片語學起來會非常實用喔。

What should I do?
我該怎麼辦才好？
和 What to do? 幾乎是同樣意思。

get over ～
克服、度過～
根據 get 後面接的介系詞不同，意思會截然不同。

週末沒有任何安排

No plans for the weekend…

中文日記

這個週末我完全沒有安排……

但我又不想待在家裡。

大介出差了，也不在。

有沒有哪個人有空呢……

英文填空日記

I have _____ plans for this weekend…
這個週末我完全沒有安排……

But I don't wanna _____ at home.
但我又不想待在家裡。

Daisuke is _____ on a business trip.
大介出差了，也不在。

I wonder if there is someone _____…
有沒有哪個人有空呢……

英文日記

I have no plans for this weekend…

But I don't wanna stay at home.

Daisuke is away on a business trip.

I wonder if there is someone free…

- - - - - - - - - - 常用單字片語集 - - - - - - - - - -

have no plans
沒有安排
plan 經常做為「預定、計畫」來使用。

stay at home
待在家裡
留意 home 前面擺放的介系詞。

be away
不在
雖然 away 也有「離開」的意思，但也可以像這樣做為形容詞使用。

someone free
有空的人
根據情境不同，也可以改用 anyone。

265

今天晚餐要煮什麼好呢？

What to make for dinner

中文日記

今天晚餐要煮什麼好呢？

雖然我有點想吃豬排，

但晚上不適合吃太油膩的……

好，那就改做薑汁燒肉吧！

英文填空日記

What should I make　　　　　 dinner tonight?
今天晚餐要煮什麼好呢？

I feel　　　　 eating Tonkatsu,
雖然我有點想吃豬排，

but it's not good to eat something　　　　 at night...
但晚上不適合吃太油膩的……

Okay, I'll make Shoga-yaki,　　　　 !!
好，那就改做薑汁燒肉吧！

英文日記

What should I make for dinner tonight?

I feel like eating Tonkatsu,

but it's not good to eat something heavy at night...

Okay, I'll make Shoga-yaki, then!!

常用單字片語集

What should I make for dinner?
晚餐要煮什麼好呢？
What should I ～？就是「我該做什麼好呢？」的意思。

feel like -ing
想～
feel 可以和各種單字組合。

something heavy
太油膩、太重口味的東西
something 大多時候不一定會翻譯出來。

then
那麼
then 也有「那時候」的意思。

20 朋友在巴黎遇到扒手了

Pickpocketed in Paris

中文日記

我朋友在巴黎遇到扒手了！

她在搭火車的時候，有人打開了她的包包。

但她完全沒發現。

太恐怖了。

英文填空日記

My friend got _____ in Paris!
我朋友在巴黎遇到扒手了！

When she was _____ the train, someone opened her bag.
她在搭火車的時候，有人打開了她的包包。

But she didn't _____ at all.
但她完全沒發現。

That's so _____.
太恐怖了。

英文日記

My friend got pickpocketed in Paris!

When she was on the train, someone opened her bag.

But she didn't notice at all.

That's so scary.

常用單字片語集

get pickpocketed
遇到扒手
pickpocket 就是「扒手、偷竊」的意思。

on the train
火車上
這種情況下用的是 on 而不是 in。

notice
發現、注意
想表示「發現」有人對自己做什麼事的時候可以用這個單字。

scary
恐怖的
也有 I'm scared.（我好怕）的用法。

看見一頂很適合大介的帽子

Found a nice cap for Daisuke

中文日記

我看見一頂很適合大介的棒球帽！

我自己是覺得很適合他啦，

但我不確定他喜不喜歡……

或許我應該先問問他的意見。

英文填空日記

I found a nice _____ for Daisuke!!
我看見一頂很適合大介的棒球帽！

I think it _____ him,
我自己是覺得很適合他啦，

but I'm not _____ if he'll like it…
但我不確定他喜不喜歡……

Maybe I should ask him _____ .
或許我應該先問問他的意見。

英文日記

I found a nice cap for Daisuke!!

I think it suits him,

but I'm not sure if he'll like it…

Maybe I should ask him first.

常用單字片語集

cap
棒球帽
有帽簷的帽子叫做 hat。

not sure if～
不確定是否～
運用 sure（確定）這個單字的片語。

It suits ～ .
很適合～。
也可以説 It looks good on ～。

first
首先、一開始
first 會根據情境和前後文有不同的意思。

十一月 22 本來打算預訂餐廳

All tables are already taken!?

中文日記

我本來要為朋友的生日預訂餐廳，

但客滿了！

我也問過其他餐廳，但全都被預訂光了……

要是早一點訂位就好了！

英文填空日記

I tried to　　　　　a restaurant for my friend's birthday,
我本來要為朋友的生日預訂餐廳，

but it was　　　　　!!
但客滿了！

I tried other restaurants, but they were also booked…
我也問過其他餐廳，但全都被預訂光了……

I should　　　　　done it earlier!
要是早一點訂位就好了！

英文日記

I tried to book a restaurant for my friend's birthday,

but it was full!!

I tried other restaurants, but they were also fully booked…

I should have done it earlier!

常用單字片語集

book
預訂
book 可以是名詞「書」或動詞「預訂」，兩種意思都學起來吧。

full
客滿
表示餐飲店客滿時經常用到的單字。

be fully booked
預訂全滿
由 fully（完全）和 book（預訂）組合而成的表現手法。

I should have done it earlier.
要是早一點做就好了。
should have ～是「早應該～」的意思。

269

最近愛上栗子口味的零食
I've been into chestnut flavor

中文日記

羅蘋咖啡店的栗子塔是我吃過最好吃的！

現在我超愛栗子的。

我還想試試其他栗子口味的甜點！

我還真是嗜甜如命。

英文填空日記

The chestnut tart at Robin's café was the _____ ever!!
羅蘋咖啡店的栗子塔是我吃過最好吃的！

Now I'm _____ on chestnut.
現在我超愛栗子的。

I wanna try other sweets with chestnut _____!
我還想試試其他栗子口味的甜點！

I have a real sweet _____.
我還真是嗜甜如命。

英文日記

The chestnut tart at Robin's café was the best ever!!

Now I'm hooked on chestnut.

I wanna try other sweets with chestnut flavor!

I have a real sweet tooth.

常用單字片語集

the best ever
最棒、最好
運用 ever（至今為止）來表達「目前為止最好的」的意思。

be hooked on ～
愛上～
也可以說 be into 或 crazy about。

flavor
口味
taste 也有「味道」的意思，但這裡不用這個單字。

have a sweet tooth
嗜甜如命、熱愛甜食
使用 tooth（牙齒）的慣用片語。

電車誤點
The train is late

中文日記

為什麼電車誤點了呀？

難道是碰到意外事故了嗎？

總而言之，我都已經遲到了，

我得拿份誤點證明才行。

英文填空日記

How come the train is   !?
為什麼電車誤點了呀？

Was there an   ?
難道是碰到意外事故了嗎？

Anyway, I'm already   late,
總而言之，我都已經遲到了，

so I need to get a delay   .
我得拿份誤點證明才行。

英文日記

How come the train is delayed!?

Was there an accident?

Anyway, I'm already running late,

so I need to get a delay certificate.

常用單字片語集

be delayed
延遲、誤點
經常用來表示交通工具誤點的單字。

accident
意外事故
有許多用法，像是 car accident（車禍）等等。

be running late
遲到
如果要表示「遲到的狀態」，則用 be running。

certificate
證明
可以和各種單字組合使用，像是 graduation certificate（畢業證書）等。

開超快的車

A car went too fast

中文日記

我在等紅綠燈的時候，

突然衝出一輛車。

車速超快的，

他應該開慢一點。

英文填空日記

When I was waiting at the　　　　　,
我在等紅綠燈的時候，

a car just came out of　　　　　.
突然衝出一輛車。

It　　　　 too fast.
車速超快的，

He'd　　　　 slow down.
他應該開慢一點。

英文日記

When I was waiting at the light,

a car just came out of nowhere.

It went too fast.

He'd better slow down.

常用單字片語集

light
紅綠燈
正式名稱為 traffic light（交通號誌），但大多會像這樣省略。

out of nowhere
突然、突如其來
使用 nowhere（沒有一個地方）的表現手法。

go too fast
開太快
主詞是人的時候，也可以說 drive too fast。

slow down
放慢速度、慢慢來
除了表示車速，也可以運用在各種情境中。

門鈴明明就響了……

Someone rang the doorbell

中文日記

我躺在床上看電視的時候，

有人按了門鈴。

我心裡想著：「是誰呀？」然後打開門，

結果外面沒有人……

英文填空日記

When I was　　　　　on the bed and watching TV,
我躺在床上看電視的時候，

someone　　　　　the doorbell.
有人按了門鈴。

I thought, "Who is　　　　　?" and opened the door,
我心裡想著：「是誰呀？」然後打開門，

but　　　　　one was there...
結果外面沒有人……

英文日記

When I was lying on the bed and watching TV,

someone rang the doorbell.

I thought, "Who is it?" and opened the door,

but no one was there...

常用單字片語集

lie on the bed
躺在床上
比起「在床上睡覺」，語意更貼近「躺在床上閒閒無事」。

ring the doorbell
按門鈴
doorbell 是「門鈴」的意思。也要留意 ring 的過去式變化。

Who is it?
是誰？
可以用在應門鈴時，表達「請問是哪位？」的情境。

no one
沒有人
注意不要和否定句一起用。

好羨慕身材很好的女演員

I wish I could be like her…

我很喜歡這齣電視劇的女演員，

她身材超好，又很時尚。

我也想變成像她那樣。

嗯，雖然聽起來就是不可能的事……

I really like the ⎯⎯⎯⎯ **on this TV drama.**
我很喜歡這齣電視劇的女演員，

She has a great ⎯⎯⎯⎯ **and a good sense of style.**
她身材超好，又很時尚。

I wish I ⎯⎯⎯⎯ **be like her.**
我也想變成像她那樣。

Well, it's impossible, ⎯⎯⎯⎯…
嗯，雖然聽起來就是不可能的事……

I really like the actress on this TV drama.

She has a great figure and a good sense of style.

I wish I could be like her.

Well, it's impossible, though…

常用單字片語集

actress
女演員
「男演員」是 actor。

have a great figure
身材好
figure 這個單字也經常用來表示「形狀」。

I wish I could ～ .
我也想～。
用過去式 could 來表示和現實相反的狀態。

～ , though
雖然
擺在句尾會有種反駁的意思。

28 好想喝酒，但今天要忍住

I shouldn't drink today

中文日記

今晚我想去喝一杯，

但我得克制一下喝酒的頻率，

因為我最近太常喝了。

我得對自己嚴厲一點才行。

英文填空日記

I feel like going　　　　　　a drink tonight.
今晚我想去喝一杯，

I need to　　　　down on my drinking
但我得克制一下喝酒的頻率，

cause I go drinking　　　　　often recently.
因為我最近太常喝了。

I gotta be　　　　with myself.
我得對自己嚴厲一點才行。

英文日記

I feel like going for a drink tonight.

I need to cut down on my drinking

cause I go drinking quite often recently.

I gotta be strict with myself.

常用單字片語集

go for a drink
去喝一杯
這種情況下的介系詞要用 for，記下來吧。

cut down on ～
克制、降低～
cut down 是「減少、刪減」的意思。

quite
太
very 和 so 也是相同意思，quite 在英式英語中經常用到。

be strict with ～
對～嚴厲
這裡的介系詞要用 with，注意不要用錯了。

275

進辦公室發現桌上很亂

My desk is a mess

中文日記

我的辦公桌超亂的！

發生什麼事了？

噢，我昨天沒關窗戶，

桌上的東西是被風吹亂了吧。

英文填空日記

My desk is so　　　　!!
我的辦公桌超亂的！

What　　　　!?
發生什麼事了？

Oh, I left the window　　　　yesterday,
噢，我昨天沒關窗戶，

so the stuff on the desk was　　　　off by the wind.
桌上的東西是被風吹亂了吧。

英文日記

My desk is so messy!!

What happened!?

Oh, I left the window open yesterday,

so the stuff on the desk was blown off by the wind.

- - - - - - - - - - - - - - **常用單字片語集** - - - - - - - - - - - - - -

messy
雜亂的
口語對話中經常用到的表現手法。

What happened?
發生什麼事了？
和 What's wrong? 一樣可以用來表示「怎麼
回事？」

leave the window open
一直開著窗戶
leave ＋形容詞是「將……一直～」的意思。

blow off ～
～被吹亂
指東西被風吹亂時所使用的片語。

鼻塞了，好難呼吸
Stuffy nose

中文日記

我鼻塞了。

很難呼吸耶！

我是不是該去看醫生呀？

不過好麻煩喔……

英文填空日記

I have a ⎯⎯⎯⎯⎯ nose.
我鼻塞了。

It's ⎯⎯⎯⎯⎯ to breathe!
很難呼吸耶！

Should I go to the doctor or ⎯⎯⎯⎯⎯?
我是不是該去看醫生呀？

But it's such a ⎯⎯⎯⎯⎯…
不過好麻煩喔……

英文日記

I have a stuffy nose.

It's hard to breathe!

Should I go to the doctor or not?

But it's such a pain…

常用單字片語集

have a stuffy nose
鼻塞
也可以說 My nose is blocked.。

It's hard to ～ .
很難～
將 hard 改成 easy 就會變成「很容易～」。

～ or not
該不該～
經常用來表示猶豫或沒有明確答案的時候。

such a pain
麻煩
還有其他很多種說法，像是 I can't be bothered 等。

DECEMBER

12 月

Christmas Day today!
今天是聖誕節！

I went to see the Christmas lights with Daisuke.
我和大介一起去看了聖誕節燈飾。

That was fantastic!!
超壯觀的！

It was the best day ever.
今天是我人生中最美好的一天。

好冷！會不會下雪呀？

Freezing today!

中
文
日
記

今天冷死人了！

早知道我就穿厚大衣出門了。

聽說明天會下雪……

可是現在才十二月初而已耶！

英
文
填
空
日
記

It's   today!!
今天冷死人了！

I should have worn the   coat.
早知道我就穿厚大衣出門了。

I   it's going to be snowing tomorrow…
聽說明天會下雪……

It's still the   of December!!
可是現在才十二月初而已耶！

英
文
日
記

It's freezing today!!

I should have worn the heavier coat.

I heard it's going to be snowing tomorrow…

It's still the beginning of December!!

常用單字片語集

freezing
冷到快結凍
想強調比 cold 還冷的時候可以用的單字。

heavy coat
厚大衣
這種情況的「厚」會用 heavy（重）這個單字，也可以用 thick。

I heard ～
聽說～、好像～
heard 是 hear（聽）的過去式。

beginning of ～
～的剛開始
不只是描述時期或季節，還可以和許多單字組合運用。

2 廣美和健司分手了

They broke up!?

中文日記

不會吧，聽說廣美和健司分手了！

或許是健司和其他女生出去的事

被廣美發現了吧……

她現在一定很低落……

英文填空日記

Oh no, I heard Hiromi and Kenji ___ up!
不會吧，聽說廣美和健司分手了！

Maybe Kenji was seeing ___ girl,
或許是健司和其他女生出去的事

and Hiromi ___ it out somehow…
被廣美發現了吧……

She must be ___ now…
她現在一定很低落……

英文日記

Oh no, I heard Hiromi and Kenji broke up!

Maybe Kenji was seeing another girl,

and Hiromi found it out somehow…

She must be down now…

常用單字片語集

break up
分手
和 break up with～（和～分手）一起學起來吧。

another
其他、另一個
如果後面接的名詞是複數形的話，要改用 other。

find it out
發現、得知
用於表示發現、知道了原本不曉得的事情。

be down
低落、消沉
down 除了表示「下方」之外，也有這些意思。

3 大介最近好像很忙

Daisuke

中文日記

我約大介一起吃晚餐，

但他説：「不行，我太忙了。」

他最近老是這個樣子！

我有點懷疑他説的是不是真的……

英文填空日記

I _____ Daisuke out for dinner,

我約大介一起吃晚餐，

but he said, "I can't. I'm _____ busy."

但他說：「不行，我太忙了。」

He's always been _____ this recently!

他最近老是這個樣子！

I _____ if he's telling the truth…

我有點懷疑他說的是不是真的……

英文日記

I asked Daisuke out for dinner,

but he said, "I can't. I'm too busy."

He's always been like this recently!

I wonder if he's telling the truth…

常用單字片語集

ask... out for ～
約……去～
除了 dinner 之外，還可以活用各種單字，像是 date 或 lunch 等。

be always like this
總是這樣
這裡的 like 並不是做為動詞，而是做為介系詞使用。

too ～
太～
和 so 意思相近，但 too 多用於負面情境。

wonder if ～
好奇是不是～
大多會翻譯成「真的是～嗎？」

十二月 4

大介很可疑
Daisuke's acting shady

中文日記

大介最近形跡可疑。

前幾天他還和一個女生通電話。

他是不是劈腿了……？

我一點都不想往那方面想呀！

英文填空日記

Daisuke has been acting lately.
大介最近形跡可疑。

He was talking to a girl on the the other day.
前幾天他還和一個女生通電話。

Is he on me…?
他是不是劈腿了……？

I don't wanna think about it!
我一點都不想往那方面想呀！

英文日記

Daisuke has been acting shady lately.

He was talking to a girl on the phone the other day.

Is he cheating on me…?

I don't even wanna think about it!

常用單字片語集

act shady
形跡可疑
shady 也有「陰暗的」的意思。

the other day
前幾天
前面不會再加介系詞，要特別留意。

cheat on ～
對～劈腿
使用時大多搭配介系詞 on，一起記下來吧。

I don't even wanna think.
我甚至不敢那麼想。
注意 even（甚至）擺放的位置。

5

爲了讓廣美打起精神

To cheer up Hiromi

中文日記

今天我們舉辦了家庭派對！

我們準備了很多廣美愛吃的食物，

好讓她打起精神來。

希望她會喜歡！

英文填空日記

We're having a ___ party today!
今天我們舉辦了家庭派對！

We ___ Hiromi's favorite foods
我們準備了很多廣美愛吃的食物，

to ___ her up!
好讓她打起精神來。

___ she likes them!
希望她會喜歡！

英文日記

We're having a house party today!

We prepared Hiromi's favorite foods

to cheer her up!

Hope she likes them!

常用單字片語集

house party
家庭派對
比起 home party，更常使用這個單字。

prepare
準備
和 prepare for ～（為了～準備）一起學起來吧。

cheer ～ up
讓～打起精神
人要擺在 cheer up 的中間。

Hope... like ～ .
希望……會喜歡～。
「喜歡」、「感到開心」都可以像這樣用 like 表示。

十二月 6

遊戲玩太久，睡眠不足

Stayed up all night yesterday

中文日記

昨天我熬夜了。

我本來在玩遊戲，

然後一玩就停不下來了！

今天肯定要喝咖啡來熬過一天了……

英文填空日記

I stayed　　　　all night yesterday.
昨天我熬夜了。

I was playing a　　　　game,
我本來在玩遊戲，

and　　　　stop it!
然後一玩就停不下來了！

I'm　　　　I can't survive without coffee today...
今天肯定要喝咖啡來熬過一天了……

英文日記

I stayed up all night yesterday.

I was playing a video game,

and couldn't stop it!

I'm sure I can't survive without coffee today...

常用單字片語集

stay up all night
熬夜
stay up 是「醒著」的意思。

video game
電動遊戲
英文裡用的是 video game，而不是 TV game。

couldn't ~
沒辦法~
會話中通常會直接縮略 could not。

I'm sure (that) ~
肯定要~
加不加 that 都可以。

285

流行性感冒

A cold going around

中文日記

喉嚨好痛，

我覺得我好像感冒了。

這幾天還很冷，

今晚我早點睡好了。

英文填空日記

I have a _____ throat.
喉嚨好痛，

I think I'm coming _____ with a cold.
我覺得我好像感冒了。

It's been cold _____ days,
這幾天還很冷，

I'll go to _____ early tonight.
今晚我早點睡好了。

英文日記

I have a sore throat.

I think I'm coming down with a cold.

It's been cold these days,

I'll go to bed early tonight.

常用單字片語集

have a sore throat
喉嚨痛
也可以說 My throat hurts.。

be coming down with a cold
疑似感冒
雖然 have a cold（感冒了）是更加普遍的
說法，但也有這種說法，學起來吧。

these days
最近、這幾天
和 recently 是同樣意思，但想特別強調「這
幾天」的時候，大多會這麼說。

go to bed
睡覺
也可以說 go to sleep。

8 影印機又壞了

The copy machine got broken again

中文日記

我們的影印機又壞了！

這是我第三次聯絡維修人員了！

我是不是該拜託主管買一台新的呀？

但新機型應該很貴吧。

英文填空日記

Our copy machine got _____ again!!
我們的影印機又壞了！

This is the third _____ that I've called for repairs!!
這是我第三次聯絡維修人員了！

Should I ask my boss _____ buy a new one?
我是不是該拜託主管買一台新的呀？

But _____ latest model would be pricy.
但新機型應該很貴吧。

英文日記

Our copy machine got broken again!!

This is the third time that I've called for repairs!!

Should I ask my boss to buy a new one?

But the latest model would be pricy.

常用單字片語集

get broken
壞掉、故障
be broken 是「壞掉的狀態」，get 才能表示「壞掉」這個動作。

This is the... time that ～
這是第……次～。
that 後面要接有「主詞＋動詞」的子句。

ask... to ～
拜託……做～
教科書裡也會出現的常用句型，學起來吧。

the latest model
新機型
the latest ～是指「最新的～」，可以活用在各種情境。

十二月 9

外國人向我問路

A foreigner asked me for directions

中文日記

今天有個外國人向我問路。

我成功用英文流利地回答他了！

幸虧我這麼努力學英文！

我應該更努力學習，才能說得更加流暢！

英文填空日記

Today one foreigner asked me   directions.
今天有個外國人向我問路。

I was   to answer in English fluently!
我成功用英文流利地回答他了！

Good   I studied English so hard!
幸虧我這麼努力學英文！

I should study harder   that I can speak more fluently!
我應該更努力學習，才能說得更加流暢！

英文日記

Today one foreigner asked me for directions.

I was able to answer in English fluently!

Good thing I studied English so hard!

I should study harder so that I can speak more fluently!

常用單字片語集

ask ~ for directions
向～問路
不明指對象的話可以省略人，直接說 ask for directions。

be able to ~
成功～
和 can 一樣是「能做到～」的意思，不過是用來形容能力。

Good thing ~.
幸虧～。
日常對話中會用到的口語表現。

so that ~
才能夠～
that 後面要接有「主詞＋動詞」的子句。

發現感興趣的工作！

Found an interesting job

中文日記

我發現了一個滿感興趣的工作！

這或許就是我一直想嘗試的事。

我決定馬上投履歷過去！

開始有點期待了。

英文填空日記

I found an ___ job!
我發現了一個滿感興趣的工作！

This might be exactly ___ I've wanted to do.
這或許就是我一直想嘗試的事。

I'll send them my CV ___ away!
我決定馬上投履歷過去！

I'm ___ excited.
開始有點期待了。

英文日記

I found an interesting job!

This might be exactly what I've wanted to do.

I'll send them my CV right away!

I'm getting excited.

常用單字片語集

interesting
令人感興趣的
做為形容詞使用。be interested in ～ 是「對～感興趣」的意思。

what I've wanted to do
我一直想做的事
使用現在完成式 have。

right away
馬上
加在句尾表示急著去做某件事。

be getting excited
開始感到期待
excited 的部分可以改成其他形容詞，加以活用。

11 公司的忘年會

Bonenkai with colleagues

中文日記

今天我和同事們參加了「忘年會」。

「忘年會」是日本年末特有的聚會。

我們會大吃大喝，

忘掉一整年不愉快的事。

英文填空日記

Today we had "Bonenkai" with my _____.
今天我和同事們參加了「忘年會」。

"Bonenkai" is Japanese special _____ at the end of the year.
「忘年會」是日本年末特有的聚會。

We all eat and drink a _____,
我們會大吃大喝，

and forget all the bad things that have happened _____ the year.
忘掉一整年不愉快的事。

英文日記

Today we had "Bonenkai" with my colleagues.

"Bonenkai" is Japanese special gathering at the end of the year.

We all eat and drink a lot,

and forget all the bad things that have happened during the year.

常用單字片語集

colleague
同事
想指「公司的人」時也可以用的單字。

gathering
聚會
可以用來指各式各樣的聚會或派對。

eat and drink a lot
大吃大喝
a lot 是「很多」的意思，可以運用在各種情境中。

during the year
一整年
during 是「在～期間」的意思，後面接的一定要是名詞。

12

昨天吃的東西好像有問題

Having a stomach ache

中文日記

肚子好痛。

是因為我昨天吃了牡蠣的關係嗎？

我覺得我快要吐了。

或許我今天早退比較好。

英文填空日記

I have a _____ .
肚子好痛。

Is it _____ I ate oysters yesterday…?
是因為我昨天吃了牡蠣的關係嗎？

I feel like I'm gonna _____ up.
我覺得我快要吐了。

Maybe it's better if I leave _____ today.
或許我今天早退比較好。

英文日記

I have a stomach ache.

Is it because I ate oysters yesterday…?

I feel like I'm gonna throw up.

Maybe it's better if I leave early today.

- - - - - - - - - - - - - - - 常用單字片語集 - - - - - - - - - - - - - - -

have a stomach ache
肚子痛
想表示「肚子痛」的常用片語。

Is it because...?
是不是因為……？
because 的後面要接名詞的話，要改成 Is it
because of...?

throw up
嘔吐
vomit 也是「嘔吐」的動詞，跟 throw up
使用方式相同。

leave early
早退
可以運用在學校或工作等各種場合。

聖誕燭光晚餐上有驚喜

What a surprise!

中文日記

今天大介突然帶我到餐廳吃飯，

他幫我慶祝生日！

我超級驚喜的！

完全沒發現他做了這些準備！

英文填空日記

Today Daisuke ＿＿＿＿＿ me to a restaurant suddenly,
今天大介突然帶我到餐廳吃飯，

and he ＿＿＿＿＿ my birthday there!
他幫我慶祝生日！

It was a big ＿＿＿＿＿ to me!!
我超級驚喜的！

I didn't even ＿＿＿＿＿ he was planning this!
完全沒發現他做了這些準備！

英文日記

Today Daisuke took me to a restaurant suddenly,

and he celebrated my birthday there!

It was a big surprise to me!!

I didn't even notice he was planning this!

常用單字片語集

take... to ～
帶……去～
如果把 take 換成 bring 會變成「帶來」的意思。

celebrate
慶祝
名詞的 celebration（慶祝）也很實用，可以一起學起來。

It was a big surprise.
我又驚又喜。
和 I was surprised. 意思相同，想稍微改變句型時，可以這麼說。

notice
注意、發現
和 realize 是相同意思。

原來大介沒有劈腿

He wasn't cheating

4月
5月
6月
7月
8月
9月
10月
11月
12月
1月
2月
3月

中文日記

前陣子和他通電話的女生

原來只是餐廳的店員。

他是為了我打電話去訂位而已。

真是天大的誤會！

英文填空日記

The girl he was talking to ___ **the phone**
前陣子和他通電話的女生

was ___ **a staff member of the restaurant.**
原來只是餐廳的店員。

He was just making a ___ **for me.**
他是為了我打電話去訂位而已。

I totally ___ **!**
真是天大的誤會！

英文日記

The girl he was talking to on the phone

was just a staff member of the restaurant.

He was just making a reservation for me.

I totally misunderstood!

常用單字片語集

on the phone
電話裡
talk on the phone 則是「講電話」的意思。

just
只是
也有「剛好」的意思。

make a reservation
預約、訂位
餐廳訂位時經常用到的片語。

misunderstand
誤會、誤解
要特別留意過去式的拼字是 misunderstood。

大掃除！

Spring cleaning

中文日記

今天我的房間得大掃除才行。

日本人通常是在每年年底做這件事，

所以我們稱之為「年底大掃除」。

好，開始動工吧！

英文填空日記

Today I have to _____ -clean my room.
今天我的房間得大掃除才行。

Japanese do this at the _____ of each year,
日本人通常是在每年年底做這件事，

so we _____ it "year end cleaning."
所以我們稱之為「年底大掃除」。

Alright, let's _____ started!
好，開始動工吧！

英文日記

Today I have to spring-clean my room.

Japanese do this at the end of each year,

so we call it "year end cleaning."

Alright, let's get started!

常用單字片語集

spring-clean
大掃除
歐美的大掃除不是在年底，而是在初春進行，所以會這麼說。

at the end of each year
每年年底
最常用到的說法是 at the end of the year（年底）。

we call it ～
我們稱之為～
也可以用被動式 It's called ～（叫做～）。

Let's get started.
開始動工吧。
日常對話的常用句子，整句記下來吧。

不曉得狗狗過得好嗎？

On my way home, Osaka

中文日記

我正在回大阪老家的路上，

上次回去是兩個月前的事了。

我們家的狗狗不知道過得好不好……

好想快點見到牠呀！

英文填空日記

I'm on my _____ to Osaka, my hometown.
我正在回大阪老家的路上，

It's _____ 2 months since I last went back home.
上次回去是兩個月前的事了。

Wonder _____ my doggy is doing…
我們家的狗狗不知道過得好不好……

Wanna see her so _____!
好想快點見到牠呀！

英文日記

I'm on my way to Osaka, my hometown.

It's been 2 months since I last went back home.

Wonder how my doggy is doing…

Wanna see her so bad!

------------------------ 常用單字片語集 ------------------------

on my way to ～
在前往～的路上
「回家路上」則是 on my way home，要特別留意這裡不加 to。

It's been... since ～ .
自上次～已經過了……。
使用現在完成式 have 的句型。

how ～ is doing
～過得如何
How is ～ doing?（～過得好嗎？）也可以做為單純的疑問句使用。

so bad
好想、非常
簡化 so badly 的用法，用於口語對話中。

看電視看得太入迷
Can't stop watching TV

我積了好多家事要在今天做。

但我就是忍不住想看電視！

因為這部電視劇是我喜歡的男演員演的！

我超愛這部戲的！

Today I have a lot of   **to do.**
我積了好多家事要在今天做。

But I can't   **watching TV!**
但我就是忍不住想看電視！

Because my   **actor is in this TV drama!**
因為這部電視劇是我喜歡的男演員演的！

I'm really   **it!**
我超愛這部戲的！

Today I have a lot of housework to do.

But I can't stop watching TV!

Because my favorite actor is in this TV drama!

I'm really into it!

常用單字片語集

housework
家事
注意不要和 homework（功課）搞混了。

can't stop -ing
忍不住想～
這裡用的不是 to do 而是 -ing。

my favorite
我喜歡的
在聊自己喜歡的東西時經常用到的說法。

be into ～
喜歡、沉迷於～
常加上 really 來表示「沉迷得無法自拔」。

十二月 18 比預期中還費時
Took longer than I thought

中文日記

都這麼晚了！

我本來打算在中午之前完成的，

但比預期中還費時呀！

現在是咖啡休息時間！

英文填空日記

It's ＿＿＿＿＿ this time!?
都這麼晚了！

I was ＿＿＿＿＿ to finish this work by noon,
我本來打算在中午之前完成的，

but it took much longer ＿＿＿＿＿ I expected!
但比預期中還費時呀！

Now, ＿＿＿＿＿ for a coffee break!!
現在是咖啡休息時間！

英文日記

It's already this time!?

I was supposed to finish this work by noon,

but it took much longer than I expected!

Now, time for a coffee break!!

常用單字片語集

It's already this time!?
都這個時候了！
常用句子，整句一起記下來吧。

be supposed to ～
本來應該～
to 之後要接原形動詞。

比較級＋ than I expected
比預期中還要更～
也可以用 thought 代替 expected。

time for ～
～時間到了。
Time for dinner! 就是「晚餐時間到囉」。

297

今天好難上妝

My makeup doesn't sit well

中文日記

今天好難上妝啊。

可能是因為我昨天太晚睡了。

不，我的眼睛底下都有黑眼圈了！

我得用遮暇膏才行……

英文填空日記

My makeup doesn't _____ well today.
今天好難上妝啊。

Maybe because I went to _____ very late last night.
可能是因為我昨天太晚睡了。

Oh no, I got _____ circles under my eyes!
不，我的眼睛底下都有黑眼圈了！

I need to use a _____ …
我得用遮暇膏才行……

英文日記

My makeup doesn't sit well today.

Maybe because I went to bed very late last night.

Oh no, I got dark circles under my eyes!

I need to use a concealer…

------------------------- 常用單字片語集 -------------------------

One's makeup doesn't sit well.
妝感不好、不服貼
sit 除了最廣為人知的「坐下」的意思以外，也有這樣的用法。

go to bed
睡覺
「到床上」，即「睡覺」的意思。

dark circles
黑眼圈
通常會搭配 under one's eyes 一起使用。

concealer
遮暇膏
可以和動詞 conceal（掩蓋）一起學起來。

勉強趕上末班車

I almost missed it!

中文日記

勉強趕上末班車！

再晚一點就要錯過了！

要不是愛海告訴我，

我就趕不上了。

英文填空日記

I **to get on the last train!**
勉強趕上末班車！

I almost **it!**
再晚一點就要錯過了！

If Manami didn't **me,**
要不是愛海告訴我，

I couldn't **it.**
我就趕不上了。

英文日記

I managed to get on the last train!

I almost missed it!

If Manami didn't inform me,

I couldn't make it.

常用單字片語集

manage to ～
勉強～
manage 也有「管理」的意思。

inform
告知
用來表示「告知、提供資訊」。

miss
錯過
「錯過」電車或飛機時經常使用。

make it
趕上
make 除了「製作」以外還有許多用法。

和廣美去逛街
Shopping with Hiromi

中文日記

我今天和廣美去逛街了！

因為前陣子的事，她有些消沉，

希望這樣能讓她解解悶。

總之，我們逛得很開心！

英文填空日記

Today I went _____ with Hiromi!
我今天和廣美去逛街了！

She was a little down because _____ what happened the other day,
因為前陣子的事，她有些消沉，

so I hope it helped keep her _____ off it.
希望這樣能讓她解解悶。

We _____ fun, anyways!
總之，我們逛得很開心！

英文日記

Today I went shopping with Hiromi!

She was a little down because of what happened the other day,

so I hope it helped keep her mind off it.

We had fun, anyways!

--------- 常用單字片語集 ---------

go shopping
逛街
這種情況下不需要 to 等介系詞。

because of ～
因為～
～的部分要接名詞。

keep one's mind off
忘掉、不去在意
加上 help 就有「解悶」的意思了。

have fun
過得很開心
fun 可以做為名詞或形容詞使用。

流感蔓延

The flu is going around

中文日記

流感疫情在我們公司蔓延開來了。

雖然還沒有傳染到我這裡，

但感覺是時間早晚的問題。

我應該要去接種疫苗了。

英文填空日記

The flu is going ____ our office now.
流感疫情在我們公司蔓延開來了。

Nobody ____ it to me yet,
雖然還沒有傳染到我這裡，

but it's a ____ of time.
但感覺是時間早晚的問題。

I gotta get a ____ .
我應該要去接種疫苗了。

英文日記

The flu is going around our office now.

Nobody gave it to me yet,

but it's a matter of time.

I gotta get a vaccination.

常用單字片語集

go around
擴散、蔓延
使用 around（～的周圍）的片語。

give to ～
傳染給～
這個片語會把 it 夾在中間。

be a matter of time
時間早晚的問題
使用 matter（問題）的表現手法。

vaccination
疫苗接種
由 vaccine（疫苗）變化而來的單字。

23

好討厭打針……

Don't wanna get a shot…

中文日記

預計這星期要接種流感疫苗。

我超不想去的！

護理師每次都說：「可能會有一點點刺痛喔。」

那種痛根本就不叫「一點點」！

英文填空日記

I'm gonna get a _____ shot this week.
預計這星期要接種流感疫苗。

I really don't _____ do it!
我超不想去的！

They always say, "You will feel a little _____."
護理師每次都說：「可能會有一點點刺痛喔。」

It's not _____ "a little"!
那種痛根本就不叫「一點點」！

英文日記

I'm gonna get a flu shot this week.

I really don't wanna do it!

They always say, "You will feel a little prick."

It's not even "a little"!

常用單字片語集

flu
流感
和 shot（注射）結合就是「接種流感疫苗」的意思。

wanna ～
想～
簡化了 want to，口語對話中經常出現。

prick
刺
可以做為名詞和動詞使用。

even ～
根本～
也可以和 not 組合使用。

十二月 24

我有點發燒……

I have a slight fever, but...

中文日記

我有點發燒了。

這應該是接種疫苗的副作用吧。

我今天不能請假,

還是得去上班,別無選擇。

英文填空日記

I have a _____ fever.
我有點發燒了。

Maybe this is the _____ effect of the vaccination.
這應該是接種疫苗的副作用吧。

I can't _____ a day off today,
我今天不能請假,

so I have to go to work. No _____.
還是得去上班,別無選擇。

英文日記

I have a slight fever.

Maybe this is the side effect of the vaccination.

I can't take a day off today,

so I have to go to work. No choice.

------------ 常用單字片語集 ------------

slight fever
微燒
slight 是「一點點、輕微的」的意思。

side effect
副作用
聽取藥物說明時經常聽到的單字。

take a day off
請假
a day off 則是「休假、假日」的意思。

no choice
別無選擇
I have no choice. 省略 I have 的說法。

303

今天是聖誕節！

Christmas Day today!

中文日記

今天是聖誕節！

我和大介一起去看了聖誕節燈飾。

超壯觀的！

今天是我人生中最美好的一天。

英文填空日記

Christmas   **today!**
今天是聖誕節！

I went to see the Christmas   **with Daisuke.**
我和大介一起去看了聖誕節燈飾。

That was   **!!**
超壯觀的！

It was the best day   .
今天是我人生中最美好的一天。

英文日記

Christmas Day today!

I went to see the Christmas lights with Daisuke.

That was fantastic!!

It was the best day ever.

常用單字片語集

Christmas Day
聖誕節

lights
燈飾
雖然「燈飾」有另一個單字是 illumination，
但實際上更常用 lights。

fantastic
令人驚豔的、令人感動的
用於因為某件事而深受感動或感觸良多的
時候。

ever
至今為止
經常搭配像 the best 等最高級的表現一起
使用。

家族溫泉旅遊

Family trip to hot springs

中文日記

我和家人要一起去箱根旅遊啦！

這是我們家族每年的例行活動。

每年我們都會住進高級旅館好好享受溫泉！

我超興奮的啦！

英文填空日記

My family and I are going　　　　　　a trip to Hakone!
我和家人要一起去箱根旅遊啦！

This is one of our　　　　　events.
這是我們家族每年的例行活動。

Every year, we stay at a nice hotel and enjoy hot 　　　!
每年我們都會住進高級旅館好好享受溫泉！

I'm　　　　　excited!!
我超興奮的啦！

英文日記

My family and I are going on a trip to Hakone!

This is one of our annual events.

Every year, we stay at a nice hotel and enjoy hot springs!

I'm super excited!!

常用單字片語集

go on a trip to ～
去～旅遊
也可以不加 to，只說 go on a trip。

annual event
每年的例行活動
使用 annual（一年一度的、每年的）的表現手法。

hot spring
溫泉
國外有些地方會稱為 spa。

super
超級、非常
口語對話中經常使用的表現手法。

塞車了
Stuck in traffic

我們正在前往箱根的路上，

但我們現在塞在車陣裡。

要花多少時間才能脫離啊！

天啊……！

We're on the _____ to Hakone,
我們正在前往箱根的路上，

but _____ in traffic now.
但我們現在塞在車陣裡。

I wonder how long it will take to _____ out of this!
要花多少時間才能脫離啊！

_____ grief…!
天啊……！

We're on the way to Hakone,

but stuck in traffic now.

I wonder how long it will take to get out of this!

Good grief…!

常用單字片語集

on the way to ~
前往~的路上
屬於常用片語，整句一起記下來吧。

be stuck in ~
卡在、陷在~裡
stuck 是 stick 的過去式及過去分詞。

get out of ~
掙脫、脫離~
也有其他用法，像是 Get out of here!（從這裡滾出去）。

Good grief!
天啊！
面對負面狀況的感嘆句。

終於抵達箱根

In Hakone, finally!

中文日記

我們終於到了！

比想像中更耗時間。

總之，我肚子餓了，

去吃點東西吧！

英文填空日記

we are!! Finally!!
我們終於到了！

It took　　　　　longer than I expected.
比想像中更耗時間。

Anyway, I'm　　　　　now,
總之，我肚子餓了，

so let's　　　　　something to eat!
去吃點東西吧！

英文日記

Here we are!! Finally!!

It took much longer than I expected.

Anyway, I'm starving now,

so let's have something to eat!

常用單字片語集

Here we are.
我們到了。
形態會根據主語變化，像是 Here I am. 等，是相當常用的句子。

much -er
還、更加
強調比較級的時候要用 much。

be starving
肚子餓
運用 starve（飢餓）的表現手法。

have something to eat
吃點東西
把 eat 改成 drink 就會變成「喝點東西」。

星冰樂客製化特調
Customizing Frappuccino

中文日記

我很喜歡點星冰樂客製化特調。

我的最愛是焦糖口味，

然後我會再追加焦糖醬和鮮奶油。

超級推薦！

英文填空日記

I like　　　　customize a Frappuccino.
我很喜歡點星冰樂客製化特調。

My　　　　is the caramel one,
我的最愛是焦糖口味，

and I always add some caramel　　　　and extra whipped cream.
然後我會再追加焦糖醬和鮮奶油。

This is highly　　　　!!
超級推薦！

英文日記

I like to customize a Frappuccino.

My favorite is the caramel one,

and I always add some caramel drizzle and extra whipped cream.

This is highly recommended!!

常用單字片語集

like to ～
喜歡做～
也可以說 like -ing。

my favorite
我的最愛
經常會說 This is my favorite.（這是我最喜歡的）。

drizzle
淋醬
指淋出細線條的醬汁。

highly recommended
超級推薦
用 highly（非常地、高度地）來加以強調。

點眼藥水

Putting eye drops

中文日記

每次點眼藥水，

我總是無法好好睜著眼睛。

我真是個膽小鬼。

真丟人啊……

英文填空日記

Every time I put eye ____ in my eyes,
每次點眼藥水，

I can't ____ my eyes open.
我總是無法好好睜著眼睛。

I'm such a ____.
我真是個膽小鬼。

This is ____…
真丟人啊……

英文日記

Every time I put eye drops in my eyes,

I can't keep my eyes open.

I'm such a coward.

This is embarrassing…

常用單字片語集

put eye drops in one's eyes
點眼藥水
也可以用 apply 取代 put。

keep one's eyes open
睜著眼睛
「keep＋形容詞」是「維持～狀態」的意思。

coward
膽小鬼、懦夫
結合 such a～，語感會更貼近「真是個膽小鬼」。

embarrassing
丟臉的、難為情的
也可以說 I'm embarrassed.（我真丟人）。

和大介一起跨年
New Year's Eve with Daisuke

中文日記

我要和大介一起跨年。

我們開始交往到現在已經五個月了，

真不敢相信！

時間過得真快。

英文填空日記

I'm _____ New Year's Eve with Daisuke.
我要和大介一起跨年。

It's already been 5 months since we started _____!
我們開始交往到現在已經五個月了，

I can't _____ it!
真不敢相信！

Time _____ by so fast.
時間過得真快。

英文日記

I'm spending New Year's Eve with Daisuke.

It's already been 5 months since we started dating!

I can't believe it!

Time goes by so fast.

常用單字片語集

spend
度過
這個單字有「度過、花費時間」的意思。

start dating
開始交往
date 是「交往、約會」的意思。

I can't believe it.
不敢相信、難以置信
經常用來表現發生令人難以相信的事情，整句一起學起來吧。

time goes by
時間經過
go by 是「經過、通過」的意思。

有關「時尚」的十大表現手法

第1名	**What should I wear today?** 今天該穿什麼好呢？	should I～? 的句型是「該怎麼～才好呢？」的意思，可以用在猶豫或迷惘的時候。What should I do?（我該怎麼做才好呢？）也是常用句子，可以一起學起來。
第2名	**I got a new dress.** 我買了一件新洋裝。	日文中常用的 one piece 屬於和製英語，英文是說 dress。
第3名	**It's too tight for me.** 對我來說太緊了。	試穿衣服或鞋子的時候經常會用 too small（太小），可以把相反情況的 too loose（太鬆）、too big（太大）也一起學起來。
第4名	**It looks good on him.** 很適合他。	直接對對方說的 You look very nice. 也是日常對話的常用句子。look 的意思不只是「看」而已，也經常用於這種語感。
第5名	**I don't like the color.** 我不喜歡這個顏色。	I don't like ～. 或 I like ～. 都是常用句型，在聊到自己的喜好時，一定會用到的表現手法。I don't like it.（我不喜歡。）也是實用句型。
第6名	**I bought many winter clothes.** 我買了好多冬裝。	I bought ～. 是寫日記時的必備句型。可以和 I'm gonna buy ～.（我要買～）還有 I gotta buy ～.（我得買～）一起學起來。
第7名	**I went to the sale in Ginza.** 我去了銀座的特賣會。	活用句型 I went to ～.（我去了～）的表現手法。後面接的部分單字不需要加 to 這些介系詞，像是 I went there. 要特別留意。其中，there、here、home 又是最具代表性的三個單字。
第8名	**I gotta take out my winter clothes.** 我得把冬季衣物拿出來了。	片語 take out 是「拿出來」的意思。除了「拿取」以外，take 還有其他意思，像是 take him there（帶他去那裡）。
第9名	**The soles of my shoes are getting worn out.** 我的鞋底被磨掉了不少。	日常生活有許多情況不一定有直接對應的英文，而「鞋底磨損」可以用 worn out（消耗）來表示。
第10名	**I spilled coffee on my sweater!** 我把咖啡灑到毛衣上了！	spill ～ on ...（把～灑到……上），把介系詞 on 一起記下來會方便許多。像是 I spilled red wine on the carpet.（我把紅酒灑到地毯上了）。

Best 10

JANUARY

Today is the first day of the New Year!
今天是新年的第一天！

My New Year's resolution is to lose 3 kg more!
今年的抱負是再瘦三公斤！

Also I'll get a new job!
還有找到新工作！

I gotta stop spoiling myself!!
我不能再繼續縱容自己了！

新年抱負
My New Year's resolution

中文日記

今天是新年的第一天！

今年的抱負是再瘦三公斤！

還有找到新工作！

我不能再繼續縱容自己了！

英文填空日記

Today is the _____ day of the New Year!
今天是新年的第一天！

My New Year's _____ is to lose 3 kg more!
今年的抱負是再瘦三公斤！

Also I'll _____ a new job!
還有找到新工作！

I gotta stop _____ myself!!
我不能再繼續縱容自己了！

英文日記

Today is the first day of the New Year!

My New Year's resolution is to lose 3 kg more!

Also I'll get a new job!

I gotta stop spoiling myself!!

常用單字片語集

the first day
第一天
大多會用 the first day of ～來表示「～的第一天」。

New Year's resolution
新年抱負
也可以用 goal 來表示目標，但這個情況大多會使用 resolution。

get a new job
找到新工作
動詞也可以用 find，但 get 更有強調「找到新工作並取得工作機會」的意思。

spoil oneself
縱容自己
除了搭配動詞 stop 使用之外，還有許多種表現手法。

2 好姊妹聚餐去了義式餐廳

Girls' night out

中文日記

今天是我們好姊妹聚餐的日子！

我們訂了一直很感興趣的義式餐廳。

那裡的披薩超好吃的！

下次我還想吃看看他們的義式冰淇淋⋯⋯

英文填空日記

A　　　　　night out today!
今天是我們好姊妹聚餐的日子！

We booked an Italian restaurant we had always　　　　to go to.
我們訂了一直很感興趣的義式餐廳。

The pizza　　　　　was really good!
那裡的披薩超好吃的！

I wanna　　　　　their gelato next time…
下次我還想吃看看他們的義式冰淇淋⋯⋯

英文日記

A girls' night out today!

We booked an Italian restaurant we had always wanted to go to.

The pizza there was really good!

I wanna try their gelato next time…

常用單字片語集

a girls' night out
好姊妹聚餐
也有「女孩聚會」的意思。

have always wanted to go
一直很想去
這裡的 always 是表示「一直」的意思。

～ there
那裡的～
there 直接接在名詞後面。

try
吃看看
直譯可能會想成 try to eat，但不需要加上 to eat。

315

晒到一半的衣服掉到路上

My laundry got muddy

我在外面晒衣服的時候，

衣服掉到路上了！

唉，我的白色衣服都沾滿了泥。

不知道這種髒汙清不清得掉⋯⋯

When I was _____ my laundry outside,
我在外面晒衣服的時候，

my shirt _____ on the street!!
衣服掉到路上了！

Oh no, my white shirt got _____.
唉，我的白色衣服都沾滿了泥。

I don't know if this _____ can be removed...
不知道這種髒汙清不清得掉⋯⋯

When I was hanging my laundry outside,

my shirt fell on the street!!

Oh no, my white shirt got muddy.

I don't know if this stain can be removed...

常用單字片語集

hang one's laundry
晒衣服
hang 有「晒、掛、吊」的意思。

fall on ～
掉到～
要注意 fall 的過去式是 fell。

get muddy
沾滿了泥
mud（泥）的形容詞是 muddy。

stain
髒汙
描述泥土或液體潑灑到衣物上時，會用這個單字。

冬季特賣會

Winter sale

中文日記

今天是冬季特賣會第一天！

好多商品都有五〇%以上的折扣！

所以我買了很多件冬裝。

我又要窮困潦倒了。

英文填空日記

Today was the first day of the winter　　　　　　!
今天是冬季特賣會第一天！

Many items were over 50%　　　　　!
好多商品都有五〇%以上的折扣！

So I bought many winter　　　　　.
所以我買了很多件冬裝。

I'm going to be　　　　　again.
我又要窮困潦倒了。

英文日記

Today was the first day of the winter sale!

Many items were over 50% off!

So I bought many winter clothes.

I'm going to be broke again.

- - - - - - - - - - - - 常用單字片語集 - - - - - - - - - - - -

winter sale
冬季特賣會
summer sale 就是「夏季特賣會」。

50% off
五〇%折扣
加上 over 就會變成 over 50% off（五〇%
以上的折扣）。

winter clothes
冬裝
summer clothes 就是「夏裝」。

be broke
沒有錢的
be low on cash 也是同樣意思。

一月 5 開工
The first day of work

今天要開工了。

好鬱悶啊……

而且天氣還很糟。

電車還因為大雪誤點了。

I'm   **at work from today.**
今天要開工了。

So   **…**
好鬱悶啊……

The   **is also really bad.**
而且天氣還很糟。

The train is   **because of heavy snow.**
電車還因為大雪誤點了。

I'm back at work from today.

So depressed…

The weather is also really bad.

The train is delayed because of heavy snow.

- - - - - - - - - - 常用單字片語集 - - - - - - - - -

be back at work
回工作崗位、開工
直譯是「回到工作崗位或職場」的意思，但也可以用來表示假期過後「重新開工」。

depressed
憂鬱的、鬱悶的
完整句子應該是 I'm so depressed. ，但經常會像這樣省略主語。

The weather is bad.
天氣很糟。
可以像本文一樣加上 really 應用。

be delayed
誤點
描述電車等交通工具的延遲會用 delayed 而不是 late。

某間公司邀我去面試！

Got an invitation from a company

中文日記

我收到一間公司的面試邀約！

我是上個月投履歷的，然後他們邀我去面試了！

我現在就已經覺得緊張了，

但我會全力以赴的！

英文填空日記

I got an _____ for the interview from the company!
我收到一間公司的面試邀約！

I sent them my _____ last month, and they called me!
我是上個月投履歷的，然後他們邀我去面試了！

I'm already so _____,
我現在就已經覺得緊張了，

but I'll do my _____!!
但我會全力以赴的！

英文日記

I got an *invitation* for the interview from the company!

I sent them my *CV* last month, and they called me!

I'm already so *nervous*,

but I'll do my *best*!!

常用單字片語集

invitation
邀請
invitation letter 則是「邀請函」的意思。

CV
履歷
也可以說 résumé。

be nervous
感到緊張
I'm getting nervous.（我開始緊張了）也是常用表現手法。

do one's best
全力以赴
I'll do my best. 是最常用的句子，整句一起學起來吧。

忘了帶傘

Forgot my umbrella

中文日記

完了，我忘記帶傘出門了！

天氣預報說下午開始會下雨。

雖然雨勢還沒有很大，

但我得趕在變成傾盆大雨前回家。

英文填空日記

Oh no! I forgot to _____ my umbrella!

完了，我忘記帶傘出門了！

The weather _____ said it was going to rain this afternoon.

天氣預報說下午開始會下雨。

It's not that _____,

雖然雨勢還沒有很大，

but I gotta go home before it starts _____.

但我得趕在變成傾盆大雨前回家。

英文日記

Oh no! I forgot to bring my umbrella!

The weather forecast said it was going to rain this afternoon.

It's not that heavy,

but I gotta go home before it starts pouring.

常用單字片語集

forget to bring ～
忘記帶～
也常說 forget to take ～（忘記帶～去）。

weather forecast
天氣預報
大多會說 The weather forecast said ～.
（天氣預報說～）。

heavy
嚴重的
可以用 heavy 來表示雨勢或雪勢「大」的狀態。

pour
傾盆大雨
It's pouring. 就是「下起傾盆大雨」的意思。

8 逛街時看見了可愛的錢包

Hanging around the city with Daisuke

中文日記

我和大介去街上閒晃了。

我們去百貨公司的時候，

看見了一個很好看的錢包！

要不要買呢？

英文填空日記

Daisuke and I were hanging ___ the city.
我和大介去街上閒晃了。

When we were at the department ___,
我們去百貨公司的時候，

I found a really nice ___!
看見了一個很好看的錢包！

Should I buy this or ___…?
要不要買呢？

英文日記

Daisuke and I were hanging around the city.

When we were at the department store,

I found a really nice wallet!

Should I buy this or not…?

常用單字片語集

hang around ～
在～閒晃
也可以説 walk around。

department store
百貨公司
只説 depart 是無法表達清楚的。

wallet
錢包
也可以説 purse。

Should I ～ or not?
我該不該～呢？
日常生活中經常用到的口語表現。

史密斯先生誇獎我的英文

My English is getting better!

中文日記

今天我和美國分公司的史密斯先生開會了。

他說：「你的英文進步好多！」

這麼努力學習是值得的！

我會繼續努力學習，說得更加流利！

英文填空日記

I had a meeting with Mr. Smith _____ the US branch today.
今天我和美國分公司的史密斯先生開會了。

He said, "Your English has _____ a lot!"
他說：「你的英文進步好多！」

It was _____ studying a lot!
這麼努力學習是值得的！

I'll study harder to be more _____.
我會繼續努力學習，說得更加流利！

英文日記

I had a meeting with Mr. Smith from the US branch today.

He said, "Your English has improved a lot!"

It was worth studying a lot!

I'll study harder to be more fluent.

常用單字片語集

Mr. ... from ～
來自～的……先生
from 後面可以接公司名稱。

improve
進步、改善
可以說 I wanna improve my English.（我想加強英語能力）。

be worth doing ～
做～是值得的
也有「做～是有價值的」的意思。

fluent
流暢的、流利的
這個單字是形容詞，副詞變化是 fluently。

10

終於要去面試了！

Today's the day!

中文日記

就是今天了，

我要去面試新工作。

我得早點出門才不會遲到。

應該沒有忘了帶什麼東西吧？

英文填空日記

Today's the _____ .
就是今天了，

I'm going _____ an interview for a new job.
我要去面試新工作。

I gotta leave early _____ to be late.
我得早點出門才不會遲到。

Do I _____ everything?
應該沒有忘了帶什麼東西吧？

英文日記

Today's the day.

I'm going for an interview for a new job.

I gotta leave early not to be late.

Do I have everything?

------- 常用單字片語集 -------

Today's the day.
就是今天了。
語感帶有「終於」、「期盼已久」的意思。

go for ～
去～
可以做各種運用，像是 go for dinner（去吃晚餐）等。

not to be late
避免遲到
注意 not 擺放的位置。

Do I have everything?
我應該沒有忘了帶什麼東西吧？
「（該帶的物品）通通都帶了吧？」，即「沒有忘記帶什麼吧？」的意思。

面試還算順利，但……

The interview was okay, but...

嗯，面試過程還算順利吧。

但還是有些地方讓我很在意，

我也說不上是為什麼，

總覺得我沒辦法融入那間公司的氛圍。

_____, I think the interview was OK,
嗯，面試過程還算順利吧。

but there's something that _____ **me.**
但還是有些地方讓我很在意，

I don't _____ **why, but I don't**
我也說不上是為什麼，

think I can _____ **into the atmosphere of the company.**
總覺得我沒辦法融入那間公司的氛圍。

Well, I think the interview was OK,

but there's something that bothers me.

I don't know why, but I don't

think I can fit into the atmosphere of the company.

常用單字片語集

well
嗯、好吧
經常用來連接句子的表現手法。

there's something that bothers me
有些事讓我很在意
運用單字 bother（困擾）的說法。

I don't know why, but...
我也說不上是為什麼……
常用句型，整句一起學起來吧。

fit into ～
融入～
可以用來表示「融入」氛圍或環境。

要不要剪頭髮呢？

Getting a haircut

中文日記

我的頭髮變長了。

長度開始讓人煩躁，

我在想要不要明天去剪頭髮，

我還想染頭髮呢。

英文填空日記

My hair has got _____ .
我的頭髮變長了。

It's getting _____ .
長度開始讓人煩躁，

I think I'm gonna get a _____ **tomorrow.**
我在想要不要明天去剪頭髮，

I also wanna get it _____ .
我還想染頭髮呢。

英文日記

My hair has got longer.

It's getting irritating.

I think I'm gonna get a haircut tomorrow.

I also wanna get it colored.

常用單字片語集

get longer
（頭髮）變長
像這種「變得～」的狀態變化通常會用 get。

irritating
讓人煩躁的
如果主語是人的話，就要改成 I'm irritated.（我很煩躁）。

get a haircut
剪頭髮
因為不是自己剪自己的頭髮，讓別人幫自己剪頭髮的情況要這樣表現。

get ～ colored
將～染色
也可以說 get my hair colored（讓別人幫我染頭髮）。

香織的歡送會
Farewell party for Saori

中文日記

今天我們舉辦了香織的歡送會。

她要去雪梨留學。

我好羨慕她呀！

我也想邁入人生的下一個階段了……

英文填空日記

We had a _____ party for Saori today.
今天我們舉辦了香織的歡送會。

She is going to study _____ in Sydney.
她要去雪梨留學。

I'm so _____ !
我好羨慕她呀！

I wanna _____ on to the next step, too…
我也想邁入人生的下一個階段了……

英文日記

We had farewell party for Saori today.

She is going to study abroad in Sydney.

I'm so jealous!

I wanna move on to the next step, too…

常用單字片語集

farewell party
歡送會
farewell 是「告別」的意思。

study abroad
留學
abroad 是「在國外」的意思。

jealous
羨慕
可以表現出各種語感的單字，也可以用來表示「好好喔～」的語感。

move on to the next step
邁向下一階段
運用片語 move on（開始新的活動）的表現手法。

14 最近睡眠不足
Not getting enough sleep

中文日記

我最近睡眠不足。

我總是太晚睡，

因為要做的事情太多了……

這個週末就在家休息好了。

英文填空日記

I haven't been getting　　　　　 sleep lately.
我最近睡眠不足。

I've stayed　　　　 so late,
我總是太晚睡，

because I've got so many things　　　　 do…
因為要做的事情太多了……

I'm going to　　　　 at home this weekend.
這個週末就在家休息好了。

英文日記

I haven't been getting enough sleep lately.

I've stayed up so late,

because I've got so many things to do…

I'm going to chill at home this weekend.

常用單字片語集

haven't been getting enough sleep
睡眠不足
get enough sleep 是「睡眠充足」的意思。

stay up late
熬夜、晚睡
很實用的表現手法，整個片語記下來吧。

get many things to do
很多事情要做
也可以用 have 取代 get。

chill at home
在家放鬆
和 relax at home 意思相同。

15 今天開始做肌力訓練

Start working out from today

中文日記

我決定開始做肌力訓練！

既然我沒時間去健身房了，

就自己來吧。

先從仰臥起坐和伏地挺身開始吧！

英文填空日記

I _____ **to start working out!**

我決定開始做肌力訓練！

I don't have _____ **to go to a gym,**

既然我沒時間去健身房了，

so I'll do it by _____ **.**

就自己來吧。

Let's start with _____ **and push-ups!**

先從仰臥起坐和伏地挺身開始吧！

英文日記

I decided to start working out!

I don't have time to go to a gym,

so I'll do it by myself.

Let's start with sit-ups and push-ups!

常用單字片語集

decide to ～
決定要～
decide 是「決定」的動詞。

I don't have time to ～ .
沒時間～。
也可以在 time 的前面加上 much 或者
enough。

do it by oneself
自己來
by oneself 是相當常用的片語，學起來吧。

sit-ups
仰臥起坐
和 push-ups（伏地挺身）一起學起來吧。

16 電車因爲下雪停駛

Trains stopped!

中文日記

雪從昨晚就一直下。

電車暫時停駛了，

什麼時候才會復駛呀？

我上班要遲到了！

英文填空日記

It's been snowing   last night.
雪從昨晚就一直下。

The trains just stopped   .
電車暫時停駛了，

When are they going to start   !?
什麼時候才會復駛呀？

I'm gonna be late   work!
我上班要遲到了！

英文日記

It's been snowing since last night.

The trains just stopped running.

When are they going to start again!?

I'm gonna be late for work!

常用單字片語集

since ～
從～一直
常和現在完成式 have 搭配使用。

stop running
停駛
「停止行駛」，即「停駛」的意思。

start again
再次開始
也可以只說 resume（重新開始）。

be late for ～
～要遲到了
上班或上課遲到時，經常用到的片語。

桌上老是亂得要命

My desk is a mess!

我得整理一下我的桌子。

亂七八糟的！

我真的很不擅長把東西整理整齊，

這一點得改進。

I have to　　　　　　my desk.
我得整理一下我的桌子。

It's such a　　　　!
亂七八糟的！

I'm so bad at　　　　things tidy.
我真的很不擅長把東西整理整齊，

I gotta　　　　it.
這一點得改進。

I have to clear my desk.

It's such a mess!

I'm so bad at keeping things tidy.

I gotta fix it.

常用單字片語集

clear
整理
clean 也有相同意思，但「整理東西」大多會使用 clear。

mess
雜亂
可以和形容詞形態 messy 一起記下來。

keep things tidy
整理整齊
翻譯就是「維持東西整齊的樣子」，即「整理整齊」。

fix
改正
描述修理物品或改正個性時會用到的單字。

一月 18

下雪了
Snowing today

中文日記

今天下雪了！

在家裡的時候完全沒注意到！

我本來還打算去做美甲的，

看來今天去不成了……

英文填空日記

It's   today!
今天下雪了！

I didn't   when I was at home!
在家裡的時候完全沒注意到！

I was thinking   getting my nails done,
我本來還打算去做美甲的，

but I don't   I can go today…
看來今天去不成了……

英文日記

It's snowing today!

I didn't notice when I was at home!

I was thinking of getting my nails done,

but I don't think I can go today…

------ 常用單字片語集 ------

snow
下雪
這裡要用的是進行式 be -ing。

notice
注意、發現
也經常做為名詞使用的單字。

think of -ing
打算要～
「本來想著要～」，即「打算要～」的意思。

I don't think I can ～ .
看來無法～了。
比 I can't ～（我無法～）在語感上更含糊的表現手法。

表弟來找我玩
My cousin came to visit me

中文日記

今天表弟來找我玩。

他比我小十歲。

真不敢相信當年那個小孩已經長這麼大了！

以前我還幫他換過尿布呢……

英文填空日記

Today my cousin　　　　　to visit me.
今天表弟來找我玩。

He is 10 years　　　　　than me.
他比我小十歲。

I can't believe that the　　　　　kid has gotten so big!
真不敢相信當年那個小孩已經長這麼大了！

I used to change his　　　　…
以前我還幫他換過尿布呢……

英文日記

Today my cousin came to visit me.

He is 10 years younger than me.

I can't believe that the little kid has gotten so big!

I used to change his diaper...

- - - - - - - - - - 常用單字片語集 - - - - - - - - - -

come to visit ～
來找～玩
除了單用 visit 以外，也有這樣的用法。

...years younger than ～
年紀比～小……歲
想表達「年長」的時候，就把 younger 換成 older。

little kid
小孩
也可以用 child 取代 kid。

change diaper
換尿布
diaper（尿布）也可以說 nappy。

連續三天都吃年糕

Rice cakes three days in a row

中文日記

我已經連續三天都吃年糕了……

這不能怪我！

是我媽一直要我吃的！

現在我不敢量體重了。

英文填空日記

I ate rice cakes three days   a row…
我已經連續三天都吃年糕了……

But it's not my   !
這不能怪我！

My mom   me to eat them!
是我媽一直要我吃的！

Now I'm   to get on the scale.
現在我不敢量體重了。

英文日記

I ate rice cakes three days in a row…

But it's not my fault!

My mom forced me to eat them!

Now I'm scared to get on the scale.

常用單字片語集

in a row
連續
row 也有「列」的意思。

not my fault
不能怪我
使用 fault（錯誤）的表現手法。

force... to ～
要求……做～
force 帶有強烈的「強迫」的意思。

be scared to ～
不敢去～
和形容詞 scary（可怕的）一起學起來吧。

意料之外的雪
Unexpected snow

中文日記

今天下雪了！

天氣預報還說是晴天的！

真是出乎意料之外。

不曉得電車有沒有行駛。

英文填空日記

It's   today!
今天下雪了！

The weather forecast said it was going to be   !
天氣預報還說是晴天的！

It's totally   !
真是出乎意料之外。

I wonder if the train is   or not.
不曉得電車有沒有行駛。

英文日記

It's snowing today!

The weather forecast said it was going to be sunny!

It's totally unexpected!

I wonder if the train is running or not.

------------------------- 常用單字片語集 -------------------------

snow
下雪
這裡要用的是進行式 be -ing。

sunny
晴天
這個單字是形容詞，所以要和 be 動詞一起使用。

unexpected
意料之外的
在 expected（意料中的）前面加上否定的 un 結合而成的單字。

train runs
電車行駛
這種情境可以使用 run（奔跑）這個單字。

愛海的老公要外派

Living by oneself

中文日記

聽説愛海的老公要外派了！

但是愛海沒有要和他一起去，

所以她老公就是單身赴任了。

他們才新婚沒多久啊……

英文填空日記

Manami's husband is going to be　　　　！
聽説愛海的老公要外派了！

And Manami is not　　　　 with him,
但是愛海沒有要和他一起去，

so he has to live　　　 himself.
所以她老公就是單身赴任了。

They've　　　 got married…
他們才新婚沒多久啊……

英文日記

Manami's husband is going to be transferred!

And Manami is not going with him,

so he has to live by himself.

They've just got married…

常用單字片語集

be transferred
外派
transfer 也可以用在「換辦公室」的時候。

go with ～
和～一起去
很常用的句型，像是 I'll go with you.（我要和你一起去）。

live by oneself
獨居、單身赴任
by oneself 是「自己一個人」的意思。

just get married
新婚
使用 just（才～沒多久）的表現手法。

錯過宅配
Couldn't receive my package

中文日記

我又沒領到包裹了！

宅配人員按門鈴的時候，

我剛好在泡澡。

太不湊巧了！

英文填空日記

I couldn't receive my _____ again!
我又沒領到包裹了！

When the delivery person _____ the doorbell,
宅配人員按門鈴的時候，

I was taking a _____.
我剛好在泡澡。

_____ timing!
太不湊巧了！

英文日記

I couldn't receive my package again!

When the delivery person rang the doorbell,

I was taking a bath.

Bad timing!

常用單字片語集

receive one's package
領取包裹
使用 package（包裹）來表現「收宅配」
的表現手法。

ring the doorbell
按門鈴
日文中常用的 intercom 屬於和製英語，要
表達「門鈴」就用 doorbell 吧。

take a bath
泡澡
和 take a shower（淋浴）一起記下來吧。

bad timing
不湊巧
「時機」使用 timing 就可以了。

吃薯條一定要沾番茄醬！

Never without ketchup!

中文日記

不會吧，番茄醬用完了！

吃薯條怎麼可以不沾番茄醬呢！

但問題是⋯⋯

薯條都已經炸好了⋯⋯

英文填空日記

Oh no, I ran _____ of ketchup!
不會吧，番茄醬用完了！

I can't eat French fries _____ ketchup!
吃薯條怎麼可以不沾番茄醬呢！

But the _____ is,
但問題是⋯⋯

I already _____ frying them...
薯條都已經炸好了⋯⋯

英文日記

Oh no, I ran out of ketchup!

I can't eat French fries without ketchup!

But the problem is,

I already finished frying them...

- - - - - - - - - - - 常用單字片語集 - - - - - - - - - - -

run out of ～
～用完了
主要用在調味料或生活用品上。

can't ～ without...
做～不能沒有⋯⋯
使用 without ～（沒有～）的表現手法。

the problem is...
問題是⋯⋯
大多會搭配 but 一起使用。

finish -ing
已經做完～
finish 不能和 to do 一起使用。

颶風來襲！沒事吧……

Worrying about a friend...

中文日記

我看見新聞報導說，

有個颶風直撲一個叫做「橘郡」的地區。

我的朋友就住在那裡！

我要去確認她是否平安無事……

英文填空日記

I saw the news that a big
我看見新聞報導說，

hit the area   "Orange County."
有個颶風直撲一個叫做「橘郡」的地區。

That's   my friend lives!!
我的朋友就住在那裡！

I have to check   she's okay...
我要去確認她是否平安無事……

英文日記

I saw the news that a big hurricane

hit the area called "Orange County."

That's where my friend lives!!

I have to check if she's okay...

- - - - - - - - - - - - - - - 常用單字片語集 - - - - - - - - - - - - - - -

hurricane
颶風
尤其在美國更容易看見颶風的新聞，這個單字經常會出現。

called ～
叫做～
「被稱之為～」，即「叫做～」。

where ～ live
～所居住的地方
the place ～ live 也是相同意思。

check if ～
確認是否～
if 也能表示「是否」，把這個用法學起來吧。

一月 26 收到的零食特產有夠難吃

Sweets from Dubai

中文日記

今天主管從杜拜帶回來一些零食，

還發給了辦公室的每個人。

但超級難吃的！

不過……我還是跟他說：「很好吃！」

英文填空日記

Today my boss　　　　 some sweets from Dubai,
今天主管從杜拜帶回來一些零食，

and 　　　　 out to everyone in the office.
還發給了辦公室的每個人。

But they 　　　　 horrible!!!
但超級難吃的！

I said to him, "It's delicious!", 　　　…
不過……我還是跟他說：「很好吃！」

英文日記

Today my boss brought some sweets from Dubai,

and gave out to everyone in the office.

But they tasted horrible!!!

I said to him, "It's delicious!", though…

常用單字片語集

bring
帶來
過去式 brought 屬於不規則變化，要多加留意拼字。

give out
發放
如果想表示「發給〜」的話，就在後面加上 to。

taste horrible
非常難吃
直譯就是「嘗起來味道很糟」，即「非常難吃」的意思。

〜 , though
雖然〜
會擺在句子的最後。

27 發現很可愛的大衣！

Found a nice coat!

中文日記

下班後，我繞去了購物中心。

我發現一件很好看的大衣！

但我前陣子已經買了很多衣服，

如果再買下去就太敗家了……

英文填空日記

When I _____ by the shopping mall after work,
下班後，我繞去了購物中心。

I _____ a really nice coat!
我發現一件很好看的大衣！

But I already bought a lot of clothes a _____ ago.
但我前陣子已經買了很多衣服，

This is too _____, I guess…
如果再買下去就太敗家了……

英文日記

When I dropped by the shopping mall after work,

I found a really nice coat!

But I already bought a lot of clothes a while ago.

This is too much, I guess…

常用單字片語集

drop by
繞去
如果要補充說明地點的話，就在 by 之後加上 at。

find
發現
過去式是 found，過去分詞也一樣是 found。

a while ago
前陣子
使用 a while（一段時間）的表現方式。

too much
做過頭
大多用來形容行為或狀況。

之前面試的公司聯絡我

The company contacted me

中文日記

今天我接到一通電話，

是之前面試的公司打來的。

他們邀我參加第二輪面試，

但我婉拒了。

英文填空日記

Today I ＿＿＿＿＿ a call from the company where
今天我接到一通電話，

I took the ＿＿＿＿＿ the other day.
是之前面試的公司打來的。

They ＿＿＿＿＿ me to a second interview,
他們邀我參加第二輪面試，

but I ＿＿＿＿＿.
但我婉拒了。

英文日記

Today I got a call from the company where

I took the interview the other day.

They invited me to a second interview,

but I declined.

常用單字片語集

get a call
接到電話
也可以用 receive（收到）來取代 get。

take an interview
參加面試
可以和 take an exam（參加考試）用同樣
方式使用。

invite... to ～
邀……參加～
也可以用在「邀請」至派對的場合。

decline
拒絕
語感更接近「婉拒、謝絕」。

最近老是偷懶沒做家事
Too lazy to do housework

中文日記

最近我老是偷懶沒做家事。

今天一整天都沒什麼事，

那我就通通做完吧！

先從洗衣服開始！

英文填空日記

Recently, I've been　　　　　corners on the housework.
最近我老是偷懶沒做家事。

I have　　　　　to do all day today,
今天一整天都沒什麼事，

so let's　　　　　up all the chores!!
那我就通通做完吧！

I'll　　　　　with the laundry!!
先從洗衣服開始！

英文日記

Recently, I've been cutting corners on the housework.

I have nothing to do all day today,

so let's finish up all the chores!!

I'll start with the laundry!!

常用單字片語集

cut corners
偷懶
也有「放水」的意思。

have nothing to do
無事可做
把 nothing 改成 something 就會變成「有些事要做」。

finish up
做完
意思和 finish 相同，但語感更接近「將做到一半的事情好好完成」。

start with ～
從～開始
結合介系詞 with（和～一起）的表現手法。

影印機的紙沒了！
No paper in the copy machine!

中文日記

影印機的紙沒了！

得補紙才行。

紙放到哪裡去了？

是放在架子後面嗎？

英文填空日記

The copy machine is _____ of paper!
影印機的紙沒了！

I have to _____ it.
得補紙才行。

Where _____ it?
紙放到哪裡去了？

Maybe _____ that shelf?
是放在架子後面嗎？

英文日記

The copy machine is out of paper!

I have to refill it.

Where was it?

Maybe behind that shelf?

常用單字片語集

be out of ～
～用光了
out 也經常用來表示「缺乏」的意思。

refill
補充
在餐飲店也可以説 Can I get a refill?（我可以續杯嗎？）

Where was it?
放到哪裡去了？
如果是回想不起來的情況，會像這樣使用過去式。

behind ～
～的後面
「～的前面」是 in front of ～。

31 今天要和大介去約會

Go on a date with Daisuke

中文日記

今天我要和大介去約會。

不過我們還沒決定要去哪裡。

讓我想想……

今天滿冷的，或許找個溫暖的地方吧？

英文填空日記

Today I'm going _____ a date with Daisuke.
今天我要和大介去約會。

But we haven't _____ where we're going yet.
不過我們還沒決定要去哪裡。

Let me _____ …
讓我想想……

It's cold today, so maybe _____ warm?
今天滿冷的，或許找個溫暖的地方吧？

英文日記

Today I'm going on a date with Daisuke.

But we haven't decided where we're going yet.

Let me see…

It's cold today, so maybe somewhere warm?

常用單字片語集

go on a date
去約會
和 go on a trip（去旅行）是同樣用法。

haven't decided yet
還沒決定
使用完成式的句型。

Let me see.
讓我想想。
思考事情時會使用的連接詞。

somewhere warm
溫暖的地方
somewhere ＋形容詞就是「～的地方」的意思。

有關 「飲食」 的十大表現手法

第 1 名	**I'm a bit hungry.** 我有點餓。	a bit 是「稍微」的意思，可以補充在各種句子裡。和 a little 是同樣意思，一起記下來會很方便。這種情況下，會擺在 be 動詞和形容詞的中間。
第 2 名	**I'm starving.** 我肚子餓得咕嚕咕嚕叫。	想誇張地形容比 I'm hungry. 更餓的狀態時，很建議使用這個句子。I'm so hungry.（我超餓的）也是同樣意思。
第 3 名	**I'll go grab a bite.** 我要去吃點東西。	go grab 是去買些東西時經常使用的片語。Let's go grab something to eat.（我們去吃點東西吧）也是日常生活中會使用的句子。
第 4 名	**I'll go get something to drink.** 我要去買點東西喝。	和 go grab 一樣頻繁用到的就是這個 go get ～ 的表現手法，常搭配 something to drink（一些喝的）、something to eat（一些吃的）一起使用，學起來吧。
第 5 名	**I don't have an appetite.** 我沒食慾。	描述身體狀況時都會用 have，在這種表達「沒有食慾」的情況也可以使用。appetite 是母音起始的名詞，冠詞要用 an 而不是 a，要特別留意。
第 6 名	**I wanna try the new flavor.** 我想試看看新口味。	在聊到食物或飲料的新口味時可以使用的句子。try 這個動詞經常用來表示「嘗試、吃看看」食物或飲料的情況，可以和 want to 的縮短形 wanna 一起使用。
第 7 名	**I want something light tonight.** 今晚我想吃點清爽的。	用 something light 來表示「清爽的東西」，相反的，「重口味的東西」則用 something heavy 來表示。在記單字或句子時，建議可以把反義詞一起記下來。
第 8 名	**I've been too lazy to cook recently…** 我最近懶得煮飯……	too ～ to...（太～以致於無法……）是在日記中也用得到的句型。這種情況的翻譯是「太麻煩以致於不想做料理」，就是「懶得煮」的意思。
第 9 名	**It was so good as expected!** 和預期中一樣好吃！	as 是具有許多意思的單字，在這個情境下，語感會更貼近「像～一樣」。除此之外，as ～ as...（和……一樣～）也是常用表現手法，一起學起來吧。
第 10 名	**I can't eat French fries without ketchup!** 吃薯條怎可以不沾番茄醬！	can't ～ without...（沒有……就無法～）這個句型乍看之下很複雜，記起來就是個簡單又實用的句型，學會這個句型就可以豐富日記和對話的內容。

Best 10

FEBRUARY

I wanna make homemade chocolates for Daisuke,

我想親手做巧克力給大介，

because Valentine's Day is coming soon.

畢竟情人節快到了。

But the problem is,

但問題是，

I've never made any handmade sweets.

我從來沒有做過甜點啊……

1

去看朋友的小寶寶

Go see my friend's baby

中文日記

朋友最近生女兒了！

因為她是第一胎，聽説花了將近二十個小時。

我簡直沒辦法想像那有多辛苦……

總之，希望她可以健康長大。

英文填空日記

One of my friends just ____ a baby girl!
朋友最近生女兒了！

She is her first child, so it took ____ 20 hours.
因為她是第一胎，聽説花了將近二十個小時。

I can't ____ how tough it was…
我簡直沒辦法想像那有多辛苦……

Anyway, I hope she will ____ up healthy.
總之，希望她可以健康長大。

英文日記

One of my friends just had a baby girl!

She is her first child, so it took almost 20 hours.

I can't imagine how tough it was…

Anyway, I hope she will grow up healthy.

- - - - - - - - - - - 常用單字片語集 - - - - - - - - - - -

have a baby
生小孩
雖然也可以説 give birth，但日常對話中更常使用這種説法。

I can't imagine ～ .
我無法想像～。
日常對話中會頻繁出現的句型，整句一起學起來吧。

almost ～
將近～
這個單字雖然也有「幾乎」的意思，但搭配時間一起使用的時候，會更偏向「將近～」的意思。

grow up
長大
用來表示人或植物「成長」的片語。

二月

找不到理想的公司……

Struggling to find a good company

中文日記

我開始找工作已經好長一段時間了，

但一直沒找到理想的公司！

是我太挑剔了嗎？

我應該問問佳奈的意見。

英文填空日記

I've been looking for a job a long time,

我開始找工作已經好長一段時間了，

but I can't any good company!

但一直沒找到理想的公司！

Am I too …?

是我太挑剔了嗎？

I think I'll ask Kana for some .

我應該問問佳奈的意見。

英文日記

I've been looking for a job for a long time,

but I can't find any good company!

Am I too picky…?

I think I'll ask Kana for some advice.

常用單字片語集

for a long time
很長一段時間
for 是用來表示「期間」的介系詞。

find
找
過去式是 found。

picky
挑剔的
語感偏向「挑東挑西的」，即「挑剔的」。

ask... for advice
向……商量、詢問意見
ask ... for ～則是「拜託……做～」，有許多運用方式。

佳奈給了一些轉職的建議

Advice from Kana

佳奈告訴我：「我也是費了好一番工夫

才確定什麼樣的工作最適合自己。

所以你可以花時間慢慢尋找你的理想工作！」

聽到這番話，我放心了不少。

Kana said, "I also had a _____ time
佳奈告訴我：「我也是費了好一番工夫

deciding which job is the _____ for me.
才確定什麼樣的工作最適合自己。

So you can take time to choose your _____ job!!"
所以你可以花時間慢慢尋找你的理想工作！」

I was _____ to hear that.
聽到這番話，我放心了不少。

Kana said, "I also had a hard time

deciding which job is the best for me.

So you can take time to choose your ideal job!!"

I was relieved to hear that.

常用單字片語集

have a hard time
辛苦、費工夫
「度過一段艱難的時間」，就是「辛苦」的意思。

the best
最好的、最佳的
要記住最高級一定要加 the。

ideal
理想的
可以做為名詞或形容詞使用。

be relieved
鬆一口氣、放心
大多會加上 to～來表示「做了～所以鬆一口氣」。

忘記丟垃圾了！

Forgot to take out the trash!

4月
5月
6月
7月
8月
9月
10月
11月
12月
1月
2月
3月

中文日記

完了，我忘記丟垃圾了！

我得把它留到星期一了……

好煩啊。

下一次我絕對不會忘記的！

英文填空日記

Oh no, I forgot to take the trash　　　　！
完了，我忘記丟垃圾了！

I have to keep it　　　　　Monday…
我得把它留到星期一了……

It's　　　　　.
好煩啊。

I won't forget next　　　　!!
下一次我絕對不會忘記的！

英文日記

Oh no, I forgot to take the trash out!

I have to keep it until Monday…

It's annoying.

I won't forget next time!!

- - - - - - - - - - 常用單字片語集 - - - - - - - - - -

take the trash out
丟垃圾
也可以用 garbage 取代 trash。

until ～
在～之前
可以用來表示「在～之前一直」的意思。

annoying
煩人的、令人煩躁的。
irritating 也是同樣意思。

next time
下一次
this time 則是「這次」的意思。

351

表弟考上高中啦！
Congrats!!

中文日記

聽說我表弟考上高中啦！

很高興聽見這個好消息！

他可是拼了命地讀書，

所以他現在肯定也很高興！

英文填空日記

My cousin just passed his high school　　　exam!
聽說我表弟考上高中啦！

So　　　to hear that!
很高興聽見這個好消息！

He's been studying so　　　,
他可是拼了命地讀書，

so he　　　be so happy now!!
所以他現在肯定也很高興！

英文日記

My cousin just passed his high school entrance exam!

So glad to hear that!

He's been studying so hard,

so he must be so happy now!!

--- 常用單字片語集 ---

entrance exam
入學測驗
exam 是 examination 的省略形，日常對話中大多會用這個單字。

glad to hear that
很高興聽見這件事
完整句子應該為 I'm so glad to hear that.，這裡是省略 I'm 的口語表現。

hard
努力、拼命
hard 也可以做為表示「堅固的」的形容詞。

must be
肯定〜
must 最常見的意思是「不得不〜」，但也有這種用途。

聽朋友抱怨丈夫

She's always complaining

中文日記

她又在抱怨她丈夫了。

景子老是在説他壞話，

煩死了！

我已經累了！

英文填空日記

She's _____ **about her husband, again.**
她又在抱怨她丈夫了。

Keiko's always saying bad _____ **about him,**
景子老是在説他壞話，

and I'm _____ **of this!!**
煩死了！

I'm _____ **tired!**
我已經累了！

英文日記

She's complaining about her husband, again.

Keiko's always saying bad things about him,

and I'm sick of this!!

I'm already tired!

常用單字片語集

complain about ～
抱怨～
complain 也有「批評」的意思。

say bad things about ～
說～壞話
語感接近「談論關於～的負面事情」，即「説壞話」。

be sick of ～
～煩死了
sick 最為人所知的意思是「生病的」，但也可用於這種表現手法。

already
已經
I'm already tired. 是很實用的表現，整句一起學起來吧。

我的天菜演員

He's just my type!

二月 7

中文日記

這部電視劇的男演員超帥的！

他叫什麼名字呀？

他簡直是我的天菜。

要是我有個像他那樣的男朋友就好了⋯⋯

英文填空日記

The _____ in this drama is so cute!!
這部電視劇的男演員超帥的！

_____ his name!?
他叫什麼名字呀？

He's my _____ type.
他簡直是我的天菜。

I _____ I could have a boyfriend like him...
要是我有個像他那樣的男朋友就好了⋯⋯

英文日記

The actor in this drama is so cute!!

What's his name!?

He's my perfect type.

I wish I could have a boyfriend like him...

常用單字片語集

actor
男演員
女演員是 actress。

What's ～ ?
～是什麼？
日常對話中經常會將 What is 縮略成 What's。

my perfect type
天菜、理想型
使用 perfect（完美的）的表現方式。

I wish I could ～
要是～就好了
使用 can 的過去式 could 來表示和現實相反的情況。

情人節就親手做巧克力吧

Homemade chocolates for Daisuke

中文日記

我想親手做巧克力給大介，

畢竟情人節快到了。

但問題是，

我從來沒有做過甜點啊⋯⋯

英文填空日記

I wanna make   **chocolates for Daisuke,**
我想親手做巧克力給大介，

because Valentine's Day is   **soon.**
畢竟情人節快到了。

But the   **is,**
但問題是，

I've   **made any handmade sweets.**
我從來沒有做過甜點啊⋯⋯

英文日記

I wanna make homemade chocolates for Daisuke,

because Valentine's Day is coming soon.

But the problem is,

I've never made any handmade sweets.

常用單字片語集

homemade
親手做的
如果是指食物以外的東西，可以改用
handmade。

the problem is...
問題是⋯⋯
日常生活中常用的表現手法，整句記下來就
可以學以致用了。

～ is coming soon.
～快到了。
可以用來表示某個季節或特定的日子「即將
來臨」。

have never ～
從來不曾～
never 後面要接過去分詞的動詞。

355

做瑜伽紓解壓力！

Yoga makes me feel refreshed!

中文日記

今天休假！

我要先去做瑜伽，

然後洗完衣服，再打掃房間！

房間也需要通風一下了。

英文填空日記

Today's my day !
今天休假！

I'm going to yoga ,
我要先去做瑜伽，

then finish my **and cleaning!**
然後洗完衣服，再打掃房間！

I gotta air **the room, too.**
房間也需要通風一下了。

英文日記

Today's my day off!

I'm going to yoga first,

then finish my laundry and cleaning!

I gotta air out the room, too.

常用單字片語集

Today's my day off.
今天休假。
還有許多種說法，像是 I'm off today. 等。

first
首先
在許多用法中，first 會搭配介系詞，但在這種情境中，簡單的一個單字就夠了。

finish one's laundry
洗完衣服
「洗衣服」會說 do one's laundry。

air out the room
讓房間通風
air 做為名詞是「空氣」的意思，也可以做為動詞使用。

一整天困在會議室裡

Stuck in the meeting room

中文日記

我今天一整天都被困在會議室裡。

有開不完的會議……

我甚至連午餐都沒時間吃！

肚子餓得咕嚕咕嚕叫了……

英文填空日記

I've been ＿＿＿＿＿ **in the meeting room all day today.**
我今天一整天都被困在會議室裡。

＿＿＿＿ **many meetings…**
有開不完的會議……

I can't ＿＿＿ **have lunch!**
我甚至連午餐都沒時間吃！

I'm ＿＿＿＿＿ **now…**
肚子餓得咕嚕咕嚕叫了……

英文日記

I've been stuck in the meeting room all day today.

Too many meetings…

I can't even have lunch!

I'm starving now…

- - - - - - - - - - - - - - - - **常用單字片語集** - - - - - - - - - - - - - -

be stuck in ～
被困在～
stuck 有「陷入、動彈不得」的意思。

too many ～
太多～
完整句子為 I have too many meetings，但可以像這樣省略主詞。

even ～
甚至～
中文不太會在口語上說「甚至～」，但在英文裡是會頻繁用到的單字。

be starving
肚子餓
想形容比 be hungry 還要餓的狀態時，大多會使用這樣的表現手法。

把半天都睡掉了

Wasted half a day...

中
文
日
記

糟了，我睡太久了！

都已經十一點了！

我本來打算今天早上要去跑步的！

我把半天都浪費掉了……

**英
文
填
空
日
記**

Oh no, I slept too _____!
糟了，我睡太久了！

It's _____ 11!?
都已經十一點了！

I _____ going to go jogging this morning!
我本來打算今天早上要去跑步的！

I wasted _____ a day...
我把半天都浪費掉了……

**英
文
日
記**

Oh no, I slept too much!

It's already 11!?

I was going to go jogging this morning!

I wasted half a day...

------------------------- 常用單字片語集 -------------------------

sleep too much
睡太久
too much 是經常用來表示「～過頭」的表現手法。

It's already ～ .
已經～點了。
可以和 It's only ～ .（才～點）一起記下來。

I was going to ～ .
我本來打算要～。
be going to 的過去式句子。

half a day
半天
注意 half 的位置。

在書店被搭訕

Hitting on girls at a bookstore!?

中文日記

我在書店打發時間的時候，

有個男人向我搭話。

他問我：「要不要去喝杯咖啡呀？」

嚇我一跳！

英文填空日記

When I was _____ time at a bookstore,
我在書店打發時間的時候，

a _____ talked to me and said,
有個男人向我搭話。

"Do you wanna _____ a coffee with me?"
他問我：「要不要去喝杯咖啡呀？」

What a _____ !
嚇我一跳！

英文日記

When I was killing time at a bookstore,

a guy talked to me and said,

"Do you wanna grab a coffee with me?"

What a surprise!

------------------------ 常用單字片語集 ------------------------

kill time
打發時間
在一般日常對話中會用到的表現手法。

guy
男人
比 man 更加口語化的説法，口語會話中經常出現。

grab a coffee
喝杯咖啡
Do you wanna grab a coffee? 也可以對朋友使用，想隨興地説一句「要喝杯咖啡嗎？」的時候，非常方便實用。

What a surprise!
嚇我一跳！
語感更接近「呼，嚇死我了！」的感嘆句。

小腿撞到桌角

Hit my shin on the corner

中文日記

我的小腿撞到桌角了！

痛死我了！

一定會瘀青的。

我偶爾就會出一次這種醜。

英文填空日記

I hit my ＿＿＿＿＿ on the corner of the table!
我的小腿撞到桌角了！

It ＿＿＿＿＿ a lot!
痛死我了！

I'm sure it's getting a ＿＿＿＿＿.
一定會瘀青的。

I ＿＿＿＿＿ do this.
我偶爾就會出一次這種醜。

英文日記

I hit my shin on the corner of the table!

It hurts a lot!

I'm sure it's getting a bruise.

I sometimes do this.

- - - - - - - - - - **常用單字片語集** - - - - - - - - - -

hit... on ～
……撞到～
hit 的過去式一樣還是 hit。

It hurts.
好痛。
把 it 改成其他單字就可以表示「～很痛」。

get a bruise
瘀青
bruise 是大家較為陌生的單字，趕快學起來吧。

sometimes
偶爾
和 often 一樣是日常對話中的常用單字。

嘗試親手做巧克力！

Homemade chocolates for Daisuke

中文日記

雖然我失敗了好幾次，

但我總算是做出要給大介的巧克力了！

他還說很好吃呢！

呼！鬆了一口氣。

英文填空日記

I messed up a _____ of times,
雖然我失敗了好幾次，

but _____ to make chocolates for Daisuke!
但我總算是做出要給大介的巧克力了！

And he said it was really _____!
他還說很好吃呢！

Phew! I'm _____.
呼！鬆了一口氣。

英文日記

I messed up a couple of times,

but managed to make chocolates for Daisuke!

And he said it was really good!

Phew! I'm relieved.

常用單字片語集

a couple of ～
好幾次～
of 後面要接複數形的名詞。

manage to ～
總算是～
日常對話中的常用表現，學起來吧。

good
好吃
good 除了「好的」以外，也可以用來形容食物「好吃的」。

be relieved
放心、鬆一口氣
用來表示在不安的心情解除過後，鬆了一口氣的樣子。

鞋底磨損了
My shoes are getting worn out

我的鞋底開始磨損了，

畢竟我也穿了快三年了。

我是不是該買一雙新的呢？

還是要修理一下呢……？

The soles of my shoes are getting   out.
我的鞋底開始磨損了，

I've been wearing them for   3 years.
畢竟我也穿了快三年了。

Should I buy new   ,
我是不是該買一雙新的呢？

or get them   …?
還是要修理一下呢……？

The soles of my shoes are getting worn out.

I've been wearing them for almost 3 years.

Should I buy new ones,

or get them repaired…?

常用單字片語集

worn out
用舊、磨損
worn 是 wear 的過去分詞。

for almost ~ years
將近~年
almost 的意思是「幾乎」，所以「幾乎~年」，即「將近~年」的意思。

new one
新的
one 除了「一、一個」以外，也經常做為這種用途。

get ~ repaired
修理~
repair 是用來表示「修理衣物、鞋子、機械類」的意思。

二月 16

在路上巧遇一樹

Bumped into Kazuki!

中文日記

我在街上閒晃的時候，

偶然遇見了一樹！

我們稍微聊了幾句，

但有點尷尬……

英文填空日記

When I was walking _____ the city,
我在街上閒晃的時候，

I _____ into Kazuki!
偶然遇見了一樹！

We just had a small _____,
我們稍微聊了幾句，

but that was kinda _____…
但有點尷尬……

英文日記

When I was walking around the city,

I bumped into Kazuki!

We just had a small chat,

but that was kinda awkward…

常用單字片語集

walk around ～
在～閒晃
和 hang around 意思相同。

bump into ～
偶然遇見～
也可以說 run into。

have a small chat
稍微聊幾句
have a chat（聊天）加上 small 以後，語感就會偏向「稍微聊幾句」。

awkward
尷尬的
在感覺到「尷尬、彆扭」時可以使用的表現方式。

363

17

好懶得煮飯……

Too lazy to cook

今天好懶得煮飯啊！

所以我決定要吃外食了！

今天是想吃點垃圾食物的心情，

下班後，我要直接去漢堡店！

I'm   lazy to cook today!!
今天好懶得煮飯啊！

So I decided   eat out!
所以我決定要吃外食了！

I feel   eating some junk food,
今天是想吃點垃圾食物的心情，

so I'm going   to the hamburger shop after work!
下班後，我要直接去漢堡店！

I'm too lazy to cook today!!

So I decided to eat out!

I feel like eating some junk food,

so I'm going directly to the hamburger shop after work!

常用單字片語集

too ～ to...
太～以致於無法……
「太麻煩以致於不想做料理」，即「懶得煮飯」的意思。

decide to ～
決定要～
使用 decide（決定）的表現手法。

feel like eating ～
想吃～的心情
加上 some（一點、一些），對話會顯得更加自然。

directly
直接地
形容詞為 direct（直接的），一起學起來吧。

怎麼沒什麼有趣的節目？

Nothing good on TV...

中文日記

我好無聊啊……

電視上有沒有什麼有趣的節目呀？

嗯……沒有。我該做什麼好呢？

不然我來看 DVD 之類的好了。

英文填空日記

I'm   ...
我好無聊啊……

Is there   good on TV?
電視上有沒有什麼有趣的節目呀？

Well... nothing good.   do I do...?
嗯……沒有。我該做什麼好呢？

Maybe I'll watch some DVDs   something.
不然我來看 DVD 之類的好了。

英文日記

I'm bored...

Is there anything good on TV?

Well... nothing good. What do I do...?

Maybe I'll watch some DVDs or something.

常用單字片語集

be bored
無聊的、閒暇的
要留意和 boring（無趣的）如何區分使用。

anything ～
～的東西
若是肯定句的話，就將 anything 改為 something。

What do I do?
我該做什麼？
和 What should I do? 的意思幾乎相同。

～ or something
～之類的
無法斷言，想含糊帶過的時候經常會用到。

二月 19

回老家奔喪
Back in my parents' house

我有一個親戚過世了，

所以我要去參加葬禮。

本來想搭飛機回去的，但航班都客滿了。

只好搭新幹線了……

One of my relatives has _____ away,
我有一個親戚過世了，

so I'm going to attend the _____.
所以我要去參加葬禮。

I wanted to go back _____ plane, but the flights were full.
本來想搭飛機回去的，但航班都客滿了。

I gotta go by _____ train…
只好搭新幹線了……

One of my relatives has passed away,

so I'm going to attend the funeral.

I wanted to go back by plane, but the flights were full.

I gotta go by bullet train…

常用單字片語集

pass away
過世
比 die 更委婉的說法。

funeral
葬禮
把 attend a funeral（參加葬禮）這個片語學起來吧。

by plane
搭飛機
基本上會用 by 來表示交通手段。

bullet train
新幹線
通常指日本的高速列車，有時候用 Shinkansen 也能表達。

辦公室裡的外遇謠言

Someone having an affair!?

中文日記

我聽八卦説岡田先生外遇了！

是真的嗎？

他都已經結婚，還有兩個小孩了。

如果是真的，那就不可饒恕了。

英文填空日記

I heard a rumor that Mr. Okada is having an　　　　!
我聽八卦説岡田先生外遇了！

Is that　　　　!?
是真的嗎？

He's　　　　, and has two kids.
他都已經結婚，還有兩個小孩了。

It cannot be　　　　if it's true.
如果是真的，那就不可饒恕了。

英文日記

I heard a rumor that Mr. Okada is having an affair!

Is that true!?

He's married, and has two kids.

It cannot be forgiven if it's true.

常用單字片語集

have an affair
出軌、外遇
「劈腿、花心」則是用 cheat。

Is that true?
是真的嗎？
用來表示對於對方或自己所説的話產生「那是真的嗎？」的疑問。

be married
已婚
若要補充説明對象的話，後面就會接 to ～。小心不要錯成 with 了。

cannot be forgiven
不可饒恕
也可以在肯定句裡用 unforgiven。

同事因為盲腸炎住院了

My colleague got hospitalized

中文日記

吉野小姐因為盲腸炎住院了！

我和其他同事一起去探望她。

她說她已經動過手術了，

不過現在看起來精神還不錯。

英文填空日記

Ms. Yoshino was ＿＿＿＿＿ for appendicitis!
吉野小姐因為盲腸炎住院了！

I went to ＿＿＿＿＿ her with my colleagues.
我和其他同事一起去探望她。

She said she had ＿＿＿＿＿,
她說她已經動過手術了，

but she looked ＿＿＿＿＿ now.
不過現在看起來精神還不錯。

英文日記

Ms. Yoshino was hospitalized for appendicitis!

I went to see her with my colleagues.

She said she had surgery,

but she looked fine now.

常用單字片語集

be hospitalized
住院
由 hospital（醫院）衍生而來的單字。

go to see ～
去探望～
「去見面」，即「去探望」的意思。

have surgery
動手術
也可以用 operation 取代 surgery。

look fine
看起來精神不錯
也可以用 OK 取代 fine。

二月 22 外遇謠言是假的

It was not true

中文日記

說岡田先生外遇的謠言居然是假的！

只是有人看見岡田先生和田中小姐在外面聊天，

就誤以為他們兩個在搞婚外情了。

我就知道他不是那種人！

英文填空日記

The rumor that Mr. Okada is having an affair was not ___ !

說岡田先生外遇的謠言居然是假的！

Somebody saw Mr. Okada ___ with Ms. Tananka outside,

只是有人看見岡田先生和田中小姐在外面聊天，

and she ___ that they were having an affair.

就誤以為他們兩個在搞婚外情了。

I knew he's not that ___ of person!

我就知道他不是那種人！

英文日記

The rumor that Mr. Okada is having an affair was not true!

Somebody saw Mr. Okada chatting with Ms. Tananka outside,

and she misunderstood that they were having an affair.

I knew he's not that kind of person!

- - - - - - - - - - - - - - - - 常用單字片語集 - - - - - - - - - - - - - - - -

not true
不是真的、假的
That's not true！（騙人！）也是常用表現。

see ~ -ing
看見~在……
語感更接近「偶然撞見」，所以不用 watch 或 look，而是用 see。

misunderstand
誤解、誤會
由 understand（理解）衍生而來的單字。

not that kind of person
不是那種人
「不是那種類型的人」，即「不是那種人」的意思。

煮菜手藝進步了
Getting good at cooking

中文日記

前陣子做了巧克力以後，

我又挑戰做料理好幾次。

其實滿好玩的！

下次要做什麼好呢……？

英文填空日記

After I made chocolates the   day,
前陣子做了巧克力以後，

I've tried cooking a   of times.
我又挑戰做料理好幾次。

**   , I really like it!**
其實滿好玩的！

What am I gonna make   …?
下次要做什麼好呢……？

英文日記

After I made chocolates the other day,

I've tried cooking a couple of times.

Actually, I really like it!

What am I gonna make next…?

常用單字片語集

the other day
前陣子、前幾天
這種情況下不用加 on 這些介系詞。

a couple of times
幾次
a couple of ～就是「好幾個」的意思。

actually
其實
這個單字可以活用在各式各樣的情境中，一定要學起來。

next
下次
也常說 next time（下一次）。

吉野小姐出院了

Congrats to Ms. Yoshino!

中文日記

吉野小姐出院了。

她説：「雖然只是短短幾天，

但我快無聊死了！」

我以前也住院過，很能理解她的心情。

英文填空日記

Ms. Yoshino was   from the hospital.
吉野小姐出院了。

She said, "It was just for a   days,
她説：「雖然只是短短幾天，

but I was so bored to   !!"
但我快無聊死了！

I've been hospitalized too, so I   how she feels.
我以前也住院過，很能理解她的心情。

英文日記

Ms. Yoshino was discharged from the hospital.

She said, "It was just for a few days,

but I was so bored to death!!"

I've been hospitalized too, so I know how she feels.

常用單字片語集

be discharged from hospital
出院
discharge 也有「卸貨」的意思。

a few days
幾天
a few（一些）是很常用的量詞，一定要學起來喔。

be ~ to death
快～死了
使用 death（死亡）的句型。

I know how ~ feel.
我懂～的心情。
know 除了「知道」以外，還經常用在表示「理解」的情況。

下下星期有場大型會議

A big meeting

中文日記

下下星期有場大型會議。

主要議題是討論新專案，

我們一直致力於這件事情上，

如果成功的話，我們會賺取龐大的收益！

英文填空日記

We'll have a big meeting the week　　　　　next.
下下星期有場大型會議。

The　　　　　topic is about the new project,
主要議題是討論新專案，

and we've been working　　　　　it for a long time.
我們一直致力於這件事情上，

It would be a big　　　　　if we succeed!
如果成功的話，我們會賺取龐大的收益！

英文日記

We'll have a big meeting the week after next.

The main topic is about the new project,

and we've been working on it for a long time.

It would be a big profit if we succeed!

- - - - - - - - - - - **常用單字片語集** - - - - - - - - - - -

the week after next
下下星期
也可以說 in two weeks。

main topic
主要議題
使用 main（主要的）的表現方式。

work on ～
致力於～
work 除了表示「工作」之外，還有像這樣的豐富用法。

profit
利益
和 benefit 是相同意思。

二月 26 菜刀切到手了

Cut my finger with a knife

中文日記

我拿菜刀切到食指了！

噢，都流血了。

我把 OK 繃放到哪裡去了？

我實在是太笨手笨腳了！

英文填空日記

I cut my   finger with a knife!
我拿菜刀切到食指了！

Oh no, it's   .
噢，都流血了。

Where did I   bandages?
我把 OK 繃放到哪裡去了？

**   clumsy I am!**
我實在是太笨手笨腳了！

英文日記

I cut my index finger with a knife!

Oh no, it's bleeding.

Where did I put bandages?

How clumsy I am!

常用單字片語集

index finger
食指
可以和 thumb（大拇指）、middle finger
（中指）一起學起來。

bleed
流血、出血
大多會用進行式 be bleeding（正在流血）
來表現。

Where did I put ～ ?
我把～放到哪裡去了？
關鍵在於要使用過去式 did。

How ～ !
真是太～ !
how 的後面要接肯定句，不接疑問句。

腳抽筋了

Got a cramp!

我的腳抽筋了！

我睡覺的時候偶爾會發生這種事。

或許是因為我最近運動不足吧。

工作也讓我很疲憊。

I got a _____ in my leg!
我的腳抽筋了！

This sometimes _____ when I'm sleeping.
我睡覺的時候偶爾會發生這種事。

Maybe because I've been _____ of shape recently.
或許是因為我最近運動不足吧。

Also I've been _____ with work.
工作也讓我很疲憊。

I got a cramp in my leg!

This sometimes happens when I'm sleeping.

Maybe because I've been out of shape recently.

Also I've been tired with work.

常用單字片語集

get a cramp in one's leg
腳抽筋
cramp 有「痙攣」的意思。

happen
發生
What happened?（發生什麼事了？）也是
常用句子。

be out of shape
運動不足
無關體型，用來表示動不動就覺得累、身體
不太好的情況。

be tired with ～
因為～很疲憊
要注意介系詞是 with。

皮膚好乾燥

Dry skin

中文日記

我的皮膚好乾燥啊。

我需要好好保養才行。

雖然我有開加溼器，

但房間還是會很乾燥。

英文填空日記

My skin is   .
我的皮膚好乾燥啊。

I need to   care of it better.
我需要好好保養才行。

I've been using a   ,
雖然我有開加溼器，

but it's   dry in the room.
但房間還是會很乾燥。

英文日記

My skin is dry.

I need to take care of it better.

I've been using a humidifier,

but it's still dry in the room.

常用單字片語集

My skin is dry.
皮膚乾燥。
也可以說 I have dry skin.。

take care of ～
保養～
這個片語也有「照顧」的意思。

humidifier
加溼器
由 humid（溼潤的）衍生而來的單字。

still
還是
日常對話中經常使用的單字。

MARCH

Wow, a lot of snow piled up!
哇，積了好厚一層雪。

It's unusual to snow like this in this season.
這個季節下這麼大的雪是很罕見的。

Anyway, I wonder if the train is running now.
總之，不曉得電車有沒有行駛。

I don't know if I can even walk to the station.
我甚至不知道自己能不能走到車站。

三月 1

積雪了

A lot of snow from yesterday

哇，積了好厚一層雪。

這個季節下這麼大的雪是很罕見的。

總之，不曉得電車有沒有行駛。

我甚至不知道自己能不能走到車站。

Wow, a lot of snow ＿＿＿＿＿ up!
哇，積了好厚一層雪。

It's ＿＿＿＿＿ to snow like this in this season.
這個季節下這麼大的雪是很罕見的。

Anyway, I ＿＿＿＿＿ if the train is running now.
總之，不曉得電車有沒有行駛。

I don't know ＿＿＿＿＿ I can even walk to the station.
我甚至不知道自己能不能走到車站。

Wow, a lot of snow piled up!

It's unusual to snow like this in this season.

Anyway, I wonder if the train is running now.

I don't know if I can even walk to the station.

常用單字片語集

pile up
累積
也經常用於「堆積」的意思。

It's unusual to ～ .
～是很罕見的。
unusual 是 usual（平常的）的反義詞。

wonder if ～
不知道是否～
「很好奇是否～」，即「不曉得有沒有～」
的意思。

I don't know if I can ～ .
不知道自己能不能～。
常用句型，整句一起學起來吧。

三月 2 和大介去一日遊

A day trip with Daisuke

中文日記

我和大介去一日遊了。

我們本來想去富士山，但沒什麼時間。

所以我們去了箱根。

那裡的溫泉真的很棒！

英文填空日記

I went　　　　　a day trip with Daisuke.
我和大介去一日遊了。

We wanted to go to Mt. Fuji, but we didn't have time.
我們本來想去富士山，但沒什麼時間。

**　　　　　we went to Hakone.**
所以我們去了箱根。

The hot　　　　there was really good!
那裡的溫泉真的很棒！

英文日記

I went on a day trip with Daisuke.

We wanted to go to Mt. Fuji, but we didn't have much time.

So we went to Hakone.

The hot spring there was really good!

------------------------ 常用單字片語集 ------------------------

go on a day trip
去一日遊
「一日遊」可以說是 a day trip 或 one-day trip。

didn't have much time
沒什麼時間
time 屬於不可數名詞，所以要用 much 而不是 many。

so
所以
口語對話中經常用到的連接詞。

hot spring
溫泉
日本的溫泉會用這個單字表示，歐美有些地方會用 spa 代替。

3 去一間不錯的公司面試了

Found a good company

中文日記

我去了一間公司面試，

他們錄取我了。

那裡的工作正是我心目中的理想工作！

我終於找到了！

英文填空日記

I had an ⎯⎯⎯⎯⎯ with the company
我去了一間公司面試，

⎯⎯⎯⎯⎯ offered me a job.
他們錄取我了。

The job there was ⎯⎯⎯⎯⎯ what I've wanted to do!
那裡的工作正是我心目中的理想工作！

Finally, I found the ⎯⎯⎯⎯⎯!
我終於找到了！

英文日記

I had an interview with the company

which offered me a job.

The job there was exactly what I've wanted to do!

Finally, I found the one!

常用單字片語集

have an interview with ~
去~面試
interview 是母音起始的名詞，所以前面的冠詞要用 an。

which
關係代名詞
像這裡的 which 指的就是 company。

exactly
正是
有時候也可以只用單字表達 Exactly!（正是如此！）

I found the one.
終於找到了。
the one 用來指「尋覓、追求已久的東西」。

三月 **4**

在車站被人撞到

Bumped into someone

中文日記

我撞到一個人的肩膀，

差點就要跌倒了。

但撞到我的男人連個道歉都沒有！

真惡劣！

英文填空日記

I _____ into someone's shoulder.
我撞到一個人的肩膀，

I _____ fell down.
差點就要跌倒了。

But the guy who bumped into me didn't _____!
但撞到我的男人連個道歉都沒有！

So _____!
真惡劣！

英文日記

I bumped into someone's shoulder.

I nearly fell down.

But the guy who bumped into me didn't apologize!

So nasty!

- - - - - - - - - - - - - - - 常用單字片語集 - - - - - - - - - - - - - - -

bump into ～
撞到～
也有「偶然遇見人」的意思。

apologize
道歉
可以說 Apologize to me!（向我道歉！）

nearly
幾乎、差一點
和 almost 意思相近。

nasty
惡劣的、可惡的
日常對話中經常出現，用來表示「令人不愉快的～」。

三月 5

媽媽的家常菜
My mom's cooking is the best!

我回老家一趟了，

因為有點事要處理。

媽媽的家常菜是最好吃的。

我要怎麼做才能擁有這樣的廚藝呢？

英文填空日記

I went back to my _____ house
我回老家一趟了，

because _____ just came up.
因為有點事要處理。

My mom's cooking is the _____.
媽媽的家常菜是最好吃的。

How can I be _____ this!?
我要怎麼做才能擁有這樣的廚藝呢？

英文日記

I went back to my parents' house

because something just came up.

My mom's cooking is the best.

How can I be like this!?

-------- 常用單字片語集 --------

go back to one's parents' house
回老家
其他說法像是 go back to my hometown。

something comes up
有事
大多會和 just 一起使用。

the best
最棒的
「good-better-best」，best 是 good 的最高級。

like this
像這樣的
如 like this/like that，like 有「像～的」的意思。

三月
6

爸爸的衣服……

How my dad wears a T-shirt

中文日記

我爸老是把衣服前後穿反，

偶爾甚至會穿錯面！

嗯，不過我有時候也會忘了穿內衣。

沒資格說別人啦。

英文填空日記

My dad always wears a T-shirt＿＿＿＿.
我爸老是把衣服前後穿反，

It's even ＿＿＿＿ out sometimes!
偶爾甚至會穿錯面！

Well, I also forget to wear a ＿＿＿＿ sometimes.
嗯，不過我有時候也會忘了穿內衣。

I can't ＿＿＿＿ for others.
沒資格說別人啦。

英文日記

My dad always wears a T-shirt backwards.

It's even inside out sometimes!

Well, I also forget to wear a bra sometimes.

I can't speak for others.

常用單字片語集

backwards
前後反轉
也可以說 back to front。

inside out
裡外相反
用 inside（內側）和 out（外側）來表示。

bra
內衣
正式名稱為 brassiere，但大部分的人都會略稱為 bra。

I can't speak for others.
沒資格說別人。
很實用的表現手法，可以整句記下來。

新幹線的人潮比想像中多

It's so crowded!

中文日記

新大阪車站人好多啊。

不曉得訂不訂得到對號座……

早知道就先預訂了。

我不知道這個時段人會這麼多。

英文填空日記

　　　　　　　　are so many people at Shin-Osaka station.
新大阪車站人好多啊。

I don't know if I can get a　　　　　seat…
不曉得訂不訂得到對號座……

I should have booked it　　　　　.
早知道就先預訂了。

I didn't know it's　　　　　this time of day.
我不知道這個時段人會這麼多。

英文日記

There are so many people at Shin-Osaka station.

I don't know if I can get a reserved seat…

I should have booked it beforehand.

I didn't know it's crowded this time of day.

常用單字片語集

There is/are ～ .
有～。
學校也會教的基礎表現句型，根據 be 動詞後面的名詞是單數或複數，選擇要用 is 或 are。

reserved seat
對號座
自由座是 non-reserved seat。

beforehand
事前、預先
如果只有 before 的話是「前面的」的意思，這種情況要用 beforehand。

be crowded
人潮擁擠
用來表示人擠人的場面。

雨水弄髒了我心愛的鞋

My favorite white shoes

中文日記

我不知道今天會下雨，

所以穿了我心愛的白鞋出門！

就算我有撐傘，

也一定會弄髒的啦！

英文填空日記

I   know it was going to rain today,
我不知道今天會下雨，

so I put   my favorite white shoes!
所以穿了我心愛的白鞋出門！

**   if I use an umbrella,**
就算我有撐傘，

they are going to be dirty   sure!!
也一定會弄髒的啦！

英文日記

I *didn't* know it was going to rain today,

so I put *on* my favorite white shoes!

Even if I use an umbrella,

they are going to be dirty *for* sure!!

常用單字片語集

I didn't know ～ .
我不知道～。
完整句子應該是帶有連接詞的 I didn't know
that ～，但 that 在日常對話中經常省略。

put on
穿
不只是穿鞋，穿洋裝也可以用這個片語。

even if ～
即便～
把這兩個單字做為一組記下來吧，是很常用
到的表現手法。

for sure
絕對
想強調「一定會～」的時候，可以在句尾加
上 for sure。

老家寄來一大箱橘子

Too many oranges!

中文日記

我爸媽寄了一個大箱子過來，

裡面是……一大堆橘子！

不過，這麼多怎麼可能吃得完啦！

只能分送給朋友了……

英文填空日記

My parents sent   a big box.
我爸媽寄了一個大箱子過來，

What are inside…   of mandarin oranges!!
裡面是……一大堆橘子！

You know, it's   to finish all these!!
不過，這麼多怎麼可能吃得完啦！

**   I can do is to give them to my friends…**
只能分送給朋友了……

英文日記

My parents sent me a big box.

What are inside… tons of mandarin oranges!!

You know, it's impossible to finish all these!!

All I can do is to give them to my friends…

- - - - - - - - - - 常用單字片語集 - - - - - - - - - -

send ＋人＋東西
把東西寄給人
如果要把東西移到前面的話，就是 send a box to me，要加上介系詞 to。

tons of ～
大量的～
語感上是比 many 還要「大量的」。

It's impossible to ～.
～是不可能的。
也可以說 It's impossible!（不可能會是那樣的！）

All I can do is to ～.
我只能～。
語感偏向「我能做得到的事就只有～」，即「我只能～」。

廣美遇見心儀的人

Good news from Hiromi

中文日記

我問廣美：「最近過得怎麼樣？」

她說：「我有心儀的人了。」

我的第一反應是：「什麼？是誰？」

我好興奮啊！

英文填空日記

I asked Hiromi, "＿＿＿＿ new?"
我問廣美：「最近過得怎麼樣？」

And she said, "I have a ＿＿＿ on someone."
她說：「我有心儀的人了。」

I was ＿＿＿ "What!? Who's that!?"
我的第一反應是：「什麼？是誰？」

I got so ＿＿＿!!
我好興奮啊！

英文日記

I asked Hiromi, "What's new?"

And she said, "I have a crush on someone."

I was like "What!? Who's that!?"

I got so excited!!

------------------------------ 常用單字片語集 ------------------------------

What's new?
最近過得如何？
想問對方近況的時候經常用到的句子。

have a crush on ～
喜歡、在意～
「喜歡」有很多種表現方式，但這個片語是
日常生活中常用到的表現手法。

I was like ～.
我的反應就像是～。
like 後面可以加上像是 Oh my god! 之類的
感嘆句，用法很多。

get excited
興奮
be excited 是表示「感到興奮」的狀態，但
如果要說「興奮起來」這個動作的話，大多
會用 get。

今天工作沒什麼進展

I messed up today…

中文日記

今天工作沒什麼進展。

我現在就想回家喝口冰冰涼涼的啤酒！

我覺得最近壓力太大了，

今天我要在浴缸裡好好泡一會兒。

英文填空日記

I didn't _____ much done at work today.
今天工作沒什麼進展。

I wanna go home and have an _____ -cold beer now!
我現在就想回家喝口冰冰涼涼的啤酒！

I've been _____ stressed recently.
我覺得最近壓力太大了，

I'll have a good _____ in the bath today.
今天我要在浴缸裡好好泡一會兒。

英文日記

I didn't get much done at work today.

I wanna go home and have an ice-cold beer now!

I've been feeling stressed recently.

I'll have a good soak in the bath today.

常用單字片語集

didn't get much done
沒有進展
也可以運用在工作以外的各種情境中。

ice-cold
冰冰涼涼的
「像冰塊一樣涼」的意思。

feel stressed
壓力很大
也可以直接說 I'm so stressed!。

have a good soak in the bath
在浴缸裡好好泡澡
soak 有「浸泡、吸收」的意思，也可以做為動詞使用。

12

太好了！我瘦了兩公斤！

Lost 2 kg!

中文日記

太好了！我瘦了兩公斤！

不過，我在春節期間胖了三公斤，

所以我得再瘦一公斤才行。

我要注意別吃太多甜食了。

英文填空日記

Yay! I _____ 2 kg!
太好了！我瘦了兩公斤！

But I _____ 3 kg during the New Year's holidays,
不過，我在春節期間胖了三公斤，

so I gotta lose 1 kg _____ .
所以我得再瘦一公斤才行。

I gotta be _____ not to eat too many sweets.
我要注意別吃太多甜食了。

英文日記

Yay! I lost 2 kg!

But I gained 3 kg during the New Year's holidays,

so I gotta lose 1 kg more.

I gotta be careful not to eat too many sweets.

常用單字片語集

lose ～ kg
瘦了～公斤
lose 的過去式和過去分詞都是 lost。

gain ～ kg
胖了～公斤
也可以用 put on 取代 gain。

lose ～ kg more
再瘦～公斤
使用 more（更加）來表示「還有」的意思。

be careful not to ～
注意別～
要留意 not 擺放的位置。

聽說會下雨
I heard it would rain

聽說會下雨我才帶傘出門的。

但看看這個天氣，

萬里無雲啊！

到底是誰說今天會下雨的！

I _____ my umbrella because I heard it would rain.
聽說會下雨我才帶傘出門的。

But _____ at this weather.
但看看這個天氣，

It's a _____ day!
萬里無雲啊！

_____ said it's going to rain today!?
到底是誰說今天會下雨的！

I brought my umbrella because I heard it would rain.

But look at this weather.

It's a clear day!

Who said it's going to rain today!?

常用單字片語集

bring
帶
bring 的過去式 brought 拼字有些複雜，要多加注意。

Look at ～ .
看看～。
也可以只説 Look.（你看）。

It's a clear day.
萬里無雲。
指一朵雲都沒有的晴朗天氣。

Who said ～ ?
是誰説～？
也可以説 Who said that?（誰説的？）

14 今天是白色情人節

White Day today

中文日記

大介送了我白色情人節禮物！

我完全沒有料想到，

所以讓我好驚喜呀！

大介，謝謝你送我這麼可愛的項鍊。

英文填空日記

Daisuke　　　　　　me a White Day present!
大介送了我白色情人節禮物！

I　　　　　expected that,
我完全沒有料想到，

so it　　　　　　me a lot!
所以讓我好驚喜呀！

Thanks　　　　　the cute necklace, Daisuke.
大介，謝謝你送我這麼可愛的項鍊。

英文日記

Daisuke got me a White Day present!

I never expected that,

so it surprised me a lot!

Thanks for the cute necklace, Daisuke.

常用單字片語集

get... ～
把～送給……
give 也有相同意思，但也能像這樣用 get 取代。

never
完全沒有～
never 本身就有否定的意味了，注意不要和 not 這些否定形併用。

surprise
令人驚喜
要分清楚和 be surprised（驚訝）的區別。

Thanks for ～
謝謝～
也可以把 Thanks 改成 Thank you。

發薪日要犒賞自己

Payday today!!

中文日記

今天是發薪日！

所以我要買稍微高級一點的肉！

平時我都只買便宜貨而已……

偶爾也要善待自己！

英文填空日記

             today!!
今天是發薪日！

So I'll buy some   **-class beef!**
所以我要買稍微高級一點的肉！

         , I can buy only cheap ones…
平時我都只買便宜貨而已……

Sometimes it's good to   **myself!**
偶爾也要善待自己！

英文日記

Payday today!!

So I'll buy some high-class beef!

Usually, I can buy only cheap ones…

Sometimes it's good to treat myself!

常用單字片語集

payday
發薪日
省略了 It's payday today. 的 It's。

high-class
高級的
也可以說 high-quality。

usually
通常、平時
不只是在日常對話裡，在各種情境都會出現的單字。

treat oneself
善待自己
語感和 spoil oneself（縱容自己）相近。

收到錄取通知了！

Ok, I'll do it!

中文日記

今天那間公司聯繫我了。

他們說：「希望你能成為敝公司的一員。」

他們提供的條件也很棒，

就這麼決定了！

英文填空日記

Today I got ⟨　　　⟩ by that company.
今天那間公司聯繫我了。

They said, "Please be a ⟨　　　⟩ of our company."
他們說：「希望你能成為敝公司的一員。」

The ⟨　　　⟩ they proposed were really good,
他們提供的條件也很棒，

so I'll ⟨　　　⟩ it!
就這麼決定了！

英文日記

Today I got contacted by that company.

They said, "Please be a member of our company."

The conditions they proposed were really good,

so I'll do it!

常用單字片語集

get contacted by ～
收到來自～的聯繫
get ＋過去分詞是很常見的用法。

be a member of ～
成為～的一員
也可以用「（現在）是～的一員」來表示現在的狀態。

condition
條件、狀態
in good condition（狀態很好）也是常用的表現手法。

I'll do it.
決定了。
有表示「下定決心」的意味。

大雨……

Such heavy rain…

中文日記

雨勢好大啊。

明明說了今天的降雨機率只有三〇%的，

根本一點都不準！

我肯定要淋成落湯雞了。

英文填空日記

It's such _____ rain.
雨勢好大啊。

They said the _____ of rain today was only 30%.
明明說了今天的降雨機率只有三〇%的，

That was _____ wrong!
根本一點都不準！

I'm _____ I'm gonna get soaked.
我肯定要淋成落湯雞了。

英文日記

It's such heavy rain.

They said the chance of rain today was only 30%.

That was totally wrong!

I'm sure I'm gonna get soaked.

常用單字片語集

heavy rain
大雨
可以用 heavy（嚴重的）這個單字來表示。

chance of rain
降雨機率
chance 有「機會、可能性」的意思。

totally
完全
經常和 wrong（錯誤的）一起使用。

I'm sure ～.
肯定會～。
使用 sure（確實的）的說法。

連日加班，身心俱疲

I'm exhausted

中文日記

這星期一直加班，我要累死了。

這個週末我要在家裡好好放鬆。

我要先睡個午覺，

然後再去租 DVD。

英文填空日記

I'm　　　　from overtime work this week.

這星期一直加班，我要累死了。

I'll just　　　　at home this weekend.

這個週末我要在家裡好好放鬆。

I'll take a　　　　first.

我要先睡個午覺，

Then go　　　　DVDs later.

然後再去租 DVD。

英文日記

I'm exhausted from overtime work this week.

I'll just relax at home this weekend.

I'll take a nap first.

Then go rent DVDs later.

常用單字片語集

be exhausted
筋疲力盡的
比 tired 更加疲憊的說法。

relax at home
在家放鬆
也可以用來表示「在家閒閒沒事做」。

take a nap
睡午覺
日常生活中經常出現的表現手法，整個片語一起學起來吧。

rent DVDs
租 DVD
borrow 是無償借用，rent 是有償租借。

櫻花怎麼還不開呀？
Waiting for spring

中文日記

櫻花什麼時候才要開呀。

聽說今年會比往年開得更早，

最近越來越暖和了，

希望可以快點看到。

英文填空日記

I wonder when the cherry blossoms are starting to ＿＿＿＿.
櫻花什麼時候才要開呀。

I heard they will bloom ＿＿＿＿ than usual this year.
聽說今年會比往年開得更早，

It's getting ＿＿＿＿ lately,
最近越來越暖和了，

so I hope ＿＿＿＿ see them soon.
希望可以快點看到。

英文日記

I wonder when the cherry blossoms are starting to bloom.

I heard they will bloom earlier than usual this year.

It's getting warmer lately,

so I hope to see them soon.

常用單字片語集

bloom
開花、綻放
和 full in bloom（盛開）一起記下來吧。

earlier than usual
比以往早
使用比較級的表現手法。

be getting warmer
越來越暖和
get 除了「得到、抓住」以外，也有這種用法。

hope to ～
希望可以～
使用 hope（期望）的句型。

絲襪脫線了

Oh no, my pantyhose…

中文日記

我的絲襪脫線了！

但我今天沒有帶備用的來……

慢著，我的置物櫃裡搞不好有！

我要去確認一下！

英文填空日記

I've got a　　　　　　in my pantyhoses!
我的絲襪脫線了！

But I don't have any　　　　　today…
但我今天沒有帶備用的來……

Wait, I　　　　have some in my locker!
慢著，我的置物櫃裡搞不好有！

I gotta go　　　　　!
我要去確認一下！

英文日記

I've got a run in my pantyhoses!

But I don't have any extra today…

Wait, I might have some in my locker!

I gotta go check!

---------------- **常用單字片語集** ----------------

get a run in one's pantyhose
絲襪脫線
絲襪在英式英語中叫做 tights。

extra
替換的、備用的
可以説 extra ～（備用的～）。

might ～
搞不好～
用來表示不確定的事。

go check
去確認
將 go to check 縮簡成 go check。

好想出國旅遊！

Wanna go abroad

好想出國旅遊啊！

去年五月我去了美國，

這次我想去歐洲！

不知道有沒有人要和我一起去？

I wanna go travel　　　　　!
好想出國旅遊啊！

I went to the US　　　　　May,
去年五月我去了美國，

so I'm going to Europe this　　　　　!
這次我想去歐洲！

Is there　　　　　who can go with me…?
不知道有沒有人要和我一起去？

I wanna go travel abroad!

I went to the US last May,

so I'm going to Europe this time!

Is there anyone who can go with me…?

常用單字片語集

travel abroad
出國旅遊
也可以加 go 變成「去國外旅遊」。

last ~
上個~
和 this ~（這個~）一起記下來吧。

this time
這次
next time 就是「下次」的意思。

anyone
任何人
也可以用 someone 取代。

三月 22 決定這次一個人去旅行！

I'll go travel alone this time

中文日記

我找不到可以和我一起出國的人，

好吧，這次我就一個人去吧。

一個人旅行也不錯。

可以去所有自己想去的地方！

英文填空日記

I cannot find anyone ...
我找不到可以和我一起出國的人，

OK, I'll go **this time.**
好吧，這次我就一個人去吧。

Traveling by **might be nice, too.**
一個人旅行也不錯。

Because I can go **I want!**
可以去所有自己想去的地方！

英文日記

I cannot find anyone available…

OK, I'll go alone this time.

Traveling by myself might be nice, too.

Because I can go anywhere I want!

常用單字片語集

available
有空的
也可以用在座位或人等各種事物上。

go alone
一個人去
alone 也可以改成 by oneself。

travel by oneself
一個人旅行
也可以說 travel solo。

anywhere
任何地方
這種情況下，go 的後面不加介系詞，要特別留意。

都已經三月下旬了

It's already late March, but...

中文日記

還是有點冷，都已經三月下旬了耶！

每年都這樣的嗎？

我已經受夠冷天氣了。

希望春天快點來啊！

英文填空日記

Still pretty cold. It's already　　　　　　March!?
還是有點冷，都已經三月下旬了耶！

Is it　　　　　　this every year?
每年都這樣的嗎？

I'm tired　　　　　this cold weather.
我已經受夠冷天氣了。

I want　　　　　to come soon!
希望春天快點來啊！

英文日記

Still pretty cold. It's already late March!?

Is it like this every year?

I'm tired of this cold weather.

I want spring to come soon!

常用單字片語集

late ~
～下旬
可以和 early～（～上旬）一起記下來。

like this
像這樣
在許多對話中都可以用到的表現手法。

be tired of ~
已經受夠～
使用 tired（疲憊的）的慣用句型。

want... to ~
希望……做～
通常……裡填的都是人，但這時候是填進 spring。

我決定要去巴黎旅行了！

Going to Paris!

中文日記

我決定下個月要去巴黎了！

巴黎有好多我想去的地方，

羅浮宮、艾菲爾鐵塔、香榭麗舍大道……

還有逛街也是必去行程！

英文填空日記

I   to go to Paris next month!!
我決定下個月要去巴黎了！

There are too   places I wanna go to in Paris!
巴黎有好多我想去的地方，

The Louvre   , the Eiffel Tower, Champs-Élysées…
羅浮宮、艾菲爾鐵塔、香榭麗舍大道……

And shopping is a   !
還有逛街也是必去行程！

英文日記

I decided to go to Paris next month!!

There are too many places I wanna go to in Paris!

The Louvre Museum, the Eiffel Tower, Champs- Élysées…

And shopping is a must!

常用單字片語集

decide to ～
決定要～
to 後面一定要加原形動詞。

too many ～
好多～
接不可數名詞的時候要改成 too much。

museum
博物館
小心不要拼錯字了。

～ is a must.
～是絕對必要的。

石田小姐休產假

My colleague going on maternity leave

中文日記

石田小姐要休產假了。

她已經懷孕九個月了。

預產期就快到了！

希望她可以產下健康的寶寶。

英文填空日記

Ms. Ishida is _____ on maternity leave.
石田小姐要休產假了。

She's already 9 months _____.
她已經懷孕九個月了。

It's almost the _____ date!
預產期就快到了！

Hope she'll _____ a healthy baby.
希望她可以產下健康的寶寶。

英文日記

Ms. Ishida is going on maternity leave.

She's already 9 months pregnant.

It's almost the due date!

Hope she'll have a healthy baby.

常用單字片語集

go on maternity leave
休產假
leave 是「休假」的意思。

pregnant
懷孕
～ month(s) pregnant 就是「懷孕～個月」的意思。

due date
預產期
預產期也可以說 baby due。

have a healthy baby
產下健康的嬰兒
「生產」可以像這樣用 have 或 deliver 來表示。

他太一板一眼了吧

How methodical he is...

中文日記

我問他：「現在幾點了？」

他一開始回答：「九點。」

沒多久又說：「等一下，正確來說是九點五分。」

好，那不重要好嗎！

英文填空日記

When I asked him, "   **the time?",**
我問他：「現在幾點了？」

     he said, "It's 9."
他一開始回答：「九點。」

But after that, he said, "Wait, it's 9:05 to be   **."**
沒多久又說：「等一下，正確來說是九點五分。」

Well,   **.**
好，那不重要好嗎！

英文日記

When I asked him, "What's the time?",

first he said, "It's 9."

But after that, he said, "Wait, it's 9:05 to be exact."

Well, whatever.

常用單字片語集

What's the time?
現在幾點？
除了 What time is it now? 以外還有很多種說法。

first
一開始

to be exact
正確來說
使用 exact（正確的）的片語。

whatever
無所謂、不重要
有些敷衍的時候所用的單字。

403

櫻花盛開

The cherry blossoms in full bloom

中文日記

終於！櫻花盛開了！

我上班途中就看見了。

我最喜歡這個季節了！

這週末要不要去公園走走呢。

英文填空日記

Finally! The cherry blossoms are in   bloom!

終於！櫻花盛開了！

I found them on the   to work.

我上班途中就看見了。

I like this season the   !

我最喜歡這個季節了！

**   I'll go to the park this weekend.**

這週末要不要去公園走走呢。

英文日記

Finally! The cherry blossoms are in full bloom!

I found them on the way to work.

I like this season the best!

Maybe I'll go to the park this weekend.

常用單字片語集

in full bloom
盛開
可以用在櫻花季的片語。

on the way to work
上班途中
on the way（在……途中）是常用表現手法，學起來吧。

like ~ the best
最喜歡~
使用 the best（最）的最高級表現。

Maybe I'll ~ .
要不要~呢。
maybe（或許）可以用在許多情境中。

聽說在巴黎買精品很便宜
Shopping in Paris

中文日記

聽說巴黎有很多精品店。

我好想去 LV 的總店啊！

我一定會花很多錢的！

不太妙啊……

英文填空日記

I heard there are many   **brand shops in Paris.**
聽說巴黎有很多精品店。

I wanna go to the   **store of Louis Vuitton!**
我好想去 LV 的總店啊！

I'm sure I'm gonna   **a lot of money!**
我一定會花很多錢的！

This is   **…**
不太妙啊……

英文日記

I heard there are many luxury brand shops in Paris.

I wanna go to the main store of Louis Vuitton!

I'm sure I'm gonna spend a lot of money!

This is bad…

常用單字片語集

luxury brand
精品品牌
也可以說 high-end brand。

main store
總店、總部
用 main（主要的）來表示。

spend
使用、花費
用在表示「花費」金錢或時間的時候。

This is bad.
不妙、不行
多用於自言自語的句子。

我忘記爸爸的生日了！

It was my father's birthday yesterday!

中文日記

糟了！我忘得一乾二淨，

昨天是爸爸的生日！

我沒有傳祝賀訊息給他，

他可能生悶氣了。

英文填空日記

Oh no! I totally   **that**
糟了！我忘得一乾二淨，

it was my father's   **yesterday!**
昨天是爸爸的生日！

I didn't   **him a message,**
我沒有傳祝賀訊息給他，

so he might be   **.**
他可能生悶氣了。

英文日記

Oh no! I totally forgot that

it was my father's birthday yesterday!

I didn't send him a message,

so he might be sulking.

--- 常用單字片語集 ---

totally forget that ～
把～忘得一乾二淨。
that 之後要接由主詞起始的句子。

it's ～'s birthday
～的生日
要表示日子的時候，句子通常會以 it's 開頭。

send a message
傳訊息
Send me a message.（再傳訊息給我）也是常用句子。

be sulking
生悶氣
moody 這個單字也是同樣意思。

和大介去看電影

What I eat at cinema

中文日記

今天我和大介去看電影了。

平時我總是會在電影開演前

就把爆米花吃完了。

我真是愛吃鬼啊。

英文填空日記

I went to a movie with Daisuke today.
今天我和大介去看電影了。

I always finish popcorn
平時我總是會在電影開演前

before the movie .
就把爆米花吃完了。

I'm such a .
我真是愛吃鬼啊。

英文日記

I went to see a movie with Daisuke today.

I always finish eating popcorn

before the movie starts.

I'm such a foodie.

常用單字片語集

go to see a movie
去看電影
也可以說 go see a movie 或者 go to the cinema。

finish -ing
做完～
finish eating 就是「吃完」的意思。

before ～
在～之前
可以和 after（在～之後）一起記下來。

foodie
愛吃鬼
「很喜歡吃東西的人」，即「愛吃鬼」。

三月步入尾聲
Already the end of March

三月已經要結束了！

我今年就要三十歲了⋯⋯

這是我步入三十代的第一年，

所以我要打造成最棒的一年！

It's already the _____ of March!
三月已經要結束了！

Finally, _____ be 30 this year…
我今年就要三十歲了⋯⋯

It's the first year of my _____,
這是我步入三十代的第一年，

so I'll make the _____ of it!
所以我要打造成最棒的一年！

It's already the end of March!

Finally, I'll be 30 this year…

It's the first year of my 30s,

so I'll make the best of it!

常用單字片語集

the end of ～
～的尾聲
end 可以做為名詞，也可以做為動詞使用。

I'll be ～ this year.
我今年就～歲了。
用未來式 will 來表示。

30s
三十代
只要在 20、30、40 後面加上 s 就是分別表示「二十代」、「三十代」、「四十代」的意思。

make the best
打造成最棒的
使用最高級 the best（最棒的、最佳的）的表現手法。

有關「金錢」的十大表現手法

第 1 名
I spent a lot.
我花了好多錢。

在有關金錢的話題裡，最常使用的就是 spend（使用、花費）這個動詞，過去式 spent 屬於不規則變化，要特別留意。

第 2 名
How cheap!
好便宜喔！

How cheap it is! 省略後的句子。只要記得 How ＋形容詞的句型，就可以在各種情境中活用的感嘆句，是個很方便也很實用的表現手法。

第 3 名
It's on sale.
這在特價。

on sale 是在表示商品降價時最簡單的表現方式。容易混淆的是另一個片語 for sale，這個片語是「這是販售商品」的意思，注意不要用錯了。

第 4 名
That's too expensive.
太貴了。

That's too ～.（ 太 ～ ）和 That's so ～.（很～）語感相近，兩種都能活用的話，可以豐富日記內容並增加變化。

第 5 名
I have to save money.
我必須存錢。

have to 也可以改成 gotta。save 雖然有「幫助、拯救」的意思，但這時候會用來表示「存錢」的意思，還有另一種說法 save up。

第 6 名
I'm broke.
我要破產了。

想表示「窮困」的狀態時，這個句子再適合不過了。簡短又好念，大家可以學起來。也可以和 I spent a lot.（我花太多錢了）一起使用。

第 7 名
I don't know how much I spent.
我不記得自己花多少了。

I don't know how much I spent. 等同 I spent a lot.，兩個句子語感相同，都記下來就可以避免老是用同樣的句子，也能增加變化。

第 8 名
I wonder how much it costs.
很好奇那要多少錢。

I wonder ～（很好奇～）是寫日記時最常使用的句型，可以用在一個人自言自語的時候。大多會搭配 if 使用，像是 I wonder if ～。

第 9 名
It was 30% off!
那可是有三〇％折扣呢！

在討論特價商品的時候經常用到的句子。一般都是用過去式，所以會用 is 的過去式 was。

第 10 名
Payday today!!
今天是發薪日！

payday（發薪日）是常用單字，是將 It's payday today. 縮簡後的句子。除了 payday 以外，也可以說 It's my birthday today!（今天是我生日！）有許多運用機會。

Best 10

常用單字、片語、句型索引

（依首字筆畫排序）

Easy 輕鬆學系列 034

一天一篇短日記，寫出英文強實力
シンプル穴埋め式 365 日短い英語日記

作　　者　mami
譯　　者　林以庭
總 編 輯　何玉美
責任編輯　陳如翎
封面設計　張天薪
內頁版型　theBAND・變設計── Ada

出版發行　采實文化事業股份有限公司
行銷企劃　陳佩宜・馮羿勳・黃于庭・蔡雨庭・陳豫萱
業務發行　張世明・林踏欣・林坤蓉・王貞玉・張惠屏
國際版權　王俐雯・林冠妤
印務採購　曾玉霞
會計行政　王雅蕙・李韶婉
法律顧問　第一國際法律事務所　余淑杏律師
電子信箱　acme@acmebook.com.tw
采實官網　http://www.acmebook.com.tw
采實臉書　http://www.facebook.com/acmebook01

I S B N　978-986-507-238-4
定　　價　450 元
初版一刷　2021 年 1 月
劃撥帳號　50148859
劃撥戶名　采實文化事業股份有限公司
　　　　　104 台北市中山區南京東路二段 95 號 9 樓
　　　　　電話：(02)2511-9798　傳真：(02)2571-3298

國家圖書館出版品預行編目資料

一天一篇短日記,寫出英文強實力 / mami 著;林以庭譯.
-- 初版 .-- 台北市:采實文化事業股份有限公司, 2021.01
　　面;　公分 .--(輕鬆學系列;34)
　　譯自:シンプル穴埋め式 365 日短い英語日記
　ISBN 978-986-507-238-4(平裝)
　1. 英語 2. 寫作法

805.17　　　　　　　　　　　　　　　109018425

SIMPLE ANAUMESHIKI　365NICHI MIJIKAI EIGO NIKKI
© mami 2019
First published in Japan in 2019 by KADOKAWA CORPORATION, Tokyo.
Complex Chinese translation rights arranged with KADOKAWA CORPORATION,
Tokyo through Keio Cultural Enterprise Co., Ltd.
Traditional Chinese edition copyright ©2021 by ACME Publishing Co., Ltd.
All rights reserved.